W9-BXM-875

A Year to the Day

ALSO BY ROBIN BENWAY:

Emmy & Oliver

Far from the Tree

A Year to the Day

ROBIN BENWAY

An Imprint of HarperCollinsPublishers

Library of Congress Control Number: 2022930399
ISBN 978-0-06-285443-8

Typography by Ellice M. Lee
22 23 24 25 26   PC/LSCH   10 9 8 7 6 5 4 3 2 1

First Edition

For Marguerite

A Year to the Day

AUGUST 17
365 DAYS AFTER

ON THE MORNING of the first anniversary of her older sister Nina's death, Leo wakes up, looks at her mussed, tangled bedsheets, and bursts into tears.

The house is quiet around her, almost too quiet, like it's holding a secret, or maybe it's still mourning like the rest of them—missing Nina between its walls, Nina thundering down the stairs, slamming the door behind her before bursting back in a few hours later, her voice echoing into the rafters. It sort of reminds Leo of when her parents got divorced and her dad moved out, his presence making him feel like a ghost even though he was still alive and living just a few miles away with Leo's stepmom, Stephanie.

"Leo?"

Leo sits up a little and pushes her hair out of her face and wipes at her cheeks. The day already feels warm and bone-dry, even with the windows all closed. "Yeah?" Her voice is scratchy and raw, and she clears her throat. "Come in."

Her mom opens the door. Her hair is all tangled, too, and she's got a robe wrapped tightly around her, a mug of tea in her hands. "You awake?"

"Well, my eyes are open, so I guess technically, yes," Leo replies, but scoots over so her mom can come sit down next to her. In the doorway, Denver, their corgi, peeks into the room and then waddles in before turning around three times and settling himself on a pile of Leo's dirty laundry.

"How are you doing?" her mom asks.

Leo just shrugs.

"Yeah, me too," her mom says with a sigh. "It's like I've been waiting for this day and dreading it at the same time."

"Worst finish line ever," Leo says, which makes her mom smile a little.

"Your dad texted me this morning," her mom says. "He and Stephanie are going to bring the baby over a little early just to see if they can get her down for a nap first."

Leo feels her heart twitch at the mention of her three-month-old half sister, the surprise addition who has become a steady joy. "Cool," she says. "East said he'd come over a little bit early, too, just if we need help."

"That's nice," her mom says, nodding absently at the mention of Nina's old boyfriend. "He can maybe help move the rosebush into the backyard."

They had all gone back and forth about an appropriate tribute for Nina, as if there was anything in the world that could adequately honor her. Leo's dad had suggested releasing balloons, which Leo and her stepmom, Stephanie, quickly shot down. "That is *so* not okay for the environment," Leo had said, while Stephanie took the more practical approach: "Who's going to transport two hundred balloons from the store to the house, hmm?"

Finally, they decided on a rosebush, and they met at a fancy gardening store to choose one. Leo had had no idea that there were so many different kinds of roses, but she, her dad, her mom, and Stephanie had all finally agreed on the Daring Spirit rose, which was a fancy kind of rose that looked tie-dyed and chaotic. "It's perfect," Leo had said as soon as she heard the name, and all of the adults murmured in agreement.

The baby had been there, too, bundled in a complicated-looking piece of fabric that wrapped around Stephanie's middle, and when they all finally agreed on the rose, she let out a squawk of approval and then fell asleep.

There's a hole in the ground of the backyard now, waiting for the tribute planting. Leo can see it from her window.

"It's going to be a beautiful day," Leo's mom says, leaning over the bed so she can move the curtain a bit.

Leo rests her head against her mom's shoulder. "Kind of wish I could just stay in bed all day, though."

Her mom smiles ruefully, then pats Leo's knee. "Me too, sweetheart."

Her mom's hired a caterer for the memorial and the house is as clean as it's going to get, so Leo hops on her bike and heads over to her dad and stepmom's house to keep an eye on the baby so they can get ready. "I've never been happier to see you in my life," Stephanie says when she opens the door. Half her hair is in hot rollers and she's holding the baby, who looks at Leo with a suspicious gaze.

But once Leo's inside, Stephanie says, "You doing okay?" and gives Leo a one-armed squeeze as her dad comes around the corner. He looks tired but still gives her a smile and a hug, which Leo returns. "I brought you something for the nursery," Leo says to Stephanie as she lets go of her dad. "You said you were looking for a photo but couldn't find something."

"Oh, that's wonderful!" Stephanie says. "Here, let's give this bundle of terror to your dad and then we can head up."

Leo's not sure she'll ever get used to hearing her dad talk to a baby, how his voice goes high and stupid like he's been sucking on helium balloons for fun. "He's such a mush around her," Stephanie whispers as they go upstairs.

"He sounds unhinged," Leo whispers back.

"I know, it's so cute."

The nursery is, of course, completely tasteful and done up in grays and creams with just a little bit of pink here and there. Leo sees the old dresser that they went to pick up last March, now clean and polished and looking brand-new.

Stephanie runs a big Instagram account, @SweetHomeBySteph, that has over 300,000 followers and focuses mostly on "rustic, time-less" furniture, and free things are always showing up at their house, rugs and housewares and, once, even a sectional sofa. There are never any shoes tossed in a heap by the front door at their house, or a fine layer of corgi fur on everything. "Where's the dust?" Nina used to say whenever they came over.

"So I hope this is okay," Leo says. "If it's not, you can totally say no, my feelings won't be hurt at all."

(Her feelings will absolutely be hurt, of course, but Leo decides to worry about that part later.)

"I'm sure I'm going to love it," Stephanie says.

Leo takes a deep breath and then digs it out of her bag. "I put some tissue paper around it so it wouldn't get scratched," she says, and Stephanie carefully folds back the paper to reveal the framed photograph that East had taken and printed and given to Leo on Christmas Eve, the one that had made her cry.

Stephanie's eyes immediately fill.

"It was taken, well, today. Or at least, a year ago today," Leo rushes to explain. "East took it and he gave it to me, but I thought maybe it'd be better here than in my room." From the frame, Nina's face beams up at them.

"This is beautiful," Stephanie breathes, then reaches for Leo to give her another hug. "Truly. East is so *talented*, look at this."

Leo just nods as Stephanie sets it on the shelf next to a stuffed elephant wearing a tutu. "It's perfect," Stephanie murmurs.

Afterward, Leo plays with the baby for a bit while her dad showers and Stephanie gets dressed. "Playing" with the baby means that Leo covers her eyes and then uncovers them while the baby gives her a reproachful look, as if to say *How stupid do you think I am?* "Look,"

Leo finally says to her, "if it were up to me, we'd be watching Netflix, but apparently that will stunt your brain. I don't make the rules here," she adds when the baby narrows her eyes at Leo.

Leo's kind of glad that the baby is so skeptical. It feels, in some way, like the most fitting tribute to Nina.

Once everyone's ready, Leo's dad loads her bike into the trunk of his car so he can take her home. "I'll be right behind you," Stephanie says. "Just gotta feed the beast."

In the garage, Leo's dad tosses her the key fob. "Think fast," he says, and she does. "Why don't you drive us back?"

Leo hasn't driven at all since before Nina died and the fob feels heavy in her hands. "You know how slow I am," she says.

"You'll be fine."

"You're the one who said I was slow! You said I drive like a grandma."

Her dad shrugs. "We've got an hour and we're going two miles. That should give us just enough time."

Leo looks down at the car, then at the fob in her hands. "Fine," she says, and climbs into the driver's seat, taking the wheel in her hands. It's smooth, not like East's car, she thinks to herself, and then wonders why she knows that.

Her dad slides into the passenger seat. "You ready?" he asks.

"Always."

"Okay," he says, then smiles. "Just don't honk."

Leo has to smile at that.

His seat belt snaps into place. That sound, the harsh metal *click!* And Leo's smile fades as she shudders.

Leo feels shaky all during the memorial.

Everyone is there: Nina's old boyfriend, East, and his dad, both of them wearing collared shirts and looking somber; Leo's friend Madison and her parents; Kai and Aidan and Dylan, who has his girlfriend Sophie draped all over him; Aunt Kelly and Uncle David and a gaggle of cousins; a few of Nina's friends from school and their neighbors. Denver is there, too, proudly wearing his plaid collar and trotting after people who have helped themselves to the cheese plate. Leo even sees Brayden and his mom for a minute, but he's too far away for her to go say hello. She'll DM him later, she figures.

Across the yard, East gives her a questioning look and a thumbs-up sign, but Leo looks away and pretends to be busy with something else. She's not ready to look at him yet.

Her mom and dad stand up at the front and thank everyone for coming. Leo hasn't seen them stand together since the night of the accident and it makes her feel weirdly hollow. "We also want to say thanks to everyone who's held us up over this past year," her dad continues in a wobbly voice. "And I know that my wife, Stephanie, and Eleonora—Leo—say thank you, as well."

Leo groans as she feels all of her friends' heads immediately pivot to look at her. "Eleo*nora*?" Madison mouths at her, then giggles behind her hand.

Leo will definitely be having *words* with her dad later.

They plant the rosebush and everyone claps, which feels like a weird and yet very normal thing to do, and then there's food and drinks and hugs and tears and and smiles and laughter. East takes a few pictures with his fancy camera. Leo mostly hangs out with her friends. As the sun sets, her anxiety starts to pulse like a heartbeat even as she circulates and holds the baby for a while and stands next to her mom while they eat some vegetables and dip.

"You doing okay?" her mom asks.

"Totally," Leo says, then goes upstairs and puts her hands on the cold bathroom countertop and breathes. It's been a year and the grief still comes in waves, pulling the memory of Nina closer and then further away. Leo thought she'd be better at navigating these waters by now.

When she looks up at the bathroom mirror, it's Nina's face that she sees. She waits until she sees herself again before going back downstairs.

It's almost dark once the majority of their guests leave. Madison gives her a big hug before she goes, and Leo lets her friend hang on for as long as she wants. "I'll text you tomorrow," she says into Leo's shoulder. "Get ready for an emoji explosion."

Leo hugs her back just as tight. "Always ready," she replies.

By the time the sun has set, it's just East and his dad and some neighbors left in their yard. Stephanie and her dad have left to get the baby back home, and Leo presses a kiss to the peach fuzz on the baby's head when they go. "See you soon, raccoon," she whispers.

The baby burps in response.

East's dad is talking to Leo's mom and just beyond their fence, Leo can see East sitting on a bench out on the greenbelt, his body a shadow against the purple sky. She finds her shoes, takes a deep breath, and slips out of the gate.

"Oh, hey, *Eleonora*," he says.

"Hi, *Easton*," she shoots back.

"Hey, at least mine's just my mom's maiden name," he replies, but his voice sounds thick as Leo sits down next to him. She remembers the last time they were in her backyard together. She wonders if East remembers that evening, too.

They sit in silence for a while before Leo finally takes the plunge. "So, did you look into those classes at Coast Community?"

"Oh, yeah, yeah," East says and Leo suspects that he's as grateful as she is for the normal conversation, to be able to think about something else other than Nina and that night for a moment. "I signed up online and I start in two weeks. English Composition, Spanish, trig, and then Photography 201." He ducks his head down as he adds, "They let me into the advanced class."

"That's so cool," Leo says. "I'm really glad you're doing that. And I bet your dad is, too."

"Nobody's happier than my dad about this," East says with a small smile, but the light dies between them as they come back to the reason for the memorial, for the day.

East's fingers find Leo's and threads them together. "I keep thinking about what we were doing exactly this time last year," he says after a while. "Just, like, how possible everything felt, you know? We were so happy that night. I think that's what I keep remembering, how happy I felt."

He turns to look at Leo. "Remember?"

Leo's eyes fill with tears. They both know the answer to that question, that she doesn't remember everything, not like East does.

There is a hole in what she can see of that night, a space surrounded by shattered glass, the sound of a cry, her hair in her face as the wind blew wildly around her.

She holds East's hand and thinks about how sometimes things are gone, just like that, even as their absence still takes up space in your heart, their place carved out forever, reminding you of what has been and what will never be again.

"Hey," East says then, and when she looks up at him, he gives her a gentle grin and squeezes her hand tight.

Nina had been right, Leo thinks, about his smile.

After everyone has left and the food is packed up and put away and the flowers are wilting in their vases a bit, Leo goes into her bedroom to get something, then heads back downstairs to find her mom.

"Hey, there," her mom says when she sees her, slipping off her reading glasses and sitting up at the kitchen table. "How are you doing? Are you and East good?"

"We're good," she replies. "Can I talk to you about something, though?"

"Of course, sweetie. What's up?"

Leo reaches into her pocket and pulls out Nina's missing phone, then sets it down on the table in front of them. "Why are you giving me your—wait. Is this Nina's phone?"

Leo sits down at the table next to her. "I'm sorry I lied about not knowing where it was. I just wanted to have a part of her all to myself for a while. But Nina's not mine to keep, you know?" Leo rubs at her eyes. She's so, so tired. "You can have it if you want it. Or wipe it, cancel it, whatever."

Her mom is gently tracing the pattern of Nina's phone case, her expression soft as she moves her finger over the pink swirls and gold stars. "It's like I just saw this five minutes ago," she says, then moves her chair back from the table and reaches out to Leo. "C'mon, come sit with me."

Leo crawls into her mom's lap, letting her wrap Leo up in a one-armed hug as she settles herself. "I'm happy you're here, kid," her mom murmurs after a minute. "You know that, right?"

"Yes," Leo whispers because her throat is suddenly tight and aching. "I always knew that."

"Okay, good." Her mom presses a kiss to the side of her head, then picks up Nina's phone.

"I haven't looked at it in a while," Leo admits. "And I never went through her photos. I couldn't . . ."

Her mom rests her chin on the top of Leo's head and holds her a bit closer. "You want to look at it together?" she asks. "Seems like a good day to do it."

"Okay," Leo says. "You first."

Her mom opens the phone and they both start to laugh at the screen: a photo of Denver wearing a gaudy tiara and looking less than happy about it.

"It's you!" Leo says as her mom turns the phone to show him, but Denver doesn't look up from his bed. It's been a long day of foraging for dropped food.

Leo enters the security code by heart and then swipes to the Photos app, her finger poised to open it. "You ready?" she says to her mom.

"Nope," her mom says. "Let's do it anyway."

Leo taps the phone and Nina's life floods the screen.

It takes their breath away.

MAY 16
273 DAYS AFTER THE ACCIDENT

LEO IS UP on the fire roads with East and their friends Kai, Aidan, and Dylan when her phone dings with a text. She's busy setting up a stationary camera for East, squatting in the dirt and trying to make sure that it's steady, so she ignores it.

"Go again!" East yells to Dylan, who's hiking back up the road, skateboard in hand. East gestures with his camera and Dylan gives him the thumbs-up sign before setting up. Behind them is the thin blue line of the ocean, the sky looming overhead.

Leo's phone dings again. "Leo!" Dylan yells. "Answer your phone!"

"It's probably just Sophie looking for *you*!" she yells back.

"We broke up!" he bellows, and Kai, Aidan, East, and Leo all exchange a loaded, shared look.

"Uh-huh," Aidan mutters.

"Of course you did," East says under his breath as he checks the camera lens.

"I can hear you, you know!" Dylan shouts.

Leo's phone buzzes again and this time she goes to answer it. But before she can pick it up, it starts ringing, and when she finally digs it out of her bag, her dad's picture is on the screen.

"Oh shit," she says, and slides it open with a shaky thumb.

"Lee?" her dad says, and he sounds both elated and terrified. "This is it, babe. For real this time."

Stephanie's officially past her due date at this point, but she and Leo's dad have been to the hospital several times, with Stephanie convinced she's going to give birth in the next thirty seconds and the doctors insisting that it's false labor. Leo's gone over to their house a few times to visit, bringing a box of Popsicles with her each time. "Bless you," Stephanie always says with a sigh. "You are my favorite, did you know that? Because it's true."

"Leo?" her dad says now. "Did I lose you?"

"No," she says. "I'm here, but are you sure? Like, *really* sure?"

"Well, all of the medical professionals are sure, so I'm going to trust them." Her dad laughs, nervous and shaky. "Never thought I'd be here again."

"Okay, I'm on my way," Leo says. "And Dad?"

"Yeah?"

"You got this. So does Stephanie."

"Thanks, sweetie. Love you. Text when you're in the lobby."

When Leo hangs up, Dylan is bombing down the hill, his arms out to his sides, and Leo starts to laugh and cry at the same time.

"What's wrong?" Kai says, standing up like he can fight off whatever's upsetting her.

"My stepmom's in labor!" she cries.

She's never seen four teenage boys move so fast in her life, and in less than a minute, East has all of his camera gear loaded up and in the trunk of his dad's car, and Leo's climbing in the passenger side while Kai, Aidan, and Dylan fling themselves into the backseat. "Do you think she'll have the baby before we get there?" Kai asks. "Because that'd be a bummer, if you miss it."

"I'm pretty sure it'll take a little longer than that," East says as he starts the car and moves it out of park. He looks pretty calm, but Leo's known him long enough to know that buried under his confident tone is the tiniest hint of a wobble.

"Oh yeah? Well, how many babies have *you* had?" Kai says.

Dylan's phone dings then, and everyone in the car turns to look at him.

"What?" he says irritably. "It's probably just my mom."

"Check it," East says as he heads down the hill.

"It's fine."

Leo's phone dings now, too, and she glances at the screen, both relieved and disappointed that it's not her dad. "Madison says that Sophie wants to know why you're not answering her texts."

Kai hoots with laughter as Dylan turns crimson. "I thought we were broken up!" he insists. "I thought that meant I don't have to answer!"

"The rules seem murky," East says, then he glances over at Leo while Kai continues to tease Dylan. "You okay? You good?"

"I'm okay," she says, then smiles at him. "Seriously."

Leo is most definitely not okay.

East is nice and waits with her in the lobby, both of them sitting in uncomfortable chairs, East bouncing his knee while Leo checks and rechecks her phone. She texted her mom, but she's at the movies with Leo's aunt Kelly and they're seeing some epic World War II thing, so she doesn't expect her mom to respond until the Allies have won, which could take a while.

"Are you nervous?" East asks again. He must have phrased that question ten different ways by this point.

"I don't know what I am," she says. In the background, a siren wails and Leo pushes the memories of that night away. "I just kind of wish it wasn't happening *here*, if I'm being honest."

East nods, picking at a thread in his threadbare jeans. "I know," he says quietly. "Me too."

After a few hours of pacing and waiting and endlessly scrolling, East finally decides to go get something from the coffee bar downstairs. "Want anything?" he asks, but Leo shakes her head. The last thing she needs is a shot of caffeine. She already feels like she could power a small city with the amount of nervous energy coursing through her body. What if something happens to the baby, or Stephanie? What if her dad faints and falls and hits his head, like men always seem to do on TV and in the movies? What if there's an earthquake and they all perish in the rubble? What if, what if, what if, what if?

And of course, as soon as the elevator disappears with East inside, Leo's phone rings.

Dad:

Baby's here! Stephanie did great. Everyone's healthy and
happy. Come on up. Fifth floor maternity.

Leo flees the lobby so fast that she doesn't even think to text
East and give him the good news.

When the elevator doors open, her dad is there waiting for her.
"Hey, you," he says, and then he's wrapping her up in his arms. He
feels trembly, but not in a scary way, and Leo hugs him back as tight as
she can. "You okay?" he asks. "You ready to meet your sister?"

It takes Leo a second to realize that her dad isn't talking about
Nina, but she nods as she pulls away. "Let's go," she says.

Stephanie's in the bed, her glasses on and her hair swept back
in a long braid. She looks exhausted and thrilled and overwhelmed,
everything on her face reflecting how Leo feels on the inside. "Hi,"
she whispers, and that's when Leo sees the tiny, blanket-wrapped
bundle in her arms. "Someone here's been waiting to meet you for
a while."

Leo freezes as the blanket stirs. "It's okay," Stephanie murmurs.
"Whatever you want to do is perfectly okay."

Leo takes a deep breath, takes a step forward, and takes the baby
into her arms.

Leo's never seen an actual newborn, and the baby is squishy and
swollen and red and feels like the most fragile thing that Leo's ever
held. "Hi," she whispers. "It's me."

"This is Opal," her dad says, standing next to Stephanie. They're
holding hands, both of them with tears on their cheeks.

"Hi, Opal," Leo says. "I'm your big sister."

Opal opens her eyes and looks at her, then frowns, and Leo starts to laugh. She hasn't seen that frown in almost a year, hasn't seen those eyes glaring at her in months, and she knows then that Nina isn't gone, that she's here in this room, that she's in Opal and in Leo and everywhere and nowhere in the world, and Leo feels like her heart is soaring and collapsing all at the same time. She wants so many things that she can't have, and yet at the same time, she has so many things that she didn't even know she wanted.

"Actually, there were supposed to be two of us here today," Leo whispers to the baby, who's still frowning at her. "And I'm really sorry, but I'm the one you're stuck with. But I'm going to do my best, okay? Because I had a *really* good teacher."

Opal continues to look at her.

"Is that a yes? I think that's a yes," Leo says to her dad and Stephanie. Everyone's crying by this point, and then Opal, who will forever hate being left out of things, lets out a shout in response, and everyone laughs.

"Let the adventure begin," Leo whispers.

Leo hangs on to her sister.

She doesn't let her go.

APRIL 11
238 DAYS AFTER THE ACCIDENT

STEPHANIE'S BABY SHOWER is being held at the house of her best friend, Lisa, who lives twenty minutes away in a fancy condo complex that advertises amenities like concierge services and heated swimming pools. The building is glass and metal, and when Leo and her mom pull up a little before 3:00 p.m., the sun reflecting off the side makes it look like it's on fire.

"Well, that's not a great omen," Leo jokes, but her mom doesn't respond as she nervously taps her fingers against the steering wheel.

"Are you sure you're okay to go by yourself?" her mom asks instead.

"Mom, it's fine," Leo says. "It's just Stephanie and a bunch of her friends. It's only two hours. I'll be fine."

Her mom nods, but Leo can tell she still feels bad.

The invitations had officially arrived two weeks earlier. Normally, Leo's mom would pin it to the refrigerator door with a magnet, but she doesn't do that this time. Leo saves hers, though, tucks it into the nightstand by her bed where she keeps important things. It's understated and tasteful, very Stephanie.

"I told Lisa, *no games*," Stephanie said when Leo had dinner at her and her dad's house on Friday night. "Absolutely no games."

"What's wrong with games?" Leo asked.

Behind Stephanie's back, Leo's dad made a slashing motion across his neck and shook his head.

"They're just awful at baby showers!" Stephanie cried. "No one likes them! People are there to eat cupcakes and drink wine and ooh and ahh at all the baby presents, and that's it." She looked flustered and out of sorts, and Leo quickly switched the subject to Netflix shows.

"Yeah, she's just tired and stressed. The baby's keeping her up at night, kicking and moving around," Leo's dad told her later that night, driving her home. "Don't worry, she's really looking forward to the shower."

"She invited Mom," Leo said, even though she was sure that her dad already knew, had probably been consulted about the decision.

"I know." Her dad checked the side mirror as he changed lanes.

"She said she'd come, too," Leo added, and her dad didn't say anything after that.

Now, sitting in front of Lisa's condo complex, Leo knows the truth.

She had gone into her mom's room that morning, holding an outfit in each hand, not sure what was appropriate to wear to a baby shower. Were they fancy? Casual? Were you supposed to wear a specific color? Leo had no idea.

Her mom was sitting on the bed, looking out the window, and Leo immediately regretted stepping foot in the room. She had seen that look on her mom's face before, lost and lonely, but when she heard Leo, she turned around, her face smoothing back into something easier, calmer, less true. "Hi, sweetie," she said. "What's up?"

Leo held up her outfits. "Which one?"

"For what?"

Leo blinked. "The shower?"

"Oh, right. Um." Her mother squinted a bit, then shook her head. "Neither. You need a dress."

Leo groaned. "I have, like, exactly one dress and it's old." Leo doesn't mention the fact that she used to have two.

"But you always look nice in it."

Leo didn't know how to explain to her mom that looking "nice" isn't always at the top of a sixteen-year-old girl's priority list, so she let it go, rolling her eyes instead. "You're still going, right?" she asked. "We have to leave in an hour."

"I'm sorry," her mom said, and Leo felt that sort of dull panic, the way she had whenever she would see her mom curled up in Nina's empty bed, the way she would stare out the kitchen window for minutes at a time, the way she would seem like an entirely different person and no longer Leo's mom. "I'm happy for Stephanie, I'm happy for you, but I just can't, sweetheart. I'm sorry. You'll have your aunt and cousin there, though, right? I'll text Kelly so she knows."

"It's fine," Leo said, and when her mom held out an arm to her, she went and sat next to her on the bed, resting her head on her shoulder. Her mom felt less frail now, not as thin as she had been right after the accident. It's not as scary to hug her as it used to be, when she was so fragile that Leo was afraid to squeeze her too tight for fear that she would shatter into dust.

"I still remember both of your baby showers," her mom said, and Leo wasn't sure if she was talking to Leo or herself. "Aunt Kelly threw both of them. It was so exciting, such a happy time. Nina was at your baby shower, too. She was only two, snuck a bunch of M&M's off the table, and then got sick afterward." Her mom laughed a little. "It's funny, the things you remember. It's never really the big moments, always the little ones."

"Do you think it's weird?" Leo blurted out before she could stop herself.

"What? Nina eating the candy?"

"No." Leo pressed her face a little tighter against her mom's shoulder, searching for a comfort that wasn't quite there anymore. "That I don't remember the accident."

Her mom's arm tightened around her shoulders as she sighed, pulling Leo in a little closer. "I don't think it's weird," she said. "And I don't think *you're* weird, either."

"It just feels like I should remember," Leo continued on. "Like every part of that night should be seared into my brain, you know?"

Her mom pressed a kiss to the top of her head. "Maybe," she murmured after a minute, "those aren't memories that you want. Maybe the ones you have are the only ones you need."

Leo didn't say anything after that, but she didn't move, either. The sunlight fell through the window into their laps, a quiet bit of warmth that eventually moved and faded away.

As the elevator rises, Leo twirls Nina's ring around and around on her finger and takes a deep breath, lets it out slowly. She's holding a gift that she had wrapped herself, curling the ribbon and securing the corners with Scotch tape, but her mom had helped her pick it out. Leo has a dress on, too, a black flowered V-neck dress that the website had called a skater dress, and black sandals. She had even put on some makeup, and then leaned toward the mirror and very, very carefully applied some eyeliner.

Unsurprisingly, Lisa's condo is very nice and there's jazzy-type music playing and a champagne bar set up at the back of the living room. Leo recognizes a few of the women, who are in fact dressed up, and she's glad she took her mom's advice and wore a dress.

"I *told* you Stephanie was knocked up," someone behind Leo snorts, and she turns to see her older cousin standing behind her, a smirk on her face. She winks when Leo sees her and Leo feels some of the tension ease in her chest.

This particular cousin and Nina had been born thirteen months apart and had remained in a constant tug-of-war ever since they were big enough to push each other over in their Pack 'n Play. It all stemmed from something that wasn't even their fault, but that didn't matter. The gauntlet had been thrown down after their cousin was born first and, in their moms' family tradition, became the rightful inheritor of their maternal grandmother's first name, and she had resented it ever since the birth certificate had been officially signed.

"*Gertrude*," her mother hisses now, nudging her. "*Honestly*. Hi, sweetheart," she says to Leo, giving her a hug.

"Hi, Aunt Kelly," Leo says. "Hey, Gertie."

"Was I wrong?" Gertie asks innocently.

"You were not," Leo says, and Gertie preens a little.

"Leo!" Stephanie cries happily when she sees her, and comes over to give her a huge hug. "Is this for me? You're so sweet, you didn't have to get me anything!" But then she whispers in Leo's ear, "Carolyn is driving me up a freaking *wall*," and Leo laughs as she pulls away.

Stephanie's mother, Carolyn, is in the kitchen, and Leo can quickly tell that some of Stephanie's friends have been put on Mom Duty. Nina had always been fascinated by Carolyn, by the way she seemed to say whatever she was thinking in the moment she thought it. "It's a party now," Nina would mutter under her breath whenever Carolyn showed up at the front door or the holiday table. Leo thought it was telling that when they weren't in the same room, Stephanie referred to her mom as "Carolyn," like she was just another person in the world.

"Mom, Leo's here," Stephanie announces, and Leo immediately finds herself swept up in a hug. Carolyn's perfume is strong and flowery and Leo tries not to breathe too much of it in, but she can still smell it on her skin even after Carolyn finally releases her.

"You poor thing, how are you doing?" Carolyn asks, hanging on to her shoulders like they're best friends, like a stranger's kitchen is exactly where Leo wants to talk about the grief of losing her older sister.

"I'm fine," Leo replies, deploying her favorite word, even as she feels a tiny prickle underneath her skin. "How are you?"

"Oh, you know, just getting ready to be a grandma." She makes a face at the word. "It sounds so old, doesn't it? Like an old woman with gray hair who wears a rain bonnet. You know, Stephanie," she says, turning around. "Some people use the word 'glam-ma.' Clever, isn't it?"

Leo watches as Stephanie's knuckles whiten against her can of seltzer. "Clever," she repeats.

Leo suspects that Stephanie has heard this suggestion before.

"Where's your mother?" Carolyn says, turning back to Leo. "I thought I'd get a chance to say hello to her."

"Oh, she's, yeah." Leo twirls her ring again. "She couldn't make it after all. She said she'd text you later, Steph."

"Totally fine," Stephanie says with a smile, but Carolyn looks disappointed.

"Oh, that's a shame, I was hoping to talk to her. You know, I was watching *The View* and they had a guest on talking about grief and I thought, I absolutely *have* to tell Nicole about this because—"

"Leo, have you met Lisa yet? You should meet her," Stephanie interrupts, taking Leo by the elbow and deftly steering her out of the room. "I'm so sorry," she whispers to Leo once Carolyn is out of earshot. "You have my permission to drop-kick her if she says anything else to you."

Leo laughs, but the prickling sensation is back again.

The baby shower is fine, maybe a little boring, but Leo's only been to three parties in her entire teenage life and all of them ended with her crying, so she's probably not the best judge here. She eats a cupcake and drinks some sparkling cider, talks to Lisa about what exactly a concierge does, and listens as two of Stephanie's design friends tell her about their favorite YouTube channels.

But all Leo can think is, *Nina should be here*, and the thought pulses through her body like the throb of a headache, each beat upping the pain a little bit more. She can see where Nina would sit and stand, the people she would talk to, the people she would avoid, and her presence is so strong that when Leo goes into the kitchen to get some water, she half expects her sister to be standing there, waiting for her.

"Leo?" Lisa pokes her head in the door and smiles. "It's present time!"

"Be right there," Leo says, then rests her forearms against the cool marble countertop and tries to catch her breath before going to find a seat next to Gertie.

She almost manages to do it.

"You good?" Gertie whispers. "Do you need a real drink? I've got the good stuff in my purse."

Leo shakes her head. "M'fine."

The presents are all super cute, tiny onesies and stuffed animals and soft blankets. Gertie gives Stephanie a pair of little Converse sneakers, and everyone oohs and ahhs, even Leo. "It would have been a lot easier if you had told us what you're having!" Carolyn scolds at one point, and Stephanie just shrugs and says, "You'll have to wait and see."

When Carolyn turns away, Stephanie winks at Leo and smiles.

When it's finally time for Stephanie to open Leo's gift, she says, "This is heavy!" and Leo has a quick stab of fear that this is the wrong gift entirely, that she should have bought a little T-shirt that says "Here Comes Trouble" or something like that.

But when Stephanie unwraps it and her eyes fill with tears, Leo knows that she gets it.

"What is it, Steph?" one of her friends ask, and Stephanie turns the gift around to show the group, a framed and matted vintage print of the October night sky.

"It's from 1903," Leo hears herself explaining, "but the store said that the stars are still the same in the sky, regardless of the year, and I know you like vintage things and I thought that October, you know, is, or was, sort of important in our family and, well, yeah."

Stephanie's nodding and wiping her eyes. "This is so beautiful, Leo, truly." All of her friends are nodding and murmuring, too, and even Lisa is dabbing at her eyes with a tissue. "I can't wait to hang it up in the room."

"Well, don't put it over the crib," Carolyn chuckles. "That glass could be dangerous!"

Glass everywhere, sparkling on the ground, the sound of shattering.

"Mom." Stephanie's voice is low and dangerous.

Carolyn shrugs. "I'm just saying."

"Well, stop saying it." Stephanie glares at her.

"Where's the bathroom?" Leo has the distinct feeling that she needs to get out of there, that the walls are too close, the air too thin.

"Just down the hall on the left," Lisa says, then passes Stephanie another gift. "Oh, look, it's from me!" she says brightly, trying to lighten the mood, and Leo hears the excited murmurs as she walks on shaky legs past the bathroom and into a guest bedroom, shutting the door behind her.

It's the same thing that happened to her way back in October, her throat tightening up, her head feeling both light and heavy at the same time, her vision narrowing at the sides. When she sits on the bed and puts her head down between her knees, she feels herself almost topple over, catching herself just in time. But when she looks up, she sees her eyeliner and remembers the last time she had worn it, Nina's hands gently resting on Leo's head and face as she carefully drew the black line across her eyelid.

Stop spiraling, Nina whispers to her, her sister's voice a ghost of a memory, and Leo breathes.

Both Gertie and Stephanie knock, asking through the door if she's okay, and Leo manages to choke out a yes. After a while, she starts to hear people leave, but Leo doesn't move from the bed.

When the third knock happens, she doesn't wait for the person to say anything before she says, "I'm okay!"

"Leo?" It's her dad. "Can I come in? Please?"

She's so surprised that she doesn't say anything, which gives her dad a chance to open the door and poke his head into the room.

"Hey, kiddo," he says, and his voice is so familiar and gentle that Leo immediately bursts into tears.

Her dad sits next to her on the bed for a long time, his arm around her shoulders as Leo cries. "I know," he says, and Leo's about to say that he doesn't know, that he has no idea, but then he adds, "I'm missing her a lot today, too," and Leo dissolves into tears again.

"I totally embarrassed Stephanie," Leo says once she's gotten herself under control, but she doesn't bother to sit up.

"Stephanie is fine," her dad insists. "Besides, you've got a lot of competition with Carolyn out there." He tightens his arm around her when she laughs a little bit. "Did she behave herself today, or is Stephanie's blood pressure going to go through the roof?"

Leo makes a "so-so" motion with her hand. "She wasn't awful."

"And what about you?" he asks. "You having a hard time?"

"It's just like I feel she should be here, you know?" Her dad's wearing a collared shirt, which is nice, and the worn cotton is soft against her cheek, like a pillowcase. "Nina should be here, she should be talking to everyone and helping Stephanie get ready for the baby and I just can't believe that she's not. She's never going to be here for any of it ever again."

Her dad is quiet for a long time, still holding her, and Leo takes a deep breath and lets it out slowly. "I know she'd want me to be happy," Leo says, "but then things like this happen and I do feel happy, but then I feel guilty. I know Nina wouldn't want me to be sad, but it's like I don't know how to be happy without her."

"Oh, kid," her dad says with a sigh. "I hear you, I really do. All day, while you and Steph were here, I kept thinking of all the things she'd say about today, about the baby and the nursery that Stephanie's putting together, all of it."

"Do you talk to her?" Leo asks.

"All the time," her dad replies. "Every day. Every hour, sometimes."

"Me too," Leo whispers. "Sometimes, though, it's hard because she doesn't answer back. I don't even know if she's listening." Leo sits up a little and drags her arm across her eyes. "Do you think she can hear us where she is, wherever that is?"

Her dad smiles a little. "Kid, I don't know what the rules are wherever she is, but if there's one thing I *do* know, it's that Nina is probably breaking them right now."

Leo laughs at that, because it's true. "She's probably grounded," she says, and now her dad's laughing, too, and she can feel his chuckle rumble through his chest.

"Probably," he agrees. "I also know that she wouldn't want us, any of us, to stop going forward. Nina was always striving, right? Going to college, moving out, she was always thinking about the future. And I know how much she loved you and would want you to do the same thing."

"It's hard," Leo whispers. "It's so hard to be by myself. I know I'm not alone but . . ."

"But there will never be someone who takes her place?" her dad guesses, and Leo nods. "I know exactly what you mean."

They sit together in silence for a while, holding space for Nina, between them. "We've talked about this before," her dad says quietly, "but your mom and I think it might be time for you to talk to someone. Not her, not me, not East, but a professional."

"I'll think about it," Leo says, and her dad doesn't push it after that. "I love you, Dad."

"Love you, too, kid. We're going to get through it, I promise. No matter how messy it gets."

She nods again and hugs him tight, and for just a second, she thinks she can hear Nina laughing, just outside the door and forever out of reach.

MARCH 20
216 DAYS AFTER THE ACCIDENT

LEO AND MADISON have a presentation in their Spanish class due next Monday. It's an oral presentation where they have to have a conversation between each other about whatever topic their teacher suggests.

"This is going to be an actual disaster," Madison moans when they meet up on Friday to practice.

"We'll get through it," Leo says with false positivity, grabbing Madison's arm and shaking it a little. "I've heard you speak Spanish before and it's fine."

"Yeah, but in front of everyone? I turn into a deer in headlights, Leo. A small, adorable, baby deer in *really* bright headlights. I'm not good in public speaking situations."

Leo just holds the door for her as they walk into Starbucks. Madison had suggested meeting at the one directly across the street from their school, but Leo remembered the last time she had been to that location, how *nice* everyone had been to her. She couldn't go through that again. "They're super stingy with the whipped cream there," she said instead, and felt grateful when Madison didn't push or ask any questions.

This location is pretty busy and there's a line, so Madison and Leo wait their turns. Most of the seats are taken by people sitting alone, but there's a table near the back that has three teenagers, two girls and a boy, sitting at it, their heads together as they chat. One of the girl's drinks has a chewed-up straw in it and they're teasing her about it.

Leo turns away, tries not to think about the fact that Nina will never tease her again, will never do things like stand directly in the doorway of her bedroom and say, "But I'm not *in* your bedroom," when Leo yells at her to get out. That used to make Leo so mad, Nina's smirking face staring into her room when she just wanted to be alone, but now she would give anything to see Nina standing there again.

"Leo," Madison says, nudging her. It's their turn to order, Leo's been daydreaming, and so she says, "Oops, sorry" as she steps forward, looks at the barista, and comes face-to-face with Brayden.

It's clear he recognizes Leo immediately, his eyes going wide and round and making him look more like a little boy than the asshole guy she had seen at that disastrous Christmas party. "Hi," she says before she can stop herself. "Madison, why don't you—I'm not ready—I'm not sure what I want yet."

"Iced chai tea latte," Madison rattles off, needing no urging. She's still looking at the refrigerated section, trying to decide if she wants a cookie or not, and Leo is just praying that she doesn't remember Brayden at all.

"Holy shit!"

Leo truly has no luck sometimes.

"You're *Brayden*!" Madison continues and Brayden goes splotchy pink again, looking more like he's having an allergic reaction than an embarrassing moment in public.

"Yep," he manages to say. "What size?"

"Oh, uh, grande." Madison turns to Leo. "Remember *Brayden*?"

Leo thinks that Madison is one of the most genuinely nice people she's ever met in her life, and Leo would never advocate for violence, but in that moment, she wishes she had a shovel so she could hit Madison in the head with it and just end this entire conversation.

"Hi," Leo says again.

"Hi." Brayden actually replies to her this time, but it's clear he's not thrilled to see her. Leo can't say she blames him.

"So what are you doing here?" Madison says, then doesn't wait for Brayden to respond before she says to Leo, "What are you getting?"

"I just started—"

"I don't think I want anything," Leo says.

"What?" Madison is aghast. "C'mon! It's no fun to go somewhere to eat and then you're the only person who orders." She's about to continue but then the three kids stand up and leave their table. "Ooh, I'm going to grab it!" she says, then sets down a twenty-dollar bill and scurries over like a squirrel with her eye on a nut.

Which leaves Leo looking at Brayden.

"Uh," she says.

"And what can I get for you today?" Brayden asks in a voice that sounds both robotic and pained.

"An iced latte," Leo says. She feels like she can't order Nina's regular drink just in case Brayden recognizes it, and her mom usually gets an iced latte, so how bad could it be?

"What size?" He sounds like he'd rather be at the dentist.

Leo runs her hand over her eyes. "I don't care, okay? I really don't."

Brayden punches something into the register and then takes the twenty that Leo hands him. "Look," she finally says. "Can we talk or . . . ?"

He sighs and his shoulders sag forward a little, going from looking like a little boy to a tired old man in a blink. "I have my break in ten minutes," he says. "I usually go out in the back for a smoke."

"Cool," Leo says, even though smoking sort of grosses her out. "Can I . . . ?"

Brayden nods, but looks none too thrilled about it, and Leo carefully pulls off one of the bills from the change Brayden hands her and puts it in the tip jar. It may look generous, but she knows what it really is.

It's penance.

"Why do you think he's working here?" Madison asks in a hiss-whisper as soon as Leo sits down at the table and throws her backpack on top of it.

"Why anybody works anywhere." Leo shrugs. "He either needs or likes money."

"Needs it," Madison says. "His mom had to sell their house last month to pay for the lawyers."

Leo knows that Brayden's dad deserves every bit of justice coming to him, but still, seeing Brayden behind the counter, wearing a grimy apron, makes her understand the full weight of his sadness.

"I'm going to talk to him when he goes on his break," Leo says.

Madison glares at her over her notebook. "Are you serious? You're going to ditch me for *Brayden*?"

"Shh!" Leo says just as a coffee grinder starts, drowning out their conversation. "I'm not 'ditching you,' I'm just going to talk to him for a few minutes. We have some, um, unfinished business."

"Oh my God, did you two make out at the Christmas party?"

Leo drops her head down and bangs it on the table a few times, then regrets it when she feels how sticky it is. "No," she finally says. "We most definitely did *not* make out. He and East were in a fight."

"Yeah, I heard about that," Madison says. "I missed the whole thing, though."

"Oh, I know," Leo says, remembering Madison coming down the stairs with mussed hair and smeared lipstick, the boy behind her looking both cocky and dazed.

Madison wiggles her eyebrows at her. "Estaba ocupada," she says, then flips open her laptop and powers it on.

★

As soon as she sees Brayden leave the register, Leo slips out the side door and goes out to where the dumpsters are lined up against the curb. He's there, cupping his hands around a cigarette as he lights it, then lets out a stream of smoke that turns into a loud sigh once he sees Leo. "What?" he says to her. "You come to finish the job? I still got another kidney, you know."

"Yeeeeeaaaaah," she says, dragging the toe of her shoe in a line on the ground. "That's kind of what I wanted to talk to you about. I'm really sorry. Like, genuinely. That wasn't okay, I was just mad and, I don't know, jealous."

"Jealous?" Brayden laughs as he sits down on the curb. Leo waits a beat, then sits down next to him. When he doesn't protest, she tucks her hands under her legs. It's cold in the back.

"I never knew you dated Nina," she says quietly. "She never told me. I found out that night."

Brayden's head bobs up and down as he takes in that information. "So, what, you had a thing for me, too?"

Some of her benevolence immediately dries up. "No," she snaps. "I was jealous that you knew something about her that I didn't know. I thought I knew everything about Nina, she was my best friend. I guess it just scares me to think that there are parts of her that I'll never understand, you know? And you were one of them."

Brayden looks appropriately chastised and he nods as he drags on his cigarette. He's polite enough to aim his exhale away from Leo, which she appreciates.

"Can I ask you a question?"

"Yes, I started working here so I could help my mom make rent each month," he intones.

"No, I don't care about—well, I mean, I *do* care. But that's not my question." When he doesn't respond, she plows forward. "Why did you break up?"

For the first time since she's seen him, Brayden cracks a smile. "You mean, why did she break up with me?"

Leo feels a tiny thrill of sisterly pride. "Okay, yes, that."

"She didn't like my car. Thought it was 'ostentatious.'" His smile gets a little wider.

Leo has a dark thought and decides to share it. "I think she would appreciate the car irony here."

"Probably," Brayden says. "At least, I don't think she would've been a jerk about it. Not like everyone else."

Leo's not sure what to say to that, so she doesn't say anything.

Brayden exhales smoke again, dragging a sneakered toe along the pavement. It's like watching a wave build in the ocean, waiting for him to speak, and Leo waits.

"Look, I'm just telling you this," he says after a minute. "But Nina, she was . . . I wasn't like, in love with her or anything, but she just made me feel—I don't know, she was just special."

"You felt special when you were with her," Leo says.

"I know that makes me a total sap or whatever," Brayden says. "But she liked that other guy better, West or whatever his name is."

Leo knows full well that Brayden knows East's name, but she doesn't bother correcting him.

"She just liked him more, so what can you do?" Brayden shrugs. It sort of feels like he's not talking to her anymore, talking to himself instead. "And then she got into the fucking car with him and she died. That's what happened. You can't go back and change it.

"I was there, you know," he continues, and Leo startles, thinks of fluorescent lights, screaming, the sound of someone performing CPR. "At the funeral," Brayden adds. "I snuck in the back because I got there late, but I was there."

"I wish you would have said hello," Leo says, but he waves the thought away with his cigarette, the smoke making zigzags in the air.

"Nah, I'm not into that. Just wanted to pay my respects, you know."

"I'm glad you were there, then," Leo says quietly. "And I'm sorry about everything else. Really."

Brayden shrugs again and stomps his cigarette under the heel of his shoe. "Whatever." He sighs. "Life sucks, right?"

"Sometimes," she says.

He scoffs, then turns to go back to work. "See you around, Leo," he says, and Leo sits outside until Madison comes looking for her, hands on hips.

"Did you kiss him?" she demands.

Leo rolls her eyes. "You give him way too much credit," she tells her friend, then holds the door for her as they head back inside.

MARCH 8
204 DAYS AFTER THE ACCIDENT

WHEN LEO SEES Stephanie's name and picture come up on her phone, her stomach drops to somewhere around her knees. Who calls instead of texts, especially when they're pregnant?

"Hi!" Stephanie cries when Leo answers. She sounds breathless and urgent, and Leo's stomach goes subterranean. "Are you home? Are you doing anything?"

"Yes and no," Leo says. She's supposed to be studying for her Monday morning English quiz, which means she should probably read the book at some point today, and her mom is out at some botanical garden with Aunt Kelly. "Did she forget that I'm massively allergic to all botanical things?" her mom muttered when Kelly first texted her about it, but she loaded up on Allegra and went anyway. Leo had planned on staying home and scrolling through YouTube and her phone for most of the day, which is, she thinks, how all Sundays should be spent.

"Are you okay?" Leo asks Stephanie now. Where the hell is her dad? Shouldn't he be with his pregnant wife 24/7 at this point??

What kind of neglectful husband would—

"Oh, absolutely, sweetie. Sorry, totally sorry, I just had to walk upstairs and I'm a little breathless. Whew!" She exhales into the phone, then laughs a little. "What, did you think that I went into labor or something?"

"Or something," Leo says. She's not exactly up to speed on all the terrible things that could happen to a forty-something-year-old pregnant woman, and she'd like to keep it that way for as long as possible.

"Sorry again. But! Listen. Can I bribe you to go to San Diego to get some furniture with me? There's a dresser that just got delivered at one of the antique stores that's just a *beaut* and the owners called and gave me first dibs, but only if I can get down there today and it turns out that his assistant is out so I need someone to help me load it into the car and your dad is golfing and ugh." She huffs again. "I swear, this baby is using my rib cage as a jungle gym."

Leo looks back at her laptop, at her copy of *The Kite Runner* that, let's be honest, she probably won't pick up until at least eight o'clock that night and will skim instead of read. It's actually Nina's copy from her own sophomore year, and it's annotated, but with nothing that's actually helpful. "BOOOORING" is a word that comes up often in the margins, and Leo's pretty sure that "Did Nina enjoy this book? Why or why not?" is not going to be a question on tomorrow's quiz.

Stephanie's still talking. "I know it's last minute, you have your own life, blah blah blah, but if you could help, lunch is on me? We can stop at that one taco place you like."

"La Sirena," Leo says immediately. "I'm in."

"Be there in thirty!" Stephanie cries, and right before she hangs up, Leo can hear her whooping with joy.

Ninety minutes later, Stephanie and Leo are sitting with chips and guacamole and two giant plates of salmon tacos in front of them. It's busy because of the weekend, but they manage to snag a table in the sunshine and Leo hooks her ankles around the bench seat as they eat.

"So what exciting things were you supposed to be doing today before I interrupted you?" Stephanie asks her.

Leo shrugs. "Not much. My mom and Kelly are at the botanical gardens today so I was just going to do some homework, you know, catch up."

Stephanie smiles. "Well, you're welcome," she teases. "And I thought your mom had a bunch of allergies to everything that grew out of the ground."

"I think Kelly 'forgot.'" Leo sets down her salmon taco, which immediately collapses, and makes finger quotes around the last word. "She's trying to get my mom out of the house every so often, which is good. But maybe a museum next time."

"How's your mom doing?" Stephanie asks. "I mean, if you feel comfortable talking about it. You don't have to, of course."

Leo has always liked that about Stephanie, the way she makes space for her to say yes or no. "It's okay," she says. "And she's okay, I think." Leo thinks about the afternoon her mom picked her up at school, about Christmas Eve, about how her mom's phone lit up the other day and Leo saw a text from someone who sounded like a therapist, offering her mom an appointment at 3:30 on the following Tuesday.

"I feel like I say 'okay' so much that the word doesn't have meaning anymore," Leo adds.

"Yeah, I used to get that way about the word 'plastic,'" Stephanie says. "And I'm glad your mom is doing . . ."

" . . . okay," Leo fills in. "Wait. Are you even allowed to eat salmon when you're pregnant?"

"Occasionally," Stephanie says. "But thanks for looking out for me and the baby."

Leo's not sure that's what she was doing, but she doesn't say that.

"How's math class going?" Stephanie asks, all super casual in a way that tells Leo this is just the opening act to her bigger question.

"It's good," she says. "Calculus is harder than I thought it would be."

"I thought your dad was going to explode when you tested into that class, he was so proud." Stephanie smiles a little bit and Leo feels a sudden rush of gratitude that her dad has someone who sees his happy moments, who remembers them. "You've always been a little math whiz."

Leo waves away the compliment. "It's just numbers," she says. "Anyone can do it."

"Sure, okay." Stephanie takes a long sip of her water, her eyes looking away as she drinks. "So you never told me about how the roller skating party was."

Leo knew it.

"How were the clothes? Did you have a blast or was it just a bunch of old fogies like me and your dad?"

Sometimes, Leo wants to tell Stephanie that she doesn't have to try so hard. "You're not old," she says, even though she thinks that maybe Stephanie is a *tiny* bit old. "And yeah, it was fun. Madison's dad seems pretty cool." She remembers what Madison said about him and feels a strange, sympathetic pull in her gut.

Stephanie waits until she finishes her taco before saying, "Your dad said that East was in the parking lot when he picked you up."

"He was," Leo says slowly.

"Well, that's nice."

"Stephanie."

"Leo."

"Would you like to *ask* me something about East, maybe?"

"I don't know. Would you like to *tell* me something about East?"

Leo sighs and crosses her arms over her chest. "Oh my God. Madison's dad just hired him to be the official party photographer. I didn't even know he was going to be there."

"I bet East appreciated the job," Stephanie says.

"Probably."

"Cool."

"Cool."

Stephanie gestures with a chip toward Leo's plate. "Are you going to finish that guacamole?" she asks, and Leo pushes it toward her, no longer hungry.

"There's nothing between me and East," Leo blurts out once they're back in the car, heading south on the 5 Freeway. The Pacific Ocean is glittering on her right, palm trees dotting the horizon. "Like, not like that."

"Okay," Stephanie says gently. "I was just asking, Leo. It wasn't an accusation."

"I would never date Nina's boyfriend," Leo says, but she's not sure if that's the right word for it anymore. "Or ex-boyfriend." That doesn't sound right, either. "Whatever, you know what I mean."

"I do," Stephanie says.

"It's not like we hate each other, of course," Leo continues. Stephanie's gripping the steering wheel and looking straight ahead while she's driving, which makes it easier for Leo to keep talking. Making eye contact with someone while talking about things like love is, she thinks, just excruciating.

"I mean, I don't hate him at all. He's my friend, he's . . . I don't know, I guess more than a friend, but not like romantic or anything."

"I don't know too much about it," Stephanie says. "Nina didn't talk to me about these things, but East seems like he was a wonderful boyfriend to her, so I imagine he's a pretty good friend to have, too."

"But it's not like that," Leo says. "I think that . . ." She trails off for a minute, counting the palm trees as they rush past the car. The sunlight is bouncing off the ocean, reminding her of a disco ball, reminding her of that night on the roller rink, the song in her ears, East's sweaty hand tight in hers.

"I think I love East," she says once she gets to ten palm trees. "We were both there on"—she swallows hard—"that night, you know? He's the only person who knows how that feels, and when you take that and add in the fact that we both really love the same person, it gets all tangled up. But not like *love* love. I loved—I *love* Nina, and he loves her, too. I think all of that has to go somewhere and maybe now that Nina's not here anymore, we just share it between us instead of with her. I mean, love just doesn't disappear once someone's gone. Right?"

When Stephanie doesn't answer, Leo looks over to see her wiping at her eyes underneath her sunglasses. "Oh, crap," she says. "Are you allowed to cry when you're this pregnant?"

"I think it's the *only* thing I'm allowed to do!" Stephanie says with a shaky, wet laugh. "And I think that's a beautiful way of looking at it, Lee. Seriously."

"Okay. Just please don't go into labor when I'm the only one with you. At least wait for my dad, or at least one person who's been to medical school."

"I've got a ways to go," Stephanie reassures her. "But noted."

Once they get to the antique store, the dresser looks beat-up and dusty, like it's sat in someone's garage for the past twenty years, but both Stephanie and the antiques dealer are ecstatic, talking about rosewood and molded handles and dovetailing.

Leo smiles politely and hopes she's never this embarrassing when she's an adult.

"It's going to clean up so beautifully," Stephanie says, clapping her hands together before rubbing one palm over her stomach with a fond look on her face. "It's going in the baby's room so it'll be special."

Leo eyes the dresser again. She wouldn't let a baby anywhere near this filthy thing, but hey, she's just the muscle today.

She and the dealer heave-ho it into the back of the SUV, Stephanie standing to the side and saying words of encouragement that are more helpful in theory than in actuality. "Gus, thank you again," she says to the dealer, who's wiping his brow and looking like he'd like to pop a couple of Advil. The day has become weirdly warm and Leo's looking forward to blasting the AC in the car and drinking the Diet Coke she saved from lunch.

And that's exactly what she does. For the first thirty minutes, anyway.

They're leaning into the curve of the 5 Freeway, Stephanie humming along happily with the radio, when Leo first sees the white vapor coming from the hood of the car. "Uh, Steph?" she says.

"What—oh no."

Stephanie pulls over at a rest stop that overlooks the ocean, and it seems to Leo like this would be a better location for a five-star resort or fancy restaurant than a parking lot for a bunch of people who have to pee and stretch their legs. But at least they get a spot in the shade and Stephanie pushes her sunglasses up onto her head as she turns the car off.

"Why does it smell like toxic pancake batter?" Leo asks, wrinkling her nose.

"The car's overheating." Stephanie sighs. "Well, crap and a half, I guess we'll just have to—Leo, stop looking at me like that."

"Like what?"

"Like I'm about to go into labor, that's what. I'm *fine*, the car is the problem here, not me."

Stephanie, levelheaded as always, calls AAA and then texts Leo's dad to tell him what the problem is. "Your dad wants to know if he should leave the golf course and come rescue us," she says, sounding bemused.

"No thank you," Leo says.

"Hard agree," Stephanie replies, then texts a quick response before rolling down the front windows and letting the ocean breeze roll through. "Well, here we are," she says. "Two ladies, a broken car, and a Norwegian dresser in the trunk."

"Totally normal," Leo agrees. "Nothing to see here."

Leo scrolls through her phone for a few minutes as Stephanie looks through her Instagram comments, murmuring happily at some and rolling her eyes at others. "Ooh," she says at one point, and Leo watches as her hand comes up to her stomach again, feeling that if she has to do something, Leo doesn't know what that thing is supposed to be.

"Just kicking," Stephanie reassures her. "This one's going to be a prizefighter or at the very least, very into physical confrontation." Then she tilts her head. "Do you want to feel?"

Leo's first instinct is to say no, but she finds herself nodding and reaching out, resting her palm against the side of Stephanie's swollen stomach. There's a flutter, followed by another flurry of movement, like bubbles floating up to meet her hand.

"Lee?" Stephanie says quietly, and that's when Leo realizes she's crying.

"Sorry," she says, wiping at her cheeks, but more tears arrive and Leo thinks how much she hates grief, how she loathes this grab bag of the worst emotions. How can she be eating tacos and laughing one hour and then be crying at a roadside rest stop the next? She thinks of Nina, of her laugh and her posture and her hair and skin, how strong she seemed and how tragically fragile she actually was, how life just seems to be a series of extremes, over and over again.

"I just, what if I'm not . . . ," Leo starts to say, and then she has to put her hand over her mouth so she doesn't say the worst thing, the thing no one else can say, but it slips out anyway. "What if I'm not enough?"

"Not enough?" Stephanie frowns as she turns toward her. "What do you mean? How are you not enough?"

"Because I couldn't save Nina. I was her sister and I was there, I was *right there*, and I couldn't do anything, and now I'm going to be someone else's sister and what if the same thing happens? What if I can't protect them or help them? What if"—Leo tries to take in air as her chest shakes—"what if I lose her again?"

A dark thought underneath her words, just below the surface: *What if I do something that hurts her?*

She stops talking once Stephanie gathers her into her arms and holds her tight. She doesn't say a word, just lets Leo cry into her shoulder for as long as she needs, and when Leo finally pulls away, she's both relieved that she finally said it and embarrassed that she did.

Stephanie digs around in the console before finding a travel pack of tissues, which she presses into Leo's hand. "How long have you been thinking like this?" she asks, and Leo shrugs. The truth is much harder to explain. It's a thought that dances around the edge of her brain in the middle of the night, as thin as the end of a dream, a dark wisp that curls and cuts like a whip.

"Let me tell you something," Stephanie says, and then she's pulling away to hold Leo by the arms, not too tight, just enough to make her feel like she won't float away. "You are a wonderful sister. You are absolutely *wonderful*, Leo. You have a big heart and I know"—now it's Stephanie's turn to blink fast and swallow hard—"I don't know, actually, what Nina meant to you, and what you meant to her. That's something special between just you two, and it always will be. But I know how much you love her, and I know your kindness and your warmth and your sense of humor and I know that whoever this baby is, she'll be so, so lucky to have you in her life."

Leo freezes. "She?"

Stephanie claps a hand over her mouth. "Oh, shit."

"It's a girl?"

"Your dad is going to be *so* pissed at me."

Leo smiles a little, even though her eyes are still wet. "You're having a girl? For real?"

Stephanie nods and her smile is wobbly. "So they tell me."

Leo's still smiling, even though her chin shakes a little. It's going to take her a while before the word "sister" doesn't rock her from the core. She hopes she can get used to it by the time the baby arrives.

"But I know what you mean," Stephanie tells her. "You know, my mom and I, we don't exactly get along." An understatement if ever there was one, Leo thinks. "And she's put me through so much over the years, and sometimes I look down at this bump and this baby and I think, how am I going to be a mom, you know?" Now it's Stephanie's turn to press her palms to her eyes. "I think, what if all I do is just put this baby through all of this grief because that's all I know? What if I can't do it?"

"You're going to be a great mom!" Leo protests. "Seriously. You've always been so good with me and Nina, especially Nina—"

Stephanie laughs a little. "Your sister definitely posed a challenge at times."

"But see? That's what I mean. You never took it personally. You just loved her anyway."

Stephanie's chin wobbles as she nods. "I can still hear her all the time in our house," she says.

"Me too," Leo admits, and then they're hugging again, but it's not as sad as it was the first time, and Leo feels like something very small has been fixed, a single stitch to hold her heart in place.

"Um, excuse me, ma'am?"

Leo and Stephanie both look up to see the AAA repairman standing by the driver's-side door, sunglasses over his eyes. "What, you've never seen two women crying together inside a broken-down car?" Stephanie says with a laugh as Leo passes her the tissue pack.

The repairman smiles, warm and sure, "Ma'am, trust me, I've seen it all."

In the back of the tow truck, barreling toward home with their SUV and dresser safely attached to the back hitch, Leo reaches for Stephanie's hand, counts the palm trees again, and breathes.

THE FIRST THING Madison says when Leo arrives at the roller rink is, "Okay, you look amazing, please do not kill me."

Leo stops in her tracks. "Well, hi to you, too," she replies. She has to almost shout because the music is so loud, some girl band singing about getting the beat? Having the beat? Something like that. There's an actual disco ball over the rink, giant neon-colored palm trees painted on one wall, and Leo can hear the whoops and shouts of the skaters.

Despite Madison's initial greeting, Leo's a little excited. She hasn't been to a birthday party in, well, a long time, and she hasn't roller-skated since she was six. The person who had been truly excited, though, was Stephanie. Last week, when Leo went over to her dad and Stephanie's for their regular Friday night dinner, she had told them where she was going and Stephanie literally screamed and clapped her hands together.

"That was *my* era!" she cried. "Do you need any clothes? Hair clips? What about hair spray? You definitely need hair spray."

Leo shrugged. "I'll take whatever."

Her dad looked amused. "I can't believe that Madison's dad wants to celebrate fifty years of life by strapping wheels to his feet. Sounds risky."

Stephanie rolled her eyes and then pushed her plate away. "You're no fun. C'mon," she said to Leo, holding out her hand. "You at least need some neon." She had a harder time standing up from her chair, letting out a little "oof" as Leo helped her to her feet. "Maybe a side pony," she added as she headed for the stairs.

"Dad, I'm scared," Leo said.

"You should be," her dad calmly replied, then ate another bite of steak. "Godspeed, kiddo."

Stephanie's enthusiasm had paid off in the outfit department: Leo's wearing striped leggings, an off-the-shoulder sweatshirt that's huge on her, and about half a bottle of hair spray holding up her hair. Stephanie had also insisted on a "statement necklace," which feels way heavier than any piece of jewelry actually should.

"Why am I not going to kill you?" Leo asks Madison now.

"Where did you get those leggings?" Madison replies instead. "Are those vintage?"

Leo's not sure if Stephanie would appreciate being referred to as "vintage," so she settles on "Kind of."

Madison, of course, has a side ponytail, and a ratted-looking tutu, a studded belt, and an old Madonna T-shirt. "This was my mom's," she says, gesturing to it now. "C'mon, let's get you some skates! What size are you?"

"Wait, answer my question first."

Madison just smiles.

Leo crosses her arms.

"I swear I didn't know anything about this until today," she says. "And then I was afraid to tell you because then maybe you wouldn't come and then I'd be stuck here alone with my dad and all of his old-people friends, reliving their 'glory days' or whatever." Madison makes finger quotes around the phrase, looking both embarrassed and disgusted.

"Oh my God, is the doughnut machine broken?" Leo asks. "Because you're right, that would be a deal breaker."

"What? Oh, no, they fired it up when we first got here. My older sister, Chloe, insisted. She's the DJ." Madison gestures toward the DJ booth at the end of the rink, where a girl with long brown hair is wearing giant headphones and looking intently at the computer. "She doesn't really need the headphones," Madison adds. "It's a whole thing."

"So if the doughnuts are safe . . ." Leo trails off, looking at Madison, who's biting her lip.

"I swear I didn't know!"

"*Madison!* Just tell me!"

"East is here."

Leo feels her stomach flip and then settle somewhere around her legwarmer-clad ankles.

"I know you had this big fight or whatever, but my dad hired him to be a videographer-slash-photographer person," Madison continues, and Leo follows her gaze out to the rink, where East is gliding on skates with his camera and stabilizer, wearing a black shirt and torn black jeans, weaving in and out among the skaters, some of whom are, generously speaking, better than others. She hasn't talked to him at all since their big fight six weeks ago, has only seen him in the hallways at school. She hates the fact that she misses him, hates the way her heart jumps a little when she sees him on the rink.

But "East knows how to roller-skate?" is all she says instead.

"Guess so," Madison replies. "Does this mean you're not going to kill me?" She folds her hands and tucks them under her chin, looking both sorry and not very sorry at all.

"Not today," Leo says. "I borrowed this outfit from my step-mom. I don't want to ruin it."

Madison claps her hands together. "Excellent! C'mon, let's get some skates and get this party started!"

It takes Leo a few minutes to get used to the skates, and there's a scary moment where she first hits the rink and feels like every important part of her body is about to go out from under her, but then Madison grabs her hand and steadies her. East is still on the rink, looking both serious and bemused, and when he sees Leo, he stutters and almost falls, too. Leo just looks away, not sure how to start a conversation underneath a disco ball while Prince is singing about this thing called *life*.

She makes several loops around the rink before Leo forgets about East, forgets about her outfit and her necklace and her sister and starts to have fun. Madison's parents' friends look like they're having a blast, even the ones who are, frankly, terrible skaters, and the music is both loud and good, despite the surly DJ.

"The next person who requests 'Hotel California' by the Eagles will be ejected from the building," Chloe says at one point before starting a Cure song. Leo vaguely recognizes it from her dad always listening to the oldies radio station in the car, and it's fine enough, but the rest of the skating crowd loses their mind. "I fuckin' *love* this song!" one guy shouts as he zooms by, and both Madison and Leo laugh with joy as they try to keep up.

"That's my dad!" Madison yells over the music.

"That explains the crown he's wearing!" Leo yells back and Madison happily nods.

East is in the middle of the rink, always present but rarely noticed by anyone except Leo, and she feels the tug between them as she goes around and around, the sweat gathering at the back of her neck, her mouth dry. When a slow song comes on ("This one's for all you *looovvvveerrrsss*," Chloe purrs into the mic), Leo exits the rink and heads for the snack bar, gets herself a cherry-flavored ICEE and a doughnut, and sits down at a plastic table to catch her breath.

Madison finds her a few minutes later, fanning herself as she gets a fountain Coke, then plops down beside Leo to watch the skaters, holding up her drink for a silent "cheers."

Well, Madison watches the skaters. Leo watches East. He glances over at them a few times and Leo quickly busies herself with her doughnut, which, like all doughnuts ever, tastes fantastic. At one point, East zips over to the skate rental and switches out some equipment before coming back with another camera, weaving through the coupled-up skaters and taking some candid shots as people grin and hold up peace signs with their fingers. He looks different when he's working. He doesn't look like East, her friend, if they are still even friends. He looks professional, composed, quick glimpses of what he'll be in the future.

"Girls!" Madison's dad clomps over to them. The plastic crown on his head is slightly askew and someone's thrown some Mardi Gras beads around his neck and he looks flushed and happy and officially fifty years old. "How *amazing* is Chloe doing right now?"

"She'd be the first to agree with you," Madison replies but then smiles sweetly when her dad just presses a kiss to the top of her head.

"You doing good? You need anything? I'm Mike, Madison's dad, by the way."

"Hi," Leo says. "I'm Leo. Happy birthday. Thanks for having me."

"Hey, the more the merrier! Did you get a doughnut yet?"

Leo holds her grease-stained piece of waxed paper in response.

"Excellent!" He claps his hands down on Madison's shoulders. "Gotta get your mom a Sprite, she's parched out there," he says, then clomps away.

"Wow, your dad is . . . ," Leo starts to say, then realizes that she doesn't have the word for that kind of energy.

"He's a lot," Madison says, but she's still smiling ruefully.

"No, I was going to say that he seems really nice."

"He is," Madison agrees. "A lot of nice."

Leo uses the spoon end of her straw to scoop the rest of her drink out of the bottom of the cup. "You said that he was sick a few years ago?"

"Yeah, back when I was in middle school and Chloe was in high school." Madison shakes her Coke, the ice rattling. "It was his thyroid. Things were, uh, kind of scary for a while." She laughs a little, nervously this time. "Sorry, I feel kind of bad telling you this after, you know, Nina."

"It's okay," Leo says, because it is. "I'm glad your dad's still alive."

"Me too. But after he got the all clear, he just started saying 'yes to life,' to quote him. He quit his job, he learned how to windsurf, all of it."

"Wow," Leo says, and tries to imagine her dad either windsurfing or roller-skating. It's impossible. "That's so cool that he's open to everything."

"Yeah," Madison says, but there's a quiet ache to her voice that Leo recognizes. "But sometimes, it's like, he just goes so far. He's really good about encouraging Chloe and me, and he's a great dad, but sometimes . . ." She pauses, shakes her ice again. "Sometimes you want a dad who's going to catch you when you jump off a cliff, not jump right alongside you, you know?"

Leo nods. "Yeah," she says, and thinks of her own dad, who's probably home watching Netflix with Stephanie, probably something that aired ten years ago that everyone else has already seen. "I get it."

"Do I sound like a terrible person?" Madison says. "Because I, like, really love my dad. He's the best."

"You sound like a person person," Leo reassures her. "And your dad sounds like another person. And we all just have to figure out how to navigate around other people, you know?" She shrugs. "Just like out there. On the rink." They watch as two people almost collide, grabbing on to each other and then the wall. "Maybe a little bit better than that, though."

Madison laughs and then shakes the ice in her cup. "So is East still a person you're navigating around?" she asks, and Leo shoots her a glare.

"Tonight, East is a paid employee," Leo clarifies.

"So?" Madison takes the top off her drink and uses it to gesture toward the skating attendant who's cruising in slow circles around the rink, keeping an eye on the crowd. "That guy's a paid employee tonight, too, but Chloe's totally going to make out with him after this."

"Are you serious?"

Madison holds out her hand. "Twenty bucks. I know my sister."

Leo shakes on it.

The party seems to hit a fever pitch a little while later, with everyone on the floor singing along with the music, fist-pumping to the lyrics like they're all back in high school again. Madison and Leo join in when they know the words, and sometimes even when they don't, howling like they mean it. "Don't you want someone to care about *yooooou*?" Leo belts out at one point, just as East glides past her. She's pointing and being super exaggerated about it, and when he goes past, she stops, feeling silly and embarrassed. He doesn't acknowledge her, though, his eyes focused on his own work, and Leo's not sure if that's good or bad.

She's taking another break, leaning against the wall with Madison and waving at people who wave at them as they skate past, when the fast song starts to slow down. "Here's one last slow jam for all you wild things," Chloe says, and yeah, she's definitely making eyes at the skate attendant. Leo's going to have to borrow twenty bucks from someone.

And then Cyndi Lauper's "Time After Time" begins and all of the air leaves Leo's body as a memory rushes in, one she's never had before, something that she thought was lost forever suddenly occupying every cell in her body, transporting her back in time.

"Leo?" Madison says. "You okay?"

Nina's singing. Her beautiful, brilliant sister is in East's car and she's smiling, and for just a second, Leo can almost *feel* her, how happy they were in the moment, the music blasting and East laughing with them, singing about ticking clocks and lost people and going slow—

Madison's saying something, but she's far away from Leo now, and Leo closes her eyes against the light and the sound, grips on to the carpeted wall and feels the warm wind through the car's open window. The air smells like eucalyptus and car exhaust and chlorine, it's whipping Nina's hair around so that she has to hold it back and Leo feels herself reach out and try to touch it, to feel her sister in this memory, in this moment.

She can feel Madison's arm holding her up now, can hear some-one else saying, "I got it, Mads, I got it," and it's confusing because East is talking to her, but he's looking at her before glancing at the road and then laughs as Nina thrusts an imaginary microphone into his face, she's alive and it's like all of their hearts are beating at the same pace, at the same time.

Leo's heart is beating so, so fast.

"Leo," East says, and she opens her eyes to see that he's in front of her now, he's not driving the car anymore, even though she can still feel the music pounding through her body, she can still hear her sister's laugh.

"East," she whispers, scared by how much her voice is shaking. "I can see her." She feels Madison's arm slip from around her waist, leaving her and East on the rink, alone together, surrounded by strangers.

"We sang this song," Leo continues, and her hands are reaching for Nina's, but it's East who catches them.

"We did," he says. His eyes are shiny, almost too bright, and Leo wonders if it's the disco lights or something else. "We were together, all three of us."

"We were really happy," she says, and even though she's smiling, she can feel the tears slipping past her cheeks and over her mouth. All she can hear is this song. She can smell Nina's perfume. She can feel her own hair, tangled and wild. She can see the flashing red lights.

She can feel everything and it's too much to hold.

"It's okay to remember," East says, only his voice is shaking, too, his eyes wide and wild. "*It's okay, Leo.*"

Leo shakes her head. It's like she's woken up from a dream, the soft intimacy of the memories dissolving into a few sparse scenes, impossible to describe to anyone else who wasn't there.

But East was there. And he's here now. Leo tightens her hand around his, squeezing hard, willing him to stay with her, to hang on to her so that she doesn't slip away, too.

"Do you want to go outside?" he asks. "Maybe get some air or—?"

"No. I need to listen," Leo says just as the music soars past both of them, like a car out of control, something neither of them can or could ever stop.

"Okay, okay," East says, and then he's motioning to Madison, he's passing her his camera and she grabs it without a word as East takes Leo's hand and leads her back out onto the rink.

Leo's still crying, she knows she is, but it doesn't matter. East won't let her get lost. His hand is warm and damp against her own, his grip so tight that she can feel his pulse under his palm, and she hangs on just as tight, afraid to let go, afraid to lose him again. When she looks up at him, he keeps his eyes straight ahead and squeezes her hand. She squeezes back, their apologies exchanged and accepted as they go around in circles, bathed in the twinkling light of a false star.

East's face is wet. Leo doesn't know if it's sweat or tears. She guesses it doesn't matter. All salt water is the same, after all.

★

When they leave the roller rink, with Chloe loudly announcing, "You don't have to go home but you can't stay here!" into the microphone before the staff has to take it away from her, the coastal night air feels frigid in contrast to the overheated, humid rink. It's quiet, too, like a hotel hallway or when you get into your car after a loud concert, the absence of noise pushing against your ears, and Leo's sneakers feel weirdly smooth after being on wheels for three hours. She feels like she should glide toward the parking lot, not just walk.

East walks out with her, his camera bag over his shoulder. His face is dry now, surreptitiously wiped on his shirtsleeve as they exited the rink together. Madison was staring at them both with huge eyes, but didn't say a word when East thanked her for guarding his camera, just nodded. When he skated away, she grabbed Leo's arm. "What was *that?*" she hissed.

"It's . . . between us," Leo said, trying to sound casual even as her heart continued to pound, as her skin still felt warm and tight. Madison didn't say anything after that, but Leo could practically hear her thinking about it.

Madison stays behind to help her parents clean up, or so she says, and she gives Leo a hug before she leaves. "I'm really glad you came," she says.

"I am, too," Leo says, and she is. She had *some* fun—and it was the first time in months that she'd been able to go more than thirty minutes without thinking of Nina, of her limp arm dangling off the ambulance gurney. She spins the ring on her finger now, swallows hard, and tries to smile.

East holds the door for her as they walk out, all of Madison's dad's friends laughing and shouting their goodbyes back and forth, their words feeling like they could form a little bubble around East and Leo. They stand next to each other on the curb as the crowd disperses, as their quiet suburban world settles back down.

"You okay?" East asks her and Leo feels a tiny twinge of pleasure that he's the one who's spoken first.

"Yeah," she says. "It was just, you know, a *moment*."

East is looking at her like she's a wild animal, which is weird. It's not like she's never cried in front of him before. "Did you, uh, remember anything else?"

"No, just the song. My dad should be here soon," she adds.

East nods and says, "Yeah, same. I told him eleven just to be safe."

Leo glances at her phone. It's a few minutes before. "You didn't drive?"

"Still grounded." East shrugs. "Another week. He only let me do this because it's a paid gig."

"Oh, cool. I mean, that they paid you. Did you get some good shots?"

East laughs a little, dropping his head down so he can rub the back of his neck. "Leo, what are we——?"

"I'm sorry," she blurts out. *Smooth*, she can hear Nina's voice tell her, annoyed and amused. "Seriously, East, I'm *so* sorry. I just, I freaked out on you, and that whole fight we had last time . . . I didn't think. I don't really care *what* you do, you know? As long as you're happy."

Under the parking lot lights, East's eyes seem to glitter.

"Happy," he repeats. "Are *you* happy, Leo?"

"I don't . . ." She trails off, trying to think of how to respond to such a seemingly simple question. "I don't really know what happy is supposed to feel like anymore, I guess, so I don't know."

He looks at her, the sides of his jaw flexing. "Yeah," he says. "It's like it's not a thing that exists anymore. Not like it used to."

"Nothing is like it used to be," Leo says, and thinks of Stephanie's rounded stomach, Nina's wet hair. "But I guess, if everything had stayed the same, then she wouldn't have been that special. You're *supposed* to change, right? If you just stay the same, then what was the point of loving someone in the first place?"

East doesn't say anything for a long time after that, just looks down at the ground for a while, thumbing at his eyes. "Yeah," he finally sighs, and then he reaches out and grabs Leo, pulling her into his arms and hugging her tight. "I'm really sorry, too," he says.

Leo doesn't realize how much she's missed him until she's touching him again, can feel his sweaty shirt and his rapid pulse, the sheer *aliveness* of East. She's missed the rudder of their shared boat, now the only two people in the world who know what that song means, who once heard it under a starry sky in a brilliant, perfect world. The intimacy of that is something Leo will hold for the rest of her life, the ability to share loss without diluting it. She wonders, faintly, if grief is stronger than love, if love is so strong because the loss of it can be so sharp.

They're still hugging when East's dad pulls up, but they don't let go. It takes East's dad getting out of the car, a frown creased across his face, a frown that Leo vaguely remembers from Nina's funeral. "Easton?" he says tentatively.

East sniffles and lets go of Leo, then flings himself into his dad's arms. "Hey," his dad says, even as he's embracing him. "Hey, buddy, what's . . ."

Leo sees the familiar lights of her dad's car sweep across the parking lot. There are only a few skating stragglers left in the parking lot, all of them too absorbed in their own conversation to see East and his dad rocking back and forth. East is crying now, loud and gulping, and Leo gives a little wave to his dad before walking away so her dad doesn't have to drive up right between them.

"Is East okay?" her dad asks as soon as she gets in the car. He's wearing old dad jeans and a UCLA sweatshirt, his alma mater. The clothes are so worn and threadbare (and Leo's pretty sure there's a food stain near the collar) that they'd normally exasperate her, but now the familiarity is warm and safe.

"He's okay," she replies, then aims the heating vent toward her. "Sometimes it's just a lot, you know?"

Her dad looks at her then, giving her a sad smile that doesn't quite reach his eyes. "I do," he whispers, and Leo is about to tell him what she's remembered, the moment, the happiness, how her heart felt both thrilled and shattered, but then he says, "You want French fries? I told Stephanie I'd get her some," and the moment is gone.

"That sounds good," she says instead. "I need some salt."

"Did you have fun?"

"Yeah," she says, then sends a wicked glance his way. "A bunch of old people skating to old people music, but otherwise it was okay."

"Hey now!" her dad cries, faux insulted, and she giggles as he starts to muss up her hair. "Those are classics! Did they play Bon Jovi? I used to listen to him all the time in high school."

"Yeah, thirty years ago!" Leo says. "Like I said, *old*."

"You kids with your Tic Tac music or whatever . . ."

"Oh my God. *Dad*."

Leo can see East and his father in her dad's rearview mirror as they leave the parking lot, East getting smaller and smaller until she can't see him at all. When she turns back, her dad's hand is on the console and she reaches for it, putting her fingers around his.

"What's all this?" he asks, glancing down at her.

"Just . . . nothing," she says, then looks away when her dad raises an eyebrow.

"Okay," he replies, then tightens his own hand in hers as they drive away.

YOU *HAVE TO* come to my dad's birthday party."

Madison is talking around a mouthful of a turkey sandwich. Leo sits across from her on the brick wall at school, poking at her own hummus and carrots, which always sounded a lot more appetizing in the morning than it did at actual lunchtime.

"I'm serious." Madison swallows and continues. "If you don't, it'll just be me and my sister and parents and a bunch of middle-aged people roller-skating." She shudders dramatically.

"Well, when you put it that way," Leo teases, then smiles when Madison throws a piece of shredded lettuce at her. "Hey, watch the hair. And I haven't roller-skated in *years*."

"Me either," Madison says. "But there's a snack bar."

Leo raises an eyebrow. "Good snacks?"

"Apparently there's a doughnut machine."

"Say no more. I'll see you there," Leo replies, then smiles when Madison laughs. It's been a minute since she's had a friend and it feels nice to sit with someone at lunch.

"Good!" Madison says. "I'll text you all the info."

"It's kind of cool that your dad wants to throw a party for his birthday," Leo says. For her dad's last birthday, she and Nina and Stephanie had gotten him an ice cream cake and then watched a movie together.

"Well, it's a big birthday," Madison says, sounding like she's parroting her dad. "And you know, he's all about 'celebrating life,' especially since he's turning fifty."

"What about Sophie and Olivia?" Leo asks.

"Oh, I invited them, too," Madison says, pulling the tomato out of her sandwich with her pink-painted fingernails. "But it's Olivia's weekend with her mom and Sophie said that it's her and Dylan's six-month anniversary that Saturday."

Leo isn't exactly heartbroken by this news. "Nice," she says. "Has anyone told Dylan yet?"

Madison giggles. "I know, right? I feel like the total time they've been together is, like, six days, if you count all the days they've been broken up." She shakes her head. "The heart wants what it wants, I guess."

"Unfortunately," Leo agrees, and moves on to her green apple slices. She doesn't even like green apples that much, but they had been Nina's favorite and Leo guesses that her mom's just in the habit of buying them. Leo doesn't have the heart to tell her.

"Sooooo," Madison says. "Have you, um, talked to East at all?"

"Subtle," Leo says.

"Yeah, sorry, nuance really isn't my thing," Madison says. "But you've had lunch with me every single day so far this semester. You used to hang out with East at least half the time. You two were always together. Did you break up?"

"We did not 'break up'!" Leo immediately yelps. "There's nothing to break up! Why, is that what everyone's saying?"

"No one's saying anything!" Madison says. "They're too busy talking about Dylan and Sophie's latest fight this morning. Did you hear about it? Apparently she threw a giant-sized smoothie at his head."

"Wow."

"Yeah, I know, right? She didn't have her glasses on so she missed by like six feet, but still. They both got detention this afternoon, so they'll probably be back together by four o'clock."

"Ah, l'amour," Leo sighs, and hopes that's enough to distract Madison.

"So why don't you and East hang out anymore?"

Guess not.

"We, um, we sort of got into a fight?" Leo says it like it's a question and not something that actually happened. "But we're not together, we've never been like that. He's—he was Nina's boyfriend, not mine. We're just friends. Or we were. I don't know, it's all kind of a mess right now."

"Mess" was a pretty moderate way to describe it. They hadn't talked at all since their terrible fight in the park earlier that month, and when they saw each other at school, they both went out of their way to walk in wide circles around each other. The anger Leo had felt that day had faded into a muted stubbornness, and judging from her silent phone and the way he refused to look at her, East felt the same way.

"Well, that sucks," Madison says, then takes a sip of her water. "But you two will figure it out. I have faith."

"I'm glad someone does," Leo says. "You don't like tomatoes?"

Madison makes a face. "You want them? Help yourself."

Leo does.

"Hey! Leo!"

Leo glances up to see Kai walking toward her, his thumbs hooked under the straps of his backpack, looking almost sheepish. She hasn't seen him since that terrible Christmas party, the one where she was (if she's being truly honest here) kind of mean to him.

"Hi," she says and when she smiles, Kai's smile gets ten times bigger. "Where are you going?"

"Oh, you know, just home."

"Same," Leo says, and because she still feels bad about the party, adds, "Want to breach enemy lines and walk with me?"

Kai's eyes soften. "Yeah, sure. Of course."

They walk in a semi-awkward silence for a little bit, waiting at the intersection without talking before crossing together. Once they get toward their neighborhood, Leo finally speaks up.

"Hey. I'm really sorry I was mean to you that night at the Christmas party."

Kai frowns a little. "Mean? You weren't mean."

"I feel like I yelled at you a few times."

"Oh yeah, no. You *definitely* yelled at East, but we're cool." Kai scuffs his worn Vans on the sidewalk as they walk. "I was just riding shotgun that night anyway."

"Well, okay. If you say so." Leo looks down at her own shoes. "How's East doing?"

Kai is quiet for a short minute. "You know . . ."

"Actually, not really," she says. "We haven't talked in"—she pretends to think about it, like she doesn't know exactly how many days it's been—"a while, I guess?"

"Whoa," Kai breathes, and Leo stares at her shoes a little harder, embarrassed.

"I kind of thought something happened," Kai replies when she doesn't answer. "He never talks about you anymore. He doesn't really talk about anything, if I'm being honest."

Leo hasn't been aware that East has ever talked about her before. This is news. "Did he tell you about . . . ?"

"Yeah." Kai sounds sad and Leo understands why. "His dad is crazy pissed—sorry, sorry, his dad is *super* pissed."

Leo tries not to smile and fails miserably. "Yeah, I can see why."

"I think East is probably grounded until graduation."

"His dad grounded him?"

"For lying, yeah. His dad was totally surprised when East told him the truth about everything."

"Well, that makes two of us," Leo says. "I also, um, said a few stupid things to him. You know, in the moment and everything."

Kai shrugs. "Well, I guess everyone gets to say a few stupid things now and then."

"I brought Nina into it, though."

"Oh."

"Yeah." Leo's cheeks go red and hot, embarrassed to confess this to Kai. "I was mean."

"You're allowed to be mean. Have you said you're sorry yet?"

Leo shakes her head. "I don't think East wants to talk to me right now. And I don't know if I should talk to him."

"Well, if it makes you feel better, he's not really talking to anyone. It's not just you."

Leo pretends to think about it for a moment. "Half credit," she says, which makes Kai laugh. He has really nice teeth, she thinks, and then feels like a weirdo creeper for thinking that.

When they get to her house, Leo gestures toward it. "This is me," she says, and then feels stupid for pointing out the obvious.

But Kai frowns a little as he peers toward the front windows. "What are those things in the window?"

Leo looks at the two small, furry triangles that are peeking out of the bottom of the windowsill. "Oh, that's just Denver, our corgi. He's super short."

"That's sweet that he waits for you."

"Oh, no, he's not waiting for me. He's waiting for his archenemy, the mail carrier. He goes berserk every day. We tried to distract him a bunch at first, but now we just let him bark his head off."

In the window, the small, furry triangles of Denver's ears quiver with anticipation.

"Well, it'd be cool to meet Denver sometime," Kai says.

"I'll see what he thinks." Leo grins. "I make no promises on his behalf."

Kai laughs again and starts to walk backward. Leo thinks that maybe she should invite him in, but she's not sure if her mom's home and she has no idea what the rules are regarding boys in the house. Nina had never brought anyone to their house before, preferring to go out and do things rather than hang out at home with her mom and little sister lurking around.

"Well, see you later," Kai says.

"Yeah, see you," Leo replies, but takes her time going inside, waiting until he walks around the corner before opening the door and letting herself in.

JANUARY 6
142 DAYS AFTER THE ACCIDENT

LEO ALWAYS THOUGHT that New Year's was the most depressing holiday, mostly because it usually heralded the end of their holiday break and the thought of going back to school after two weeks of gift-giving, Christmas lights, and no early morning alarm was, quite frankly, depressing. She never looked forward to it the way some people did, clinking glasses at midnight and wearing party store top hats and silly New Year glasses. Nina, who would have had a party to celebrate Groundhog Day if their parents had let her, of course loved it. She used to come in and wake Leo up right at midnight, and Leo remembers how she used to bat her sister away, how Nina always succeeded in planting a kiss on top of her head while fondly calling her a party pooper.

But not this year.

This year, Leo actively sat up and looked through Nina's phone, waiting impatiently for the digital numbers to turn to 12:00 a.m. When they did, she cried a little, even though nothing felt different, even though it was only a second's difference between the new and the old. This was the first year of her life that she would spend entirely without her sister, and Leo wanted to rip the Band-Aid off, to move on into a new beginning even though she had no map, no plan, and no energy to do any of it.

School in January was depressing, all of the holiday decorations now removed, leaving bare cinder block walls and boring window displays in the library. Even the teachers and staff seemed grumpier than usual, everything and everyone just a little bit grayer than they had been two weeks earlier. The weather was uncooperative, too, giving them dark skies and buckets of rain for three days straight. The neighboring cities worried about mudslides, and Leo spent most days slugging through puddles of water, soaking the Converse shoes her dad and Stephanie had given her for Christmas.

It hadn't been the easiest day, but by the time they made it to Christmas afternoon, Leo felt like she could breathe a little easier. Leo and her mom had recovered from Christmas Eve, Christmas morning was over, and by the time she got to her dad's and Stephanie's house on Christmas afternoon, Leo felt like someone was waving a checkered flag at the end of a race. *You're almost through the worst holiday season ever!*

She and her dad and Stephanie exchanged gifts, including a little board book version of *Goodnight Moon* that Leo had gotten for the new baby. It felt generic, but Leo had seen it in a bookstore and found herself picking it up, reading through the words, and taking it up to the cashier. Stephanie and her dad loved it. "It's their first book!" Stephanie had said. She was getting rounder everywhere, her cheeks and belly and even her hands, her fingers looking swollen, and she seemed tired but happy. Her dad, though, just looked tired, and Leo recognized that lost sort of look in his eyes, the one he always managed to blink away whenever Stephanie looked up at him.

She recognized it in his eyes because she spent so much time seeing it in her own.

After they opened gifts, they went for a walk and then had turkey chili, Leo and her dad serving it up while Stephanie rested on the couch, scrolling through her phone. She had hired a new social media assistant who was taking care of replying to comments, and Leo could hear her annoyed *tsks* as she read through them.

"You should hire me!" Leo yelled out to her. "I can comment with the best of them!"

Stephanie laughed. "You'd write a whole paragraph every single time!"

"Nina would have responded to each one with just the puking emoji," her dad said as he cut up the onions. Leo was grating cheese and trying very hard to not grate her fingers at the same time. "Even when you tried to text her, you'd be lucky to get a thumbs-up from her."

"She preferred in-person contact," Leo agreed, but then set down the cheese and went over to her dad, wrapping her arms around his waist, hanging on in a silent question of *Are you okay?*

Her dad let her hug him, and Leo felt the shudder through his spine as he worked through it. Before, it had been so strange to see her dad cry or be sad. He wasn't some big manly, stoic, "only girls cry" type of guy, but he was reserved and protective of his feelings, the complete opposite of how Nina had been.

"Stephanie's been such a trouper," he said.

Once he was better, he wiped at his eyes and said, "Damn onions." Leo went back to her cheese and when her dad reached out to stroke her hair in a silent thank-you, she didn't duck away.

At dinner, Stephanie asked the question that had been floating around them all afternoon. "So, how was Christmas Eve with your mom? Was it . . . ?"

Leo thought of everything that had happened just one night earlier.

Her hair still smelled faintly of ash and smoke.

"Fine," she finally replied. "It was fine."

At school on the first Monday of the new year, Leo plods through the hall with her books hugged close to her chest, even though she's wearing her backpack, her new sneakers squeaking on the floor. The kids around her are shouting hellos to one another, and Leo says hi to a few of them as she makes her way to her locker.

"Leo!" someone shouts, and Leo looks up from her lock to see Madison bounding toward her. It's raining, not exactly freezing out or anything, but she's wearing both a scarf and a hat with a pom-pom on top and a giant heart knitted into the front. "Hey! How was your break?"

Madison had texted Leo a few times over the break, and Leo had politely responded, once with just emojis, something that she's sure would have made Nina proud. Madison had even tried to get together, but Leo had finally said, *Thanks, but I think I need to spend some time with my family right now,* and Madison had replied with *TOTALLY get it OMG* and then a row of pink hearts.

But here she is, looking like the human equivalent of a stuffed animal you could buy in a hospital gift shop. Nina would have rolled her eyes behind Madison's back, maybe made a snide comment about a forest missing its Bambi, but Leo finds herself liking Madison more and more. She keeps showing up and that, in Leo's mind, is no small thing.

"Hi," Leo says now. "Cute hat."

"Oh, thanks." Madison reaches up and gives the pom-pom a gentle pat. "My nana knitted it for me for Christmas. She has arthritis so, you know, a big deal." She smiles again, softer this time. "How was your Christmas, for real?"

"It was fine," Leo says. In one of the grief workbooks, right before it had burned up, she had seen a passage that talked about the word "fine" standing for "fucked up, insecure, neurotic, emotional," and Leo has decided to embrace the acronym.

"Oh, good," Madison says, and the relief on her face makes Leo feel guilty, like she's somehow responsible for all of the eye-rolling Nina would have done. "How are your mom and dad doing?"

The last thing Leo wants to do is talk about her parents and their feelings while, three lockers away, Jamie Masterson is making out with Evie Engels like they haven't seen each other since Thanksgiving.

"Um, they're good, you know," Leo says, and Madison just nods in sympathy.

"Totally," she says. "Oh my God, did you hear? Alice got into Harvard early decision."

"Wow," Leo says, even though she doesn't know who Alice is.

"Yeah, the guidance counselor is giving everyone high fives like *she's* the one who's going to Cambridge." Madison rolls her eyes a little, and it's ten times sweeter than Nina's eye rolls ever were. "But isn't that awesome? Alice is *soooo* nice, too."

"I'm really happy for her," Leo replies, and the weird thing is that she is, kind of. She's not against good things happening to people. Nina used to say, "It's nice when nice happens to nice" and Leo thinks of that now as she and Madison walk toward their English class. Good for Alice!

But by lunchtime, it hits Leo that a) she hasn't seen East all day, not even in their shared calculus class, and b) he hasn't said anything to her about his early action college applications. Wasn't he supposed to apply to a bunch, RISD and NYU and Pratt? Hadn't that been his plan, or more accurately, his and *Nina's* plan? Maybe it was bad news. Maybe he had gotten rejected from all of them. Or maybe he was just sick after the holidays and Leo was doing the brain equivalent of doom scrolling? She sends him a quick text: *You ok????*

Leo checks her phone in between classes, but he hasn't responded. There's a picture from Stephanie, though, of a crib halfway set up and her dad sitting amid the rubble, looking both frustrated and amused. *My hero*, Stephanie had texted, and Leo quickly sends back the laughing/crying emoji, even though she doesn't feel like doing either one of those things.

As soon as Leo gets home from school, she drops her bag on the kitchen table and walks over to East's house.

The rain has stopped but the skies are still puffy and gray, filled with warning that they could start dumping water at any time. The hills that surround their neighborhood are usually sun-scorched and overgrown, but today they're a brilliant green from the rare storm. It seems like she can almost feel the color in her lungs, it's so vibrant.

Her shoes, of course, get wet again. She doesn't even want to know what her hair looks like.

She knocks twice on East's front door before he finally opens it. He's got sweatpants and a long-sleeved shirt on, and a deep sleep crease on one cheek. "Hey!" Leo says. "You didn't answer any of my texts today."

"Oh, sorry." He lets out a breath as he runs his hand back and forth over his hair. "Yeah, my phone must have died."

Leo frowns a little. He could have easily texted her back from his computer. "Uh, okay," she says instead. "Do you feel all right?"

"Yeah, I'm fine."

Leo's ears perk up.

"You sure?"

"Leo, is there a reason . . . ?" He trails off, waving his hand in front of him. Behind him, the house seems eerily quiet in a way that rattles Leo. She's been in a house that quiet before, in the days after Nina died, and the way everything seems so tense that it gives her a chill. She doesn't want to be there anymore. She doesn't want *East* to be there anymore.

"Want to walk to the park?" she says instead.

East looks pained. "I can't really . . . oh fuck it," he says once Leo's face falls a little. It's like they're in a fight, but they're not. He brought her a Christmas gift, hugged her mom. People who are in fights don't do those things . . . right?

"Give me a minute," he says, and then he's shutting the front door in her face before Leo can even respond. She looks down at her wet shoes and sighs. Maybe she should have asked for rain boots instead.

It takes a few minutes before East finally opens the door again. He's wearing actual pants now, plus the ever-present pink hoodie, and has a baseball cap pulled low over his tangled hair. Leo can barely see his eyes and once he's locked the door behind him, he starts walking without even waiting for her.

Once, right before her mom and dad finally split up for good, the four of them did a puzzle as a family. The Grand Canyon, 1,000 pieces. They worked on it at night after dinner at their coffee table, but it turned out that Denver had worked on it during the day while they were all at work or school, and by the time they finished, they realized that he had eaten a few center pieces. "That was the most expensive puzzle we ever bought," her dad had sighed once they got Denver—and the bill—back from the vet. And even though it was still clearly the Grand Canyon, the missing pieces gave it a jagged, almost malicious look.

That's how Leo feels now as she trots alongside East, like she can kind of tell what's going on, but there are key pieces she doesn't have. His steps are long and fast, and she feels like a circus pony trying to keep up with him. It's not a great feeling. "Why are we running?" she teases him and he slows down after that, but even from under the brim of his hat, Leo can see that he's stone-faced.

"Where's Denver?" he asks as they wait at the crosswalk.

"Oh, he had a previous engagement," Leo says. She's trying to make him smile, but all she succeeds in doing is making herself feel stupid. Nina, for all of her bluster and chattiness and brouhaha, always knew how to stay quiet when it mattered.

Leo wonders why she can't seem to do that now.

The park isn't too crowded since school just got out an hour or so ago. There's an elderly couple toddling around the path near the playground and East and Leo follow them. They do an entire lap before Leo finally stops. East is so set on walking that he goes right past her and has to double back. "What's wrong?" he asks.

"You tell me," Leo says. "You don't respond to any of my texts for days, you weren't in school today, and now you're acting like you're mad at me or something!"

East closes his eyes for a brief second. "I told you, my phone—"

"Your phone did not die," she says. "Don't even. And we're actually face-to-face now. You don't need a working phone to talk to me."

East looks away. "I didn't feel well this morning. How was school?"

"It was school," she says, then decides to poke a little bit. "Some people got their early action acceptances over the break."

East nods. "Did Alice get into Harvard?"

"Yes! How did you—Does *everyone* know Alice?"

"She's been talking about Harvard since kindergarten. Or her mom and dad have been, anyway." East looks away again, almost like he's searching for a distraction or an escape. "Anyway. I'm not mad at you."

"Well, then, what the hell?" Leo opens her arms and then lets them slap down against her sides. "You give me this amazing Christmas gift and then *nothing*?"

"Leo," East says, so quietly that Leo can barely hear him. "It's not about you, okay?"

It stings and Leo suddenly feels small, a bratty little sister forever chasing after the older kids. "East," she says, and hates the tiny whine in her voice. "What happened? Did you . . . Did you not get in anywhere?"

East laughs a little, but it doesn't make Leo feel any better, and he collapses down onto a bench and puts his head in his hands. "No," he finally says, his voice muffled against his palms. "I didn't get in anywhere."

The weight of his words hits Leo, making her drop down next to him. She thinks of the photo he gave her on Christmas Eve, the video she watched him film up on the fire roads, him and Nina talking about college and the future, all of it done with such care and talent and love. Leo had seen a lot of amateur photographers on

Instagram, especially boys like East, but there was nothing she had seen that matched what he could do, the way he could make people feel with a photo.

"Not anywhere?" she asks before she can stop herself. "*Really?*"

East looks at her. "Yeah, that's what 'I didn't get in anywhere' means, Leo."

"No, I know, I just . . ." No matter what she says next, Leo knows it's going to be wrong. She says it anyway. "East, you're so *good*, though."

"Leo." He presses the heels of his hands against his forehead, making a low growl that reminds Leo of Denver whenever the mail carrier approaches their front door: a completely empty threat.

"Leo," he says again. "I didn't get in anywhere because I didn't *apply* anywhere."

"Well, that's not true," she says. "You were working on your portfolio. I *saw* you."

"I did work on it." He looks at her and his eyes are red and tired. "But I didn't send it in."

"But why?"

"Because!" he shouts, and that's when Leo realizes that she's been shouting, too. "Because I don't know, what if they say it's shit? What if they looked at everything and said, this guy's a fucking idiot for even trying?" East mimics an imaginary critic. "Wasn't his mom Sloane Easton, the photographer? Why is his stuff so terrible then?"

"They wouldn't say that!" Leo cries, thinking of East's mom's photos, the ones that line his bedroom wall, a quiet shrine to her. She doesn't know when she stands up, but now she's towering over him, trembling in her damp shoes but ready to fight all of East's imaginary enemies for him. "But it's not too late, right? You can just apply with everyone else. It doesn't have to be early action." This soothes her, the idea that they can finally fix something that went so wrong.

But East shakes his head. "No, Leo. I'm not going to apply. I don't want to anymore."

Leo's deeply angry all of a sudden. She hasn't felt like this since the incident at the party, that white-hot pulse pushing up under her skin. "But that was your plan—"

"No, that was *our* plan," he says. His voice is quiet, but not in a soothing way. It's quiet like the hospital after Nina died, quiet like Leo's mom passed out in Nina's bedroom. It's quiet not on purpose, but because it simply doesn't have the energy to be anything else.

"It was our plan," he says again. "Nina at UCLA, me in New York. We talked about it all the time, how we'd make it work. And now if I do it, it's like, fuck, I don't know, like I'm leaving her behind."

Leo feels her fingernails pushing into her palms and realizes that she's clenched her hands into fists. "No," she says. "It's like you're going forward, East! It's like—"

"You don't get to tell me how I feel, Leo."

"But you have to go!"

"Look!" East shouts, and now he's standing up, too. "I don't have to do *anything*, okay, and especially something that you want me to do just because Nina can't do it anymore!"

His words are a kick in the shin, but Leo doesn't flinch. "You're right!" she yells. "Nina can't do it! But you can! I thought that's what you wanted!"

"What I *want*," East huffs, "is to finally sleep at night without seeing Nina's body crumpled on the ground! What I want is to stop seeing you lying on the ground next to her, Leo! Fuck, I thought you were both, I thought that you had . . ." He's making terrible gasping sounds now, and Leo can see his hands shaking before he shoves them into his hoodie pocket.

"I miss her so much and I can't just go and do all the things we were supposed to do together because all it does is remind me that I'm doing them alone! You said it yourself that night after the party, that I'm the only one who remembers," he continues. "But I don't know what's worse, remembering it or not, because it's so fucking *lonely* being the only person in the entire world who remembers that moment."

He pushes his hood back and yanks his hat off his head, then smooths his hair back, and pulls it down again, grunting a little with the effort. "All I want to do is leave and stay at the same time and it sucks."

Leo's breathing hard, like she's the one who's just been shouting. The elderly couple who were walking around the park are now shooting worried glances in their direction. "Well, I'm sorry to be such a disappointment to you," she spits back at him. "I'm sorry that my brain is so fucking broken that I can't remember the worst moment of my entire life."

"Wait, what? We *talked* about this, Leo!" East cries. "That's not fair!"

"No, it's *not* fair," she shouts. "Nothing has been fair since that night, and it's not going to get better by just staying here!"

"Well, then, fine," East says. "What are *you* doing, Leo? Besides staying home all the time and going through Nina's phone?"

"I don't just 'stay home' all the time!" she yells, and oh yeah, the couple across the park now look officially worried, and there are a few moms at the playground who are glancing up at them, too.

In retrospect, the park was probably not the best place to have this conversation.

"I go out!" Leo insists. "Did you already forget the Christmas party? Where I had to bail *you* out? The party that you told me not to go to, remember?"

East's cheeks are flushed a deep red, the tips of his ears a dark pink. "I told you—!"

"Nina won't get to do anything ever again!" Leo yells. "Not ever again, East!"

"Do you think I don't know that?!"

"And here you are, you can do so much, you can do *anything*, and instead you do nothing? That's such bullshit!" Leo stomps at the ground even though she knows it makes her look about three years old. "She would *not* want to hear this. She—she'd be angry. She'd be disappointed."

Across the playground, a mom starts to walk over, tentative steps that make her look like a deer about to walk into a hunter's trap. *Save yourself*, Leo thinks.

"Leo." East is so close to her that she can smell his laundry detergent. "Don't. You'll fucking break me, Leo. I can't hold both her and you up at the same time."

Leo starts to cry. "Fuck you," she says. "You're in so much pain? You think I'm *not*?! And the one thing I've ever asked you for, you refuse to give me. You won't help me remember. And now, you won't do the thing you know Nina wants. You—you're ruining everything!" and she hates that she says it because she doesn't mean it at all. She wants to hug East around his waist, hang on to him, the one solid thing she has, but it feels like they've both blown it up into pieces that can never fit together again, their broken puzzle writ large.

"Everything okay over there?" the mom calls, and both East and Leo give her a thumbs-up even though there are tears on both of their cheeks. She doesn't look reassured.

"I'm going home," Leo says. "You can stay here, go there, do whatever you want. I'm out."

"Leo."

"You're wasting it!" she shouts at him, and she's not even sure what she means, but she feels both heavy and light-headed at the same time.

When she gets home, she's drenched from the clouds that finally opened up again, and her mom is in the kitchen, cleaning out the refrigerator, storage containers littering the countertops. "What happened to you?" she says, glancing up from the produce drawer.

"Forgot an umbrella," Leo mumbles, then goes into the laundry room for a towel.

"Hey, have you seen East lately?" her mom calls after her, and Leo freezes. She has no idea if there's a right answer to that question.

"Yes," she finally says.

"His dad called me today." Leo's mom holds up her phone like it's evidence. "He said that he got home after work and East wasn't there, didn't leave a note or anything. And that his phone was off."

"He probably just forgot," Leo says.

"Did you know that East didn't apply to any colleges? His dad just found out yesterday. He's really worried about him." Her mom pulls a plastic container out of the fridge and looks at it critically. "When did we last have spaghetti and meatballs?" she mutters to herself, then throws the whole thing in the trash. When she turns back to Leo, her eyes widen in alarm.

"Sweetie!" she says. "Why are you crying?"

DECEMBER 24, 10:17 P.M.
129 DAYS AFTER THE ACCIDENT

LEO HADN'T BEEN sure how Christmas Eve was going to go this year.

She knew it'd be different, to put it mildly.

She just hadn't counted on the fire department showing up.

The firefighters seem pretty unimpressed by their sooty fireplace and their now very smoky living room. Denver stands at the front door, wagging his tail and butt fiercely as they all troop in, and Leo scoops him up as the firefighters survey the living room.

If any of them notice the remnants of what was in the fireplace, they don't mention it.

"I'm so sorry," Leo's mom keeps saying. "I just completely forget to open the flue. I'm so sorry to bring you out here on Christmas Eve." Leo can't help but think that if this had happened the year before, they could have offered the firefighters Christmas cookies or hot cocoa or something. That had always been their routine when it was their turn to do the holiday with their mom: cookies, cocoa, and a new set of matching pajamas for Leo and Nina, ones that they often wore into late spring, way past the time for holiday-themed clothes. They'd take a picture in front of the fireplace every year, too, and it's not like they displayed them in frames on the wall or even looked at them that often, but Leo knew that they were all tucked away in a photo album, starting with the one where Leo was a baby and Nina was grinning into the camera and hanging on to her squirmy, bald little sister.

Nobody mentioned matching pajamas this year. Nobody took a photo in front of the fireplace. Nobody made cookies or cocoa.

Now, though, their fireplace is being inspected by three firefighters wearing reflective gear.

"Happens every year," one of them says to her mom. "You sure you don't have any smoke inhalation?"

Both Leo and her mom shake their heads. Denver wags his tail and shakes his butt, patiently waiting for a head scratch. He's rewarded for his efforts a few minutes later when the firefighters stomp out of the house. They shut off their lights and don't use the siren when they leave, which makes Leo feel grateful. The sound of a siren still sets her teeth on edge, makes her entire body tense up and wait for something that has already, tragically happened.

After they leave, and after Leo's mom wraps herself in a sweater and goes across the lawn to reassure their concerned neighbors that they're all fine and it was just a silly fireplace thing, the two of them stand in the hallway and look at each other. They don't have any smoke inhalation, but the house still smells like they're in the center of a heavily used firepit during camping season.

"Well," her mom says, then raises her arms and slaps her hands onto her hips. "What do you say to a hotel tonight?"

Leo smiles.

An hour later, they're standing in the lobby of a Westin hotel that they had driven past at least two hundred times but had never set foot in before. There's a festively lit Christmas tree just next to the check-in desk and some jazzy song that Leo keeps trying to recognize as her mom speaks with the hotel employee. Denver's standing between them, clipped to his leash and looking around with pure doggie joy on his face. Leo's not sure if he's excited at the prospect of meeting so many new people (and the prospect of these new people giving him belly rubs) or he's just happy to be out of the smoky house.

"'Joy to the World'!" Leo finally cries, and both the clerk and her mom turn to look at her. "Sorry, I was trying, the song," she says, then points up at the ceiling. "I was just . . . Anyhoodle."

They only have rooms with one king-sized bed, which means that they have to share, but then the employee passes them their room keys and says, "Room service closes at midnight tonight," and Leo's eyebrows go up a little.

Leo also hadn't envisioned her Christmas Eve involving a hotel room, with appetizers being delivered to the room, but if she's learned anything this year, it's that it doesn't matter what she thinks might happen. The universe will just take hold of the reins and charge ahead anyway.

Which is how Leo and her mom end up in matching white

bathrobes, eating mozzarella sticks and French fries on the massive king-sized bed, watching a Hallmark movie about the spirit of Christmas. Her mom gets a glass of wine and Leo orders a Coke, which comes in a glass bottle that feels fancier than just a can. They even have linen napkins, which are a step up from their normal routine of just ripping some paper towels off the roll.

Leo dips her fry in some ranch dressing before popping it into her mouth. Denver's curled up at the end of the bed, his head on his paws. He smells like peanut butter, which room service has sent up after the guy who delivered their food said that Denver reminded him of the dog he had had growing up. Denver has never had individual peanut butter packs before tonight, and Leo suspects that Denver's future was going to be disappointing once he returned home to dry kibble and the occasional teeth-cleaning treat.

"They totally filmed this in Calabasas," Leo says, pointing at the TV screen with the end of a mozzarella stick. Her mom, who had taken out her contacts and put on her glasses, raises her eyebrows over the tortoiseshell frames.

"Yeah, that snow definitely doesn't look real," she replies. "They must be sweating to death under all of those scarves and earmuffs."

"Nina and I used to sneak out of bed and watch these movies," Leo says. "You and Dad would always pass out on the couch, you never even heard us."

Her mom looks bemused. "How old were you?"

"I don't know. Maybe six and eight? It was Nina's idea. She said they were romantic."

Her mom smile gets a little bigger. "She always loved love, didn't she? Her big heart." She turns to look at Leo. "Did you like watching them?"

Leo swirls her mozzarella stick in the marinara sauce, then takes a bite. Even lukewarm mozzarella sticks are delicious, she decides. "I think it was just more fun to stay up late together. It didn't matter what we were watching.

"We were," Leo says slowly, like her mouth is trying out these words for the first time, "the only two people who knew we did that. And now I'm the only one who knows, at least until right now. But there were all these things we shared together, these adventures, and now I don't share them with anyone.

"I think that's what I miss the most about her, you know? The adventures. And the possibility of more adventures."

Leo can't tell if her mom's eyes are tearing up, or if it's just the TV light reflecting off her glasses. "I know what you mean," she says after a minute. "She was an adventure from the minute she was born, that's for sure. When she was born, she came out just staring at us. She didn't make a sound. I'm pretty sure she was judging your dad and me. And rightly so." She laughs a little. "We had no idea what we were doing. Still don't, sometimes."

Leo takes a sip of her Coke. "Mom?"

"Yes?"

"Stephanie's pregnant."

Leo had no idea she was going to say those words, but here they are, hanging between her and her mom, their presence so loaded that Leo can almost see them, as if they're in a little cartoon dialogue bubble.

Her mom blinks once, then twice. Her wineglass is halfway to her mouth. She stops, then sets it down, then picks it back up, and takes a long slug. "*Stephanie* Stephanie?" she asks.

"Dad's wife, Stephanie," Leo clarifies. "That would be the one, yes."

Her mom takes off her glasses. On the screen, an actress in a purposefully bad wig is screaming at another actress. "Well," she says, "that is . . . something. When did you find out?"

"A couple of weeks ago," Leo admits, since that's *technically* when her dad and Stephanie told her, and not when she actually found out about it. "I meant to tell you earlier, but yeah." She waves her hand behind her, gesturing toward all the things that have happened between her and her mom over the past month. "It just never felt like the right time. As opposed to now, of course," she adds. On the TV screen, the actors gasp as the joy of Christmas is revealed.

Her mom smiles a little at Leo's attempt at humor, which makes Leo feel a little less like their car is about to go over the cliff. "And how do you feel about this?" Mom asks.

Leo shrugs and reaches for another French fry. They're shoestring, Nina's least favorite variety of fry. "I shouldn't have to eat at least five French fries in order to equal one French fry!" she would complain.

Leo eats it anyway.

"I don't know," she says in answer to her mom's question. "It's fine, I guess." It's not fine, of course, and Leo knows exactly how she feels, but describing those feelings is a lot harder. All the words she has for feelings—"happy," "sad," "angry," "tired"—are black-and-white terms. There's nothing there for the grayness of it all, how she can feel all of those things at the same time and yet none of them ever seem to cancel each other out, or even blunt one another's sharpness.

It hurts, is what she would say, if she wasn't afraid that by saying that, she would hurt her mom, too.

On the TV, the two main actors embrace in a hug.

"Do they know what they're having?" her mom asks. "And was your dad planning on telling me at some point?" The second question is a little sharper than the first one.

"I don't know," Leo says. "And for what it's worth, Dad wanted to tell you a while ago."

Leo's mom opens her mouth to say something (and Leo can tell from the crease between her eyes that it's not going to be flattering toward her dad), but then Denver, nearly comatose from the peanut butter and general excitement of the evening, rolls over in his sleep and tumbles off the bed.

There's a flurry of mozzarella sticks and fries as both Leo and her mom fly off the bed after him. He's fine, though, standing on all fours and looking more embarrassed than anything else, and Leo feeds him a forbidden French fry before tugging him into her lap. He seems to accept that and then they watch "Weekend Update" and don't talk about it again.

There's really nothing else to say, Leo figures.

After, they get ready for bed, taking turns at the sink without really speaking, and then climb into the bed with Denver curled up between them. Leo suspects that if they were at home, Denver would be relegated to the floor, but they're both too tired to move him.

They lie in the dark for a while, the strange silence of the hotel room so much louder than the familiar silence at home.

"I can hear you thinking over there," her mom says after a few minutes.

"Same," Leo replies. "You first."

There's a pause before her mom sighs. "I just keep thinking, why did Nina and I fight? That last day, you remember?"

Leo remembers.

"But like, *why*?" her mom continues. "What was the point? Why did I even care? It was so stupid and I just . . . I let her go. I thought we'd figure it out. I don't know, I don't want to put this on you, Lee."

Leo thinks about that night, that last night, the party, talking to East in the kitchen, colleges and promises, the future, which seemed so definite and assured that it makes Leo want to laugh now, laugh at how stupid she was for thinking that any of it had been guaranteed.

She's about to tell her mom what East had told her at the party that night, but then her mom interrupts her. "What about you? Your turn."

Leo pauses in the dark. Between them, Denver sighs like only dogs can do. "I was just thinking, Nina would have loved tonight. The fire department, the hotel, all of the drama and everything. This would have been her favorite Christmas Eve ever."

Her mom starts to shake next to her, and Leo freezes, thinking that she's crying, that she's finally broken her mom and here they are, alone together in a hotel room and Leo will have to figure out how to fix it, but then she takes a breath and Leo realizes that she's laughing, not crying.

"She would *definitely* have loved all of this," her mom agrees. "She would've been on a first name basis with every single firefighter."

"We probably would have gotten free room service, too," Leo adds, and now they're both giggling.

"I just think you should know that . . . that night? At that party? I know we weren't supposed to go and all of that, but Nina looked so pretty and she was so *happy*. I don't remember other things, but I remember that she was beautiful."

Her mom wiggles around a bit, then slides her hand across the mattress. Leo takes it, feels her mom squeeze three times, her grip hard and steady.

"She was super in love with East that night, and she was talking to everyone, and we sat together on the diving board and she was just smiling and *alive*, you know? Like, when I think about that night, she seemed so alive that I can't believe she's dead. It doesn't seem possible. How could all of that be gone so fast?"

Her mom squeezes her hand hard.

Leo hangs on. "I like when we talk about her," she says, staring at the dark, unfamiliar ceiling. "It makes it feel like she was real."

"I like talking about her, too," her mom replies. "And she'll always be real, Leo."

"Merry Christmas, Mom," Leo whispers. "And Nina."

Her mom squeezes again in response.

The silence is softer after that.

DECEMBER 24, 6:07 P.M.
129 DAYS AFTER THE ACCIDENT

"MOM? MOM!"

Leo hurries up the stairs, looking for her mom. "Mom? Where are you?"

Her mom comes out of her bedroom. Her eyes are a little puffy but she's not crying, which is good. It had been a rough day. Not that Leo had been expecting Christmas Eve to be a party. She felt like she did the time she first went to that big roller coaster amusement park, tagging along with Nina and her friends. She had thought she could handle it, but the way her stomach had swooped once she saw the wild tracks made her think twice, and she spent most of the trip waiting for everyone at the ride's carefully marked exits.

This time, though, there's no getting off the ride. Christmas Eve has officially begun.

There are a few gifts under their tree, hastily wrapped and tied with lopsided bows. Two of them are for Denver (a new collar and a new leash), both of them purchased by Leo. Nina had always been responsible for Denver's gifts, had even put a few squeaky balls in his stocking every year, and for all of the heartbreak and pain that this year has brought to Leo, she doesn't think her heart can handle it if Denver doesn't get any presents this Christmas. She hopes he likes his new leash. It's red and has paw prints all over it. She's pretty sure Nina would approve.

She doesn't get him anything for his stocking, though, mostly because she has no idea where it even is. They didn't exactly do a lot of decorating this year. The tree is up, but not decorated, and the only reason it even has lights in the first place is that it's artificial and pre-lit. It even has a special button that changes the lights from bright colors to soft, then flashing, then fading. Denver, for reasons only he knows, likes to sleep on that button, so the tree sometimes looks like it's in the middle of a raging party, lights changing and flashing every few seconds.

Leo and her mom don't have the heart to shoo him away from the tree this year, so the tree is currently lighting up a storm.

"Whoa," her mom says now, clearing her throat a little, a sure sign that she's been crying in her bathroom. Leo decides to ignore that part. "You're in a hurry. Where's the fire?"

"East just texted me," Leo says. "He has a gift for me, I guess. Can he come over? Just for a few minutes. He has to go to his grandfather's house tonight, they go to Christmas Eve Mass and everything."

Leo can feel the weight of her words as her mom pauses. "Mom," she says again. "It's *just* a gift."

"Fine," her mom finally says. "It's fine, sure. Tell him to come over."

"But I didn't get him anything," Leo worries, picking at her cuticles again. Her mom pulls her hands apart without even mentioning it, going down the stairs and heading toward the tree. Denver's moved away so she hits the button and tiny white lights settle in the branches.

"I'm sure East will understand," her mom says.

"Will I seem like a jerk, though?"

"Lee." Her mom looks up from the tree. "You have never been a jerk in your entire life."

"That's not true," she says. "Remember when I shoved that kid in preschool and she landed facedown in the sandbox?"

"Agatha Perkins deserved it," her mom replies, which makes Leo smile.

"Probably," she agrees. Agatha had been pretty notorious in their neighborhood circles. Nobody had cried when she and her family moved away the week before third grade started.

"You are not a jerk, East will understand. Have you seen the TV remote?"

"Under the couch cushion," Leo says, then adds, "Denver was trying to chew on it so I hid it," when her mom raises a questioning eyebrow.

Denver doesn't even look up from his water bowl, where he's currently slurping like a camel. He never worries if he's a jerk or not, Leo thinks.

Their plan had been to heat up a frozen pizza and watch a non-Christmas movie. Neither of them were up for any feel-good holiday cheer about love and family and togetherness. More specifically, they were going to watch *Independence Day*. Leo had picked it out and it said a lot about her mom's current state of mind that she had agreed immediately to watch a movie about aliens on Christmas Eve. She had expected her to disagree immediately but all she said was, "Is that the one where Bill Pullman is president?" and Leo said yes even though she wasn't sure and had to look it up later on IMDb. (It was.)

Leo had FaceTimed with her dad and Stephanie earlier that night, the two of them holding up champagne glasses filled with sparkling cider. They looked happy, but their smiles were tight, and there were a few moments where the three of them pretended that the gaping silences in between their sentences were because of Wi-Fi delays and not their own inability to fill the space. "Love you guys," Leo said at the end. "All of you."

Stephanie's smile got a bit bigger, a bit more real.

Leo still hasn't told her mom about the whole baby thing. She keeps thinking that tomorrow will be best, and then tomorrow becomes yesterday and now tomorrow is Christmas and well, Leo's not an expert but she's pretty sure that today's not the best day to drop the news. Leo decides that maybe that weird week between Christmas and New Year's is best, when everyone's a little deflated and tired from the holidays but still has some jolly spirit left.

Leo tries not to think about what Nina would say if Leo ever used the phrase "jolly spirit" in front of her.

"When's East coming over?" her mom asks, her voice muffled by one of the couch cushions as she digs around for the TV remote.

Leo checks her phone. "Um, maybe in the next fifteen minutes or so?"

They both look around at the house. A fine layer of corgi hair seems to coat every available surface. There's a bunch of old drinking glasses on the coffee table and five shoes—not five *pairs* of shoes, just five shoes—lying near the front door. The tree is still leaning to the left, even though one of them has said, "We should straighten the tree" at least once a day since it's been up. Two coats are slung over the stair railing, crusty plates are stacked up in the kitchen sink, and the throw rug is cultivating its own family of dust bunnies.

"I'll get the vacuum," Leo says.

"I got the kitchen," her mom replies.

East shows up eighteen minutes later, just when Leo is literally kicking their Roomba back into the hall closet, and her mom is slamming the dishwasher shut. "We're sort of violent cleaners, aren't we," Leo says, feeling a little out of breath after their mad dash to make the house look hospitable again.

"The tree is still crooked," her mom says.

"That's part of its charm." Leo shuts the closet door and quickly puts her hair back behind her ears. "Plus it's just East," she adds. "He doesn't care what the house looks like."

"*I* care," her mom says, which is news to Leo, then starts the dishwasher. It immediately roars to life, its familiar surge and hum making the house almost feel like it did before, working in tandem with all of the people who lived in it, doing its part to create a home for them. Leo can't remember the last time they ran it. She's eaten cereal out of the same bowl for at least the last month, washing and rinsing it and leaving it to dry in the rack so she can just grab it again the following morning.

Fuck, Leo thinks to herself as her phone buzzes. She's sentimental about the *dishwasher*. If this is what Christmas Eve is going to feel like, Christmas is sure to be a disaster. She'll probably end up sobbing over her dad and Stephanie's Nest thermostat at the rate this is going.

She checks her phone. *Hello hello*, East has texted, and she can almost hear him saying the words, low and quiet and slightly bemused.

Leo looks up at her mom, who's tucking her own stray hairs behind her ears. Her mom's gone a lot grayer in the past few months and Leo has a sudden sense of time moving too fast, of her mom changing and aging and slipping through her hands. But all she says is, "East's here."

"Did he knock?" Her mom frowns, and Leo holds up her phone and wiggles it a bit.

"He can't just ring the bell?"

"Mom, nobody rings the bell. This isn't a sitcom." Leo's not even sure if she knows what their doorbell sounds like. "I'm opening the door, okay? The house looks fine. East knows that we live here with a shedding corgi. He doesn't think it's a film set."

Out of the corner of her eye, she sees her mom open a kitchen drawer and shove a pile of unopened mail inside.

True to his text, East is indeed standing at the door. He looks nice, his hair actually combed back rather than in his face. Leo thinks it looks like the kind of hairstyle a grandparent would approve of on their way to Christmas Eve Mass. He's also wearing a buttoned-up blue shirt and a zip-up gray sweater, and Leo doesn't even have to look at his shoes to know that they're black and sturdy. Sensible. It's a far cry from his checkered Vans and Nina's hoodie, and she knows her sister would tease him endlessly about his temporary new look.

But Leo is not her sister.

"You look nice," she says, standing back a little so he can come inside. "Nice shirt."

"Thanks," he says. "I like your tree."

"It leans," Leo and her mom say at the same time. Leo's almost forgotten that her mom is even there, and when she turns to look at her, Leo's surprised to see that her mom actually looks nervous?

And then she remembers that night in the emergency room, the squeak of gurney wheels in the emergency room corridor, how bright the fluorescent lights had been, her mom bursting through the door, East's wails ringing down the hall.

"Hi, Ms. Stott," East says, sounding as nervous as her mom looks. "I'm sorry to stop by in the middle of Christmas Eve and all, I just had this thing"—he gestures toward the gift in his hand—"for Leo."

"No, that's fine, that's fine," her mom says. "It's—It's good to see you, Easton."

"You too."

Her mom is the one who moves first, stepping forward and

putting her arms around East, who gingerly hugs her back. In the background, the dishwasher stops and then starts with renewed vigor, and Leo finds herself wishing she could step in between them, but also knowing that there's no place for her inside their embrace.

Her mom says something so quiet that Leo can't make it out, then East is nodding as he pulls away. Both of their eyes are wet, her mom laughing a little as she quickly wipes hers on her sleeve, and East's cheeks are flushed pink. "I'll let you two talk," her mom starts to say, but East interrupts her.

"Actually, my dad was wondering if you could come out to the car? He wanted to say hello, just like for a second." East runs his hand through his hair, but he's forgotten that it's styled and so he only just messes it up. Leo has the urge to comb it back into place with her fingers. "He also said it's okay if you'd rather not."

"No, no, I'll talk to your dad." Leo's mom pulls her cardigan tighter around her and Leo can see how her waist is thinner than it was last Christmas. No one else would have noticed, but now that it's just the two of them in the house together, Leo sees things that she otherwise would have missed.

As soon as her mom steps outside toward the driveway, East turns back to Leo. "Hi," he says. "Sorry, I look like I'm in some catalogue."

"You look nice," Leo says again. "Seriously."

"You've used the word 'nice' three times in the past minute," East points out.

"You know, we cleaned the house for you," she teases. "We even ran the dishwasher. So you could be a little nicer."

"That's four."

"East!" she screeches, and from underneath the tree, she can see Denver's head pop up as the tree's white lights begin to flash.

"That's a party right there," East says, gesturing toward the tree, and it occurs to Leo that maybe he's stalling? Because he's nervous? She's seen East be many things over the past four months, but nervous has never been one of them, and she wonders what exactly is in the gift-wrapped package in his hand.

"So did you just come over to admire our disco tree or . . . ?" Leo says.

"Oh yeah. Yeah. Sorry. I, um." East clears his throat and Leo finds herself suddenly feeling like a big sister toward him, even though she's two years younger. She wonders if this is how Nina used to feel toward her, exasperated and protective at the same time.

"So!" East says, handing her the package. "Merry Christmas. Sorry about the wrapping."

"You used duct tape," Leo says, turning it over in her hands. The paper is pretty but the silver tape makes it looks more like a threat than a present.

"Yeah, apparently we're out of Scotch tape." East shrugs and runs another hand through his hair. At this rate, he's going to show up to Mass looking like he arrived in a convertible during a hurricane. "This is all we had."

"No biggie," she says. "Can I open it now?"

"Yes, yes," East says. "Sorry, yeah. Of course. I just, I really hope you like it and if you don't, I'll get it out of here and throw it in the trash and we can forget this whole thing ever happened."

Leo smiles. It's sort of fun to see him tripping over himself. She's used to Cool East. She almost likes this version better.

"I'm sure I'll love it," she says, then tears the wrapping paper right down the middle since there's no way she can get through the duct tape.

At first, all she sees is the back of the frame, but when she turns it over in her hands, her breath catches and her hand goes to her chest like she could force the air back into her lungs.

It's a black-and-white photo of her and Nina at the party. They're together on the diving board, Leo's head tucked toward Nina's as if she was trying to hear what her sister was saying. They're both in profile, Nina's face alive in a smile as the pool lights illuminate them. There are people in the background, but they're blurred, making Nina and Leo look even sharper, almost as if someone's drawn them with a fine-tipped pen.

When Leo doesn't say anything at first, East jumps in.

"It's a silver gelatin print," he says. "I did it as a test and it looked really good. I didn't even know I had this shot until a few days ago." He clears his throat. "I know you want more memories of that night. This is how I remember it. Before everything, before . . ." He trails off as Leo grips the frame, stares into the photo like she could somehow disappear inside of it, slip back into the past before it all went wrong.

"This is my memory, Leo," East murmurs. "I want you to have this one."

Her heart thumps hard, almost like someone has reached into her chest and given it a tight squeeze. "East," she says as soon as her brain calms down long enough for her to form words. "It's beautiful. It's . . ."

"I remembered what you said about her face," East adds. "Maybe now you won't forget it."

Leo nods as her eyes fill. She's cried so much this year and still has trouble figuring out if they're happy or sad tears. These feel like both.

"I love it," she says, then reaches up and wraps her free arm around his neck, hugging him so tight that he almost loses his balance. He catches himself, though, then puts his arms around her and holds her back. Outside, Leo can hear her mom's voice, quiet but calm, and she closes her eyes and tries to imagine that everything is okay, that Nina is just upstairs, that East is here to surprise Nina with a beautiful photo of her and Leo, that Nina will absolutely love it.

"She would love it, too," Leo whispers, and feels East nod against her shoulder.

Leo's mom kindly clears her throat before she steps back through the doorway and East and Leo pull away from each other. "Hi," Leo says, then wonders why she said it. "We're fine."

"Good." Her mom smiles. "East, your dad is so excited for you and your college applications. That's almost all he could talk about. You should be hearing back in a few weeks, he said?"

East looks a little uncomfortable as he shifts his weight, and Leo wonders if he feels guilty that he's doing it alone, that Nina won't be there by his side at graduation, or for that matter, anywhere else ever again.

"Yeah," he says, then clears his throat. "He's, uh, really proud."

Leo's mom glances down at the gift. "So what'd you get?"

Leo just holds it out to her because she's not sure how to describe it, and her mom frowns as she takes the frame, holding it out a little so she can see it. Her glasses are on top of her head but Leo doesn't point that out.

"Oh," her mom says, and then "Oh" again, but this time it's slightly garbled. She glances at East, then Leo. "Is this from . . . ?"

"Yes," Leo replies, already knowing what her mom is asking. Next to them, East shifts his weight from one foot to the other and looks wary, like a kid who's not sure if he broke a major rule. "It's from that night. At the party." *Please don't freak out*, she adds silently.

But her mom doesn't freak out. She just glances up at East with watery eyes, then gives him a small smile. "It's beautiful, East," she says. "Did you take this?"

East is now clutching his hands in front of him. "Yes," he says. "And printed it, too."

Leo's mom nods as she hands the photo back to Leo, and then she reaches up and gives him a hug. It's such a simple movement that none of them seem to register it at first, least of all East, but then he's putting his arms around Leo's mom and Leo sees his face wobble and shift as she holds him tight.

Apparently forgiveness can appear in many different ways, at the most surprising times. Leo tries very hard not to think about how death can sometimes do the same thing.

They only pull apart when East chuckles under his breath, then gestures to the stack of books about grief and healing on their stairs. They've been sitting there since at least September, Leo realizes, their permanence borne out of her and her mom's steadfast refusal to acknowledge them.

"We had those, too," he says wryly. "After my mom died."

"Oh yeah." Leo's mom laughs a little, too. "My sister, Leo's aunt, sent them. So did a few other people." She shrugs. "They mean well, I guess."

"There was a dumb workbook," Leo adds.

East squints a little as he looks at the pile. "I think my dad still has the one on the bottom. That one's not too bad. No quizzes or worksheets."

Both Leo and her mom laugh at the same time, in the same way, that sharp bark of dark humor, a noise that can only truly be heard by someone who's also uttered it. East's eyes sparkle a little when he recognizes the sound. "Yeah," he says. "Lots of people mean well."

He leaves soon after and Leo waves toward his dad's car, wrapping her arms around herself as she watches the red taillights fade into the dark street. Nina would love this weather, cold but not freezing, that tiny hint of crispness that signifies a Southern California winter. "Capital W Weather," she would call it in the confident tone of someone whose closest experience with snow had been ordering Hawaiian shaved ice from a food truck every summer.

Leo leaves the front door open, waiting for her mom to tell her to shut it, that she's letting out all the warm air, that the electric bill isn't going to pay itself, all of the things she would have said to Nina if she had been there, too.

But when there's nothing, Leo turns around to see her mom standing near the stairs, staring at the books. There's five or so of them, some thin and some as thick as Nina's old AP Bio textbook, the one she had forgotten to return to the school library at the end of last summer. It was still sitting on her desk upstairs, a picture of a green, slimy-looking frog staring up with bulging, unsympathetic eyes.

"Mom?" Leo says, but she doesn't hear her at first, and Leo shuts the door with a little more force than normal, which jolts her mom out of her trance. "Sorry, it slipped," she lies.

"Kelly does mean well," her mom says, gesturing toward the stack. "These probably weren't cheap, either."

"Probably not," Leo agrees, even though she has no idea. She's still holding East's gift in her hand, almost afraid to set it down and have it disappear just like Nina did. "Did you want to watch the movie?"

"What?" her mom says. "Oh, yes. Yes, of course. The one with the aliens, absolutely. Let's do it."

They light the fireplace with one of those fake logs, heat the frozen pizza (which always seems lukewarm at best in the middle, no matter how much Leo fiddles with the oven temperature), and pour sparkling cider and bring all of it over to the coffee table. Leo grabs the remote before her mom can, which means they'll save at least ten minutes of her mom accidentally pressing the wrong button or changing the channel when she meant to turn up the volume.

It's fine at first, but Leo can feel a small timbre of tension stretching through their living room. She manages to eat a slice of pizza, then another, but her mom only takes a few bites of hers and doesn't touch the cider, either. There's a lot of exciting things happening on the screen, aliens blowing up downtown Los Angeles and Will Smith saying booming, heroic things, but Leo can feel her mind being pulled toward her mom like a child who doesn't want to leave a toy store.

Why did East have to point out the books? she thinks. They were so close—so fucking *close!*—to making it through this terrible rite of passage. A movie, a pizza, and then Leo could go upstairs and shut her door and scroll through her phone and pretend like it was just another night, that Nina was bent over her textbook down the hall, griping about homework under her breath. Leo knows it's not exactly healthy to pretend (and those books on the stairs probably each have a chapter or two on denial), but when she's alone at night, Leo can pretend, and pretending at night is what gets her through the days.

One of the aliens has just finished destroying everything and everyone in the lab when Leo's mom reaches for the remote. "Can I . . . ?" she says, and Leo sees her hand shaking a little as she hands it over. True to form, she accidentally turns the volume up a few notches before she manages to pause the movie, so the alien destruction sounds particularly piercing before they're jerked into silence.

"Mom?" Leo says. The two slices of pizza sit like rocks in her stomach. This whole thing was stupid, so stupid. She should have just gone to her dad's.

But her mom is up and off the sofa, marching with a sturdiness that Leo hasn't seen since The Before, and Leo scrambles after her, wondering if this is the moment when her mom loses it, if she's going to have to watch her mom have a complete nervous breakdown while an alien is frozen mid-snacking on a bunch of people on TV.

Leo wonders if it's too late to call an Uber and meet up with East and his family at Mass.

But her mom walks straight to the stairs, then reaches down, scoops all of the grief books up into her arms, then hands a couple to Leo. The cover on the top of her mom's stack has a resigned-looking woman staring pensively out a window, a scarf wrapped around her shoulders. *Saying Goodbye*, the title says in looped script.

"Is this what I'm supposed to look like?" Leo's mom says, holding it up and shaking it at Leo. "Like *this* woman?"

"It sort of looks like those romance novels that they sell by the cash registers at grocery stores," Leo points out, and her mom's face breaks out into a grin.

"It's just so stupid," she says, walking past Leo into the living room. Denver's head pops up as she passes him, his ears following like two tiny satellites looking for either treats or trouble. "I don't know what the hell Kelly was *thinking*. Like there's a book that could help with this!" She gestures to the overall house, but Leo understands what she means. There's nothing that could ever fill the space left behind by Nina.

And then before Leo can stop her, her mom's tossing the book into the fireplace.

"Mom!" Leo cries.

"Which ones do you have?" Her mom asks her, ignoring her outburst as the flames catch the corner of *Saying Goodbye*. The woman still looks sad and serene as her face begins to crumple into ash.

Leo holds up one of hers. It's a paperback but heavy. "*From Mourning 'til Night*," she says, holding it up.

Her mom stands back and gestures toward the fireplace. "Let 'er rip, kiddo."

Leo's read *Fahrenheit 451*, or at least enough of it back in freshman English to get the point, so this feels . . . wrong? Is it technically illegal to burn books? Nina would know, Leo thinks before she can stop herself, but Nina's not there anymore to tell her yes or no, true or false, right or wrong, and that's sort of how they got here in the first place.

Leo tosses the book on top of the last one as her mom whoops and puts her fists into the air. It's so weird to see her mom celebrating, to see her hopping up and down in her socked feet and smiling, and Leo finds herself half elated that her mom actually looks happy for once, and half terrified that her mom isn't really acting like a mom anymore.

Whatever's happening at her dad and Stephanie's tonight, Leo's pretty sure they're not doing *this*.

"What about that workbook you mentioned?" her mom asks

now, reaching for her sparkling cider and taking a big sip. "Do you still have it?"

"No, I put it in the recycling bin," Leo admits.

Her mom—*her mother!*—rolls her eyes and polishes off the cider like it's actual champagne. (And to be honest, now Leo's a little curious if her mom secretly swapped out the fake stuff for the real thing when Leo wasn't looking.) "A quiz," she mutters, shaking her head. "Unbelievable."

The Sixth Stage is next on the heap, followed by *Struggling Through Sorrow.* Her mom munches on a slice of pizza as the covers catch fire and her eyes have a glow to them that isn't just a reflection of their now very roaring fireplace. "As if anyone could ever fucking understand this," she says to herself.

This is now the second time that Leo's ever heard her mom say the word "fuck."

They stand next to each other for a few minutes, watching the flames get bigger and the room slowly begin to get smokier. "Mom?" Leo asks after a few minutes.

"Hmm?"

"Did you open that thing in the chimney, what's it called?"

"The flue?"

"Yeah." Leo coughs a little, waving a hand in front of her face. "That thing."

Her mom pauses, then shakes her head. "Huh. I'm not sure."

Leo's about to respond, but the sudden, high-pitched screech of the smoke alarm beats her to it.

LEO'S MOM IS waiting in the kitchen when Leo gets home from school that day.

They've barely spoken since their fight on Friday night, the silence hanging thick and heavy in their house over the weekend. Leo had been planning on telling her about Stephanie on Sunday night, giving her mom time to absorb the news before Christmas, but instead, Leo barely left her room all day, waiting to help herself to cereal for dinner until after her mom reheated leftovers in the microwave and had gone upstairs. Her mom was in the shower when she left for school that morning and as soon as she shut the front door behind her, Leo felt like she could take a deep breath for the first time since Friday night.

But when she sees her mom's car in the garage, that relief dissipates in a snap, and a terrible slideshow of potential worst moments flips through her head. Is Stephanie okay? Is it her dad? Does her mom have cancer? Did something happen to Aunt Kelly?

The look on her face must be obvious because her mom sees her face as she hurries inside. "Everything's fine," she says, and Leo puts a hand to her heart, like she's someone starring in a dramatic film and not a person in her own life. "Sorry, I'm sorry, everyone's okay, I just thought I'd come home early, maybe work remotely for the afternoon." Her laptop is open in front of her, her phone in her hand.

Now that Leo's been reassured, her panic gives way to annoyance.

"Maybe lead with the good news next time?" Leo says as she sets her bag down by the table. She waits for her mom to say something about taking it upstairs, but she never does.

"Sorry," her mom says again. "How was school?"

"Fine."

"Do you want a snack or . . . I think we have some granola bars in the pantry?"

Leo sits down at the table. Her mother hasn't offered her an after-school snack since the first grade. "Mom, what's going on?"

Her mom takes a deep breath as she looks out the kitchen window. "We need to talk."

Leo says nothing. The last thing she wants to do is talk, not after how their last conversation went. Why didn't she just accept the granola bar and hightail it upstairs?

"What you said . . ." Her mom begins, then stops and restarts. "I wanted you to know that I called a therapist today. Kelly recommended someone. They specialize in, um, grief counseling."

"Okay," Leo says, and thinks that must be an awful job, hearing people talk all day about their dead loved ones, their own mortality, a never-ending litany of sad thoughts and unsaid words.

"I'm seeing them later this week. I just, I wanted you to know that."

"You don't have to tell—" Leo starts to say, but then her mom leans across the table and takes Leo's hands before she can move them away.

"I need you to know something else," she says. "Part of what you said that night was true, but the other part . . . Leo, I need you to know that will *never* be true."

Leo knows this is the part where her eyes should fill with tears, where they should get up and hug and promise to be kinder to each other, to talk more, but instead her eyes and throat are completely dry, her mouth still and unwavering. She never wants to think about that conversation ever again, but the truth is that she always will.

"Never," her mother says again. "I love both of you so much, I always will, and I would never . . ." She trails off. "Well, you know."

"I know," Leo whispers, because she does. She wishes she had never said anything, wishes that she had never blurted out how she felt because of the pain in her mom's eyes now.

"When I walked into the hospital that night," her mom continues, "all I knew was that you both had been in a crash, and I didn't know . . . I thought that maybe . . ." She blinks and looks away, tucking her lips between her teeth.

Leo hasn't thought about how her mom found out about the accident, how she must have driven in a panic to the hospital. Leo's brain is already too full of her own terrible thoughts, the flashes of images that wake her up in the middle of the night, that startle her out of dreams and daydreams, but now that they're sitting together, Leo realizes that they have very different memories of that night.

"I don't know what I would have done if I had lost both of you," her mom finally says, and Leo looks down at her hands, not able to look at her mom's face anymore. "Nina was—*is*—my baby and so are you.

"I'm sorry that I've been so bad at this, Leo."

"You're not *bad* at this," Leo protests. "I don't think anyone's supposed to be *good* at it, right?"

Her mom smiles ruefully at that. "I guess not." She lets go of Leo's hands when she says that and Leo finds herself missing the contact.

"I know you were upset on Friday night about East and the driving," Leo blurts out before she can stop herself. "And I'm sorry, too."

Her mom sighs. "I was. And honestly, I still am, a little bit. I just panicked when I saw you get out of his car." She pauses before she murmurs, "You looked like just like Nina when you did that. It scared me."

Her mom reaches over and covers Leo's hand once again with hers. Her fingertips are a little cold but Leo is grateful for the touch, for the way it settles her. "I think I can still hear her sometimes," her mom says. "On the stairs or in her room at night."

"I hear her all the time," Leo admits. "Her voice in my head, telling me what to do. She's . . . really loud."

Her mom smiles at that. "So maybe she isn't really gone, right? Maybe some of that life is still here, in a way."

"Maybe." Leo looks down at her mom's hand, the way it's gripping hers. "She might also be haunting Gertie."

They both laugh out loud. "I'm sure Gertie will let us know if that's the case," her mom says.

"Also, I told Dad and Stephanie that I wanted to do Christmas Eve and Christmas morning with you this year," Leo says. The skin around her fingernails is dry and she picks at it until it starts to hurt, waiting for her mom to say something.

When she finally looks up, her mom's eyes are wide and dry. "Sweetheart," she says. "I told you, you don't have to take care of me."

"Yeah, but I kind of do, though," Leo replies, and her mom blows out a breath and glances out the window for a minute.

"And Dad was okay with this idea?"

Leo nods, trying not to think about everything else she and her dad had discussed that night. She still wasn't sure how she felt, or even if she felt anything about it. She's decided that's a problem for the new year, not now.

"He said it's fine. He understood."

Leo watches as her mom resists the urge to roll her eyes. "Okay," she says after a minute. "That'll be nice, Lee. Really. Also, stop picking at your cuticles, please." She picks up Leo's hand and shakes it, and Leo thinks all of this good energy is about to slip away, when her mom lets go of Leo's hand, stands up, and pulls her into her arms. For how much everything has changed, her mom still smells like her mom, soap and detergent and fancy powder blush from Sephora that Nina always used to steal. It's no small thing and Leo hugs her back, thankful for the familiarity, for the ability to hang on to something solid.

They hug for a minute until Leo looks up from her mom's shoulder and out the window toward their neighbor's house. "Mom?"

Her mom strokes her hair a little. "Hmm?"

"Mr. Grayer is out watering his lawn."

"Okay?"

"I don't think he's wearing pants?"

Her mom immediately releases her grip. "Time to get blinds!" she says.

Denver pads into the room to greet them, all tongue and tail and paws, and for the first time in months, the house feels a little less empty than when they left it.

THE PORCH LIGHT is on as Leo climbs up to the front porch after East drops her off, but she doesn't need her key because her mom is already there, opening up the door.

Leo waves goodbye to East as he drives away, shivering a little as she goes from the damp night air into the warm house. It smells different now that Nina's not there anymore. Her shampoo, her perfume, her spearmint-flavored gum, it's all gone. Now it smells like reheated leftovers and dry dog food and dust that has settled all over the furniture. Even their fake Christmas tree seems to be wilting to one side. It's as if the house has gone to sleep waiting for Nina to return, a slumbering fairy princess waiting for her true love's kiss.

"Who was that?" Leo's mom says before she can even shut the door behind them. "Was that Madison's mother, hmm?" It's very clear from her sarcastic tone that she knows it was most definitely not Madison's mother.

"No," she says, setting her purse down on the front table. There used to be a framed picture of Nina, Leo, and Denver there, the girls smiling and Denver giving the camera his best doggie grin. Leo doesn't know where it went. She's almost scared to ask.

"Who was it?" Her mom is wearing her robe, flannel pajamas underneath. Nina had given them to her three Christmases ago, but Nina had ended up borrowing them a lot. They had smiling, steaming mugs of coffee on them, and they look so familiar that Leo almost starts crying again.

She wants to hug her mom, tell her about the party, about the fight, about how no one would talk to her because they still don't know what to say. She wants to tell her mom how upsetting it is to remember nothing about the last moments of Nina's life and how terrified she is that at some point she *will* remember them. She wants to tell her how scared she is for the holiday season, how feaful she is about how much Christmas is going to hurt, how frightening it is to feel such pain and know that everyone else you love is feeling it, too, and how nothing feels like home anymore, not even her actual home.

Instead she says, "East drove me home," and starts to tell her mom about the fight, about Kai and Aidan, Dylan and Sophie, Brayden and his repossessed Lamborghini, but her mom cuts her off.

"East," she says, an eyebrow going up. There's a sleepy crease mark on her cheek, but the TV is still on in the living room. "*East gave you a ride home.*"

Leo has the distinct feeling that she just did something wrong without realizing it. "Yeah, Madison stayed at the party so—"

"You got into a *car* with *East*."

Oh, Leo thinks.

"Answer me, Leo!" her mom barks at her. "Why were you driving around in a car with Easton?"

"What, am I not allowed?" Leo yells.

"Did I say that he could drive you *anywhere*?" her mom yells back. Her eyes are wide and wild and Leo has a terrible memory of the emergency room, of her mom's face as she ran down the hallway.

"He gave me a ride home!" Leo cries. "Everybody was drinking at the party—"

"There was alcohol at this party?!"

Leo's pretty sure that this is the point that Nina would have closed her eyes and rubbed her forehead while sighing in Leo's direction.

"There's always alcohol at these parties!" she pushes back, not realizing until the words are out of her mouth that she's only digging a bigger hole for herself. "It's not like everyone's sitting around at a quilting bee sipping ginger ale!"

"Were *you* drinking? Was East?"

The way her mom asks the question doesn't make it sound like a question at all, more like a demand that Leo confirm her mom's worst suspicions, which makes Leo angry, which makes her irrational and scared and furious that once again, Nina has left her alone to navigate all of this by herself.

It's not fair, she knows that. She knows but she doesn't care.

"I wasn't drinking!" she lies. "And neither was East! That's why *he* gave me a ride home!"

Her mom's eyes flash for a brief second, and Leo can't help but feel a little sick at the realization that this is the first time since that unimaginable August night that her mother actually seems *alive*.

"Listen to me," her mom says now, stepping forward. "We're putting up some new rules starting. Right. Now."

Leo laughs. She can't help it. "Why?" she says, throwing her arms out to her sides. "I don't go anywhere, I don't do anything. What are you going to do, ground me? Make me stay home, in my room?" Leo rolls her eyes and starts to walk past her mom. "Oh no, anything but that."

Suddenly her mom is in front of Leo, blocking her from the stairs. "You are never, ever allowed to be in a car with East again. Do you hear me? Never again!" Her mom's hand is shaking as she points at her.

"East didn't *kill* Nina, Mom!" Leo finally shouts. "He was just driving the car!"

"Because you were coming home from a party—"

"That Nina wanted to go to!"

"—that I explicity told you both *not* to go to!"

"So this is my fault, too, now?"

Her mom wavers, falters. An illustrated latte with steam rising from its mug grins at Leo. She hates these pajamas so much, hates that her mom still wears them.

"It is not your fault," her mom says. "I'm not saying that but—"

"But you're saying that it's East's fault then, even though he wasn't even drinking? You know who *was* drinking, Mom? The drunk driver who plowed into us, that's who! That's the person who's responsible!"

"I know that, but—!"

"And you know what else? I am so tired of keeping it together for you! I am *exhausted*! I feel like I have to keep moving or else everything is just all going to fall apart. You think that I don't want to spend the day in bed, in *Nina's* bed, or in front of the TV? I can't because *you're* there." She thinks of her dad and Stephanie, of Stephanie's big news, her gently rounded stomach. "We're all walking around protecting your feelings all the time because we all have to move on, but you're not!"

"You do *not* have to do any of that, Leo—"

"You know what?" Leo continues, and much later, when she's older and grown and in a different bed in a different home in a different city altogether, she'll remember this moment and cringe. It will wake her up and not let her fall back to sleep. It will hiss around the curve of her ear, *Remember what you said to your mother that night?* and bury itself so deep in her bones that the shame will bloom under her skin and take root there, forever anchoring her adult self to her teenage life with no hope for a clean break.

"I think you're mad at Nina for dying," she says, and her mom steps back with a flinch. "You're mad because it was her and not me."

The moment hangs in the room like a photo she can never forget. Leo can see the neighbor's Christmas lights twinkling on their roof, Denver sitting up in his dog bed with his head cocked to the side, worried about the fight. The star on top of their Christmas tree is leaning to the left and looks like it's four days away from falling off. But Leo's mom's face is at the center of it all, slack and shocked and frozen in the moment.

Leo almost wishes she had hit her mom instead.

Before she can even say anything, Leo dashes upstairs and slams her door behind her. Even her bedroom feels unsafe now, like it knows what a terrible person she is, what a horrible daughter, what a useless sister. She reaches for the lamp but then decides to leave it off, almost like she's punishing herself by leaving her in the dark.

She lies on her bed for a long time, long after her mom turns off the TV and goes upstairs, long after Denver paws at her door for a few minutes before trotting on down the hall toward Nina's also-dark room. Her phone lights up a few times but she ignores it, curls up on her side, and wonders how she could say something like that to her mom.

And the darkest den of her mind wonders if it was the truth.

When she wakes up, she's still in her jacket and clothes from the party, and she's overheated and suffocated from the weight of them. She leaves the lamp off as she shrugs out of them, changes into sweatpants and an old, long-sleeved sweatshirt of her dad's that says "UCLA" on the front in peeling letters. And then she opens her door to the sound of a house that's empty in so many ways and goes down the hall to her mom's room.

She's asleep in her bed, curled up on her side away from Leo, one arm wrapped around her waist almost like she's hugging herself in her sleep. "Mom?" Leo whispers, even though she's not sure what to say or even if she would know how to say it if she did.

Her mom doesn't move, though, and Leo watches the rise and fall of her rib cage. She doesn't know if her mom can hear her or not but she still tries again. "Mom?"

Still nothing, and Leo leans against the doorframe.

It scares her sometimes, how much she hurts, but nothing scares her as much as how she can hurt someone else.

"GET IN THE car, Leo!" East yells.

Leo just keeps walking. It's cold, not only because of the season but also from the fog rolling in off the coast, and she's not wearing a jacket, but she just wraps her arms around her waist and keeps walking. The alcohol blur has worn off, leaving sharp edges in its wake, jabbing her with every step, reminding her of what she's said and done.

"Leo!" Now Kai is sitting on the ledge of the passenger window, gesturing to her from over the roof. East is driving at the same pace as Leo is walking, so he's not in any danger, but it still makes her nervous to see his body outside of the car.

"I can walk," she tells them.

"It's freezing," East points out. He's driving and keeps looking between her and the road ahead, even though the street is dark and empty.

Leo knows what he's looking for, the flash of headlights, the blinding glare, the glitter of broken glass.

"I'm fine," is all she says though.

"C'mon," he tells her.

"Don't you have someone you want to go fight with?" she yells back. She's furious with him, not even caring about whether or not it's fair to be angry with her dead sister's boyfriend. She feels like she could reach right through the window and shake East until his teeth rattle, until his eyes spin in their sockets, until he understands what it feels like to hurt the way she does.

The scratch on his cheek looks worse than it did when she walked out of the party. She hates that she cares. Or even notices.

"Okay, you're angry, fine," East says. Kai is still sitting on the passenger-window ledge, nodding sagely, like he has any idea how Leo even feels. She wishes she had another beer can in her hand, and then immediately feels bad for feeling that way in the first place. None of this is Kai's fault, after all.

"But I can't just leave you out here," East continues. "You know that."

She does know that, and she finally stops walking and turns to face them. Kai lights up a little bit but East just looks pitiful. "Where's Dylan?" she asks.

Kai gestures back toward the party. "Sophie finally showed up so he stayed."

"Of course," she says, then looks down the street. The sidewalk ends after the next block, which means she'll be walking on the side of the road, in the dark, and she's seen enough horror movies to know how that particular scenario usually ends. Nina had never been able to get through any horror movie without inserting her own brand of commentary, usually something along the lines of "Oh my God, what a dumbass" as the heroine went into the dark basement during a blackout, or carefully pried opened the creaky front door of the abandoned house.

Leo was many things, but she was not a dumbass.

"Fine," she says, and Kai smiles wider. "But I'm sitting in the back and I'm not talking to either of you."

"Fine," East agrees. "Just get in so I can finally speed up. I look like I'm leading a fucking parade."

Leo glares at him as she yanks the back door open, then slips into the backseat and fastens her seat belt. She can see East watching her in the rearview mirror, but he looks away once he hears the click.

Leo hates how warm the car is, how good it feels to be inside it.

They drop Kai off first, and he smiles again at Leo and says, "I'm still saying goodbye to you even though I know you're not talking to me," before fist-bumping East and hopping out of the front seat. East waits until Kai disappears through his front door, then looks back over the seat at Leo. "Are you not coming up to the front seat?"

Leo just stares out the passenger window.

East sighs. "I look like the world's creepiest Uber driver," he says. "Just come up here."

Leo dips her head down so now she's the one glaring at him in the rearview mirror. "No."

"Please?"

It's the "please" that gets her, the way East sounds tired and run-down. She wonders if he's sore from the fight, if he's bruised, if it hurts him to breathe as much as it hurts her.

Without a word, she gets out of the backseat and goes around the car to the front, sliding in to the passenger seat. At first she thinks it's warm from Kai's body heat, but then she sees that the seat heaters are on and feels a little less benevolent toward him.

"Thank you," East says once she's in.

"Can you please just take me home?"

East huffs out a laugh that doesn't sound funny at all. "If memory serves, that's what I've been trying to do all night."

They drive in silence through the streets, each intersection between Leo and the party making her chest feel tighter, heavier. Her hand is sore from gripping the beer can so hard, and she can feel her pulse in time with each orange streetlight they pass, the beat of her heart set to the lights as they illuminate the car over and over again.

They both see the In-N-Out at the same time, and Leo suddenly smells the warm strawberry milkshake pouring out onto the hot pavement, can see it oozing across the gravel, its sheen reflecting the ambulance lights. She tightens her hand on her seat belt, sits up a little straighter, and feels East's eyes flicking over to her.

"The milkshake spilled," she says. "That night. It was all over the ground."

East flinches a little, his mouth tightening up as he realizes what she's saying, and that's all it takes for the hard rock of anger in Leo to turn molten, the tears running out of her eyes so fast that even she's surprised. "Oh, fuck," East says. "Okay, okay, give me a minute. It's okay, you're okay."

He pulls off the street and into the parking lot of the Home Depot, which is one of the few buildings in their town that doesn't have a lingering memory of Nina attached to it. In-N-Out is behind them now, that sticky sweet scent is gone, and Leo unfastens her seat belt with a *click!* that scrapes her ears. She turns toward East, her anger so white-hot and her grief so icy that they both burn inside her.

"That's exactly it!" she cries, jabbing her finger at him. "*You* know! You're the *only person* who knows, the only other person who was there, who remembers how she . . ." The sobs catch in her throat and she drags her sleeve across her face, not caring how messy she looks. "There's no one else in the world who knows, East, not even me! And you won't *tell* me!"

East looks sad and uncomfortable, his eyes shifting between her hands folded in her lap and the cart rack outside the store. "I'm sorry," he says after a while. "I know you can't remember, but I can't forget.

"Sometimes," he adds after a second, the sound of Leo's jagged breaths cutting through the tension, "I think you're the lucky one. Because if I could cut this memory out of my brain, if I could just get rid of it, I'd do it in a second, Leo. Trust me, you don't want anything that I have."

Leo lets his words hang between them, the honesty of what he's saying sobering her up for good. "I hate that you got into a fight at that party," she says instead, because it's true but also because his words are so stark and harsh that it feels like she's looking into a bright light, something so strong that she has to blink and look away.

His face is long, his eyes round with sympathy as they reflect the Christmas lights on the light poles. "It was just a stupid fight at a stupid party, Leo," he says gently. "Sometimes guys, they show up just to fight. I know it's dumb, but it's over now." The automatic doors at Home Depot open up and a man comes out, carrying his plastic bag. The store is playing Christmas carols over its intercom system and "Hark! The Herald Angels Sing" swells and then fades as the doors shut.

"It's *not* over!" she argues. "That's the thing, this is never going to be over! It's a bunch of people just ignoring me at a party because they don't know what to say, it's *me* not knowing what to say. It was her birthday and then it was Thanksgiving and now it's Christmas and it's my parents and Stephanie and . . . and Nina's gone, her life is over, but the pain isn't. It's never going to stop hurting." Leo takes a deep, ragged breath. "This is never going to end. It's just going to keep going, and keep hurting, and I can't do it by myself, okay? I need to know there's someone else out there who gets it."

She runs a quick hand across her eyes. "I don't want anything to happen to you."

East nods slowly, not looking at her but at the back of the man who's shuffling to his car. East's elbow is on the window ledge, the backs of his fingers against his mouth.

"Okay," he finally says after two more people go into the store and another woman wheels out a cart filled with sheets of plywood. "Okay. You're right. I'm sorry." He doesn't sound sorry this time, though, more like sad and resigned.

"Stephanie's pregnant," she tells him. "They said it's still super early, but yeah."

"They finally told you?"

"Yeah. The baby's due in May."

She watches as East's jaw clenches and releases three times before he speaks. "Wow."

"Yeah." It's sometimes funny how such tiny words can have such big meanings.

"You good with that?"

"Does it matter?" She bites the inside of her cheek and looks out the window again. "I fucking hate Christmas now." The silence afterward is between them like a weighted blanket, pinning them in place, both of them too weary to move.

"I know," East finally replies.

"I don't think I can do it."

"It doesn't matter. It's going to happen either way."

He's right, which is why it hits so hard when he says it.

"The first year is the worst," he continues, still not looking at her.

His mom. He lost her a long time ago. Leo doesn't know when.

"Does it get easier after that?"

"Not easier. But at least you know how much it's going to hurt.

You can, I don't know, brace yourself." East reaches to turn the car on, then finally looks over to her. "You better now?"

Leo shrugs and wipes at her face with the cuff of her sweater.

"I'm sorry I got into that fight."

"I'm sorry I freaked out on you," she replies. "For real."

He smiles a little and Leo wonders how many times Nina saw that smile, how often she sat in the front seat of a car with him and felt like they were the only two people in the world. "Can I ask you a question?" he asks.

"Of course."

He mimes throwing something. "Who taught you to aim for the kidneys?"

Leo smiles despite herself. "Who do you think?"

"Should have known," he replies.

She laughs at that and nods. She's forgotten how good it feels to laugh after crying, like a little breeze that carries away the clouds. It makes her breathe easier, makes her chest hurt a little less, and as East drives her home, the orange lights blink through the car like a beacon, like a lighthouse, their gentle rhythm guiding her into either a port or a storm, Leo's not quite sure anymore.

THE PROBLEM WITH realizing that something is a bad idea, Leo thinks, is that by the time you realize it, it's usually too late to change course.

For her, she realizes that the Christmas party is a bad idea five minutes after she walks into it.

Madison is standing next to her, wearing angel wings and a plastic halo, even though it's not a costume party and no one else is dressed up. She's beaming like she's been placed atop someone's Christmas tree. "Cool," Madison says with an approving nod when they walk into the house. "Let's party."

The whole thing had been Madison's idea in the first place, which probably explained a lot about both Leo's and Madison's decision-making capabilities.

Leo hadn't planned on doing anything that night, maybe just watching *Elf* on her laptop upstairs with Denver or reading a book that she had read ten times already. So when Madison texted, "Hey! Eva in my bio class is having a holiday party tonight, wanna go?

My mom can drive us," followed by four Santa emojis, Leo carefully placed her book facedown on Denver's back so that she wouldn't lose her place and then texted East.

They hadn't really talked at all in the past few days. They hadn't talked because, well, Leo isn't sure what to say, how to backtrack from a stupid conversation that should never have happened in the first place.

But now she has a reason.

Leo:

Are you going to Eva's party tonight?

The response came back almost immediately.

East:
How did you hear about Eva's party????

Leo frowned.

Leo:

She invited Madison who invited me.

Are you going?

East:
Yes. But you're not.

Leo's frowned deepened. Who put East in charge? When did he start telling her what she could and could not do?

Before she could respond, he texted again.

East:
I'm serious, Leo. Stay home. Hang out with Denver.

Leo glanced over at the dog. He was snoring.

K, she wrote back, then got up and went to the landing. She could hear the home makeover show's theme music again, the living room dim save for the TV light and the glow of their semi-lopsided Christmas tree. It was fake and made the room always smell musty for a day or two. Her mom had put it up two weeks earlier, grunting and shoving all of the pre-lit branches in place. She didn't have to say that she was doing it solely for Leo, that if Leo hadn't been there, the house would go undecorated and dark, a mourning widow wearing all black, curtains drawn like a veil.

Leo both loved her mom for putting up the tree and wished she hadn't done it at all.

"Hey, Mom?" she called, leaning over the banister and scratching her arm on the garland. "Can I hang out with my friend Madison?"

There was a pause. "Who's Madison?"

"She's the one who invited me to the mall that one time, remember?" Leo decided to be judicious about how much information she handed out. "Her mom can pick me up, you don't even have to drive me."

An hour later, she was piling into the backseat of Madison's mom's car, a Lexus sedan that smelled new. "Hi there!" Madison's mom chirped.

"Hi," Leo said. Madison's mom sounded just like Madison. It was a little weird. "Thanks for the ride."

"Oh, sure, not a problem." She glanced back at them in the rear-view mirror and smiled. "This way I get to hear all the gossip."

"Oh my God, Mom." Madison groaned into her hands. "We live in the most boring town in America. There's no gossip."

"If you say so," she replied with an exaggerated wink, and Leo felt the secondhand embarrassment so deep that it made her cheeks flush. Parents who tried too hard were so much worse than the parents who didn't try hard enough. She thought of her own mom alone on the couch, their front porch dark, and wondered if she had made a mistake, leaving.

Five minutes into the party, Leo realizes that she has.

There's an energy in the room that's different from the last party she went to, a dark tension that makes Leo feel like she's about to witness something she doesn't want to see. The kids at this party look older, tougher, less familiar, and Leo sees a few faces she recognizes from school, but no one that she actually *knows*. There's a lit Christmas tree, but it's bright white and covered in shiny ornaments, almost sterile and harsh, and Leo thinks of their sad, musty little tree.

Nina, she realizes with a stomach-swooping sense of dread, would have never let her come to this party.

She and Madison stick close to each other, holding red plastic cups filled with sour-tasting wine, talking about dumb stuff over the loud music. Someone puts on Mariah Carey's "All I Want for

Christmas Is You" and people cheer and start to dance, but it's replaced after the first chorus with a Bad Bunny song and everyone cheers again, louder this time. There's beer pong happening in the kitchen and every so often, screams of rage and victory rise up over everything else, making the hair on the back of Leo's neck stand up, reminding her of her mom in the emergency room that night, an animalistic howl.

But then Madison sees the host of the party, the girl from her bio class, and so she heads over to say hello and Leo finds herself sitting on the stairs by herself, trying to look aloof and pensive and effortlessly cool, and not how she really feels, lonely and small and a little wobbly from the wine. It reminds her of sleepovers at friends' houses back in elementary school, when she'd wake up in the middle of the night and not recognize the shadows on the wall, not know where the bathroom was. She wonders if it's too late to sneak out and walk home. It's only a few miles away. Fresh air never hurt anyone. The walk would do her good. Ten thousand steps a day, after all.

"Oh, Jesus Christ."

She sees his camera before she sees him.

"Hi!" she says to East, way more enthusiastic than she wishes she was. She reminds herself of Denver when someone pulls cheese out of the refrigerator, and Leo knows it's not a great sign when she's comparing herself to the family corgi.

East, on the other hand, looks decidedly less pleased.

"I thought you were staying home," he says. "Where's Madison?"

Leo points toward the corner, where Madison's absentmindedly patting her halo while talking to a boy. A boy who is definitely *not* looking at her halo.

East groans and rubs his hand over his eyes.

"Well, it's nice to see you, too," Leo says as she stands. Now that she's up, she can see Kai and Dylan behind him. Kai's eyes go wide and happy when he sees her, but Dylan is busy texting on his phone, his frown intensified by the screen's blue light.

Leo thinks of her mom again, alone in front of the television.

"Hey, Leo," Kai says, waving a little. He has a Santa hat on and quickly wipes it off his head, leaving it on the floor.

"Hi," she says. Thirty seconds ago, she had been ready to walk home, but seeing East grumble makes her want to be the life of the party, and she's not sure why. "Do you know where the drinks are?"

"Yeah, sure, I'll show you," Kai says.

"Leo," East starts to say, but one look from Leo has him closing his mouth.

"Last time I checked, you weren't the boss of me," she tells him, and she could swear it's Nina's voice she hears and not hers. "Have a *great* time tonight."

Kai's looking back and forth between them like a kid watching his parents fight, but when Leo steps away and heads toward the kitchen, he follows her. "Just ignore him," he says.

"That's the plan," Leo replies. She has no idea where she's going or what she'll do when she gets there, but once they're in the kitchen, Kai plucks a can of beer from the ice-filled kitchen sink and hands it to her.

"Thanks," Leo says. She doesn't even like beer or drinking but it feels good to hold something cold in her hand.

Leo flashes back to East in the kitchen, the August air flowing hot through the room. Nina's laugh floating to them from across the pool.

She pops the can open and watches as the wispy foam rises like white smoke from the can's mouth, then takes a long swig and regrets it almost immediately. Leo remembers Nina's warning at the last party they went to, how she should never accept drinks from a boy, no matter what.

Too late, she thinks, and sips again.

Kai cracks open his own drink. "A tip?" he says. "Don't drink wine at these parties. The headache the next day is . . ." He winces a little.

Leo laughs at that, then "Cheers," she says.

"Cheers," Kai replies and knocks his can against hers. "So how did you end up here?"

"Someone invited me and it seemed better than staying at home with my mom. You?"

Kai nods toward the doorway, back where East had been before Leo had flounced away. "Just came to keep an eye on that guy out there."

Something very small shifts in Leo's stomach, something that doesn't make her feel any better. "East? Why?"

Kai raises his beer to his mouth and raises an eyebrow while taking a sip. "He just needed to blow off some steam."

Suddenly Dylan is there, flanked by Aidan, who reaches between her and Kai to pull two more beers out of the sink, deliberately jostling Kai as he goes. He's wearing the Santa hat now, but it had looked better on Kai, and he winks at both of them as he pulls away. "Catch you later, kids," Aidan says. "Don't wait around for me."

Dylan looks at Leo as he reaches for his own beer, and she recognizes that blazing look of protection in his eyes. It's the same one she used to see in Nina's whenever some kid was mean to Leo at school. "East came here to get fucked up," he tells her.

"East can still get fucked up," Leo says, even though her stomach is sliding around again.

Dylan just rolls his eyes and Leo realizes this is the first time she's seen him look at her and not at his phone. "He's not going to do that now that *you're* here," he tells her. "Get serious."

Leo looks over to Kai, who takes another gulp of his beer as Dylan saunters away, checking his phone again. Kai's cheeks are pinkening and she wonders if he feels as drunk as she's starting to feel, the lights softening, the room feeling nostalgic even though she's never been there before.

"So, um." Kai clears his throat. Even the tips of his ears are red. "Do you and East, um, you know? Are you . . . ? Have you ever, like, kissed or anything?" His words come out in a rush, like people stampeding for an exit.

Leo thinks for a minute, then takes a sip of her beer and carefully wipes her mouth.

"No," she lies.

It's a strange party.

Leo talks to Kai about their old middle school and how it always smelled like leftover cafeteria food and isn't that just *so weird*? After a while, Madison bounces back over and seems genuinely happy to see Leo and Kai together, and then Kai reluctantly drifts away to join East and Dylan outside.

There's a pool in the backyard, but no diving board.

After an hour, with Leo's mostly empty can of beer now warm in her hand, a huge pickup truck pulls up outside and a few guys get out. It's one of those trucks that has a step-up rail on it, exaggerated wheel wells, and an extended cab. "That truck's got hips," Nina would say whenever she saw one on the road, and would always giggle to herself afterward, not caring that she had made the joke dozens of times before.

Leo doesn't recognize any of the new boys, but there's a sudden friction in the air that she can't quite figure out. It reminds her of the time she accidentally shocked herself while plugging a lamp into an outlet, a sharp jolt that left her feeling jittery and rattled for the rest of the night. Through the sliding glass door, she sees East looking at her. She turns away, but not before seeing the look on Dylan's face, hard and steely and almost mean. He's holding a cigarette. Leo didn't even know he smoked. She wonders if Sophie knows. She wonders where Sophie *is*.

"Do you know those guys?" she asks Madison as the three guys saunter through the party, some people saying hi to them and others ignoring them outright. One of them has a funny little smirk on his face, like he's enjoying the people ignoring him more than the people saying hello, and Leo has an impulsive and childish wish that her sister was there. She would know what was happening—and what to do.

"Oooh," Madison says quietly, and Leo hates that she leans closer to her to get the scoop. "*Brayden's* here."

"Who's Brayden?" Leo whispers back, even though the music is pretty loud and no one's listening to them anyway, the two little sophomores huddled together on the couch, one of them dumb enough to wear a costume, the other dumb enough to show up in the first place.

"You know. *Brayden.*" Madison widens her eyes a little like that would somehow make Leo understand. When Leo just looks at her, she sighs and says, "Brayden Carlson? His dad was the one who got arrested for embezzlement back in September. They lost their house, that big one up on the hill by the freeway, all of their cars. They even repossessed Brayden's Lamborghini while he was in class, took it right from his school parking lot in front of everyone. I heard he's working at, like, Starbucks or something now."

Leo remembers hearing something about that, a fancy car getting towed, but all she thinks is that Brayden has lost both his car and his dad. "Where's his dad now?"

"In prison, I guess? Waiting for a trial?" Madison shrugs. "I heard he's kind of a jerk."

"A shocking twist," Leo says, the wine and beer overriding her ability to censor herself, but it makes Madison laugh.

Brayden and his henchmen (Leo can't think of a better word for the two boys skulking behind him) float through the party, helping themselves to beers in the kitchen and then grabbing a full bag of potato chips off the counter before going outside. Leo keeps talking to Madison, but she can feel East watching her through the window, can sense that Brayden is getting closer and closer to East, like an animal slowly cornering its prey, and before she knows what she's doing, Leo stands up and pulls Madison to her feet. She wobbles a bit, but Madison's arm steadies her. "C'mon," Leo says. "I need some air."

Her legs feel shaky as she heads outside, the air bracingly cold after the body heat in the house, and Madison shivers next to her. "Let me go get my coat," she says, ducking back inside, but Leo keeps moving toward East, who doesn't exactly look thrilled to see her.

"You need to go home," he says to her as soon as she's close enough.

"No way," Leo replies. Kai and Dylan aren't even looking at her, but over her shoulder toward Brayden, who's now only a few steps away.

"'Sup, East?" Brayden says. His words are slurred, his eyes hazy. Leo wonders how much he's had to drink so far tonight.

"Hey," East says. "Good to see you. You ride your bike here?"

People are starting to gather, pouring out of the house like ants streaming out of an anthill, and Kai grabs Leo's free hand and swiftly tugs her to the side, out of the way. "Hey," she says, stumbling, but he ignores her, and that's how she knows that things are about to go sideways.

"How'd *you* get here?" Brayden replies. "You drive your dad's car?"

East doesn't respond, just glances over at Leo, who's too busy remembering the feel of the car's soft interior, the *click!* of a seat belt, the music on the radio, the rush of warm air through an open window on a hot night.

"Yeah, that's what I thought." Brayden snickers when East doesn't respond. "How's the single life?"

"You tell me," East says. "Since she broke up with you first."

Leo feels like she's been dropped into a TV series where she's missed the first three episodes and has no idea what's going on, who the characters are, or how they know each other, but one thing is for sure: Nina is the star of the show.

Did her sister once date *Brayden*? Suddenly Nina seems so far away that Leo can't even feel her anymore. She wonders if she's had too much to drink, wonders if she's misunderstanding an easy situation, if the alcohol has taken something simple and complicated it into something inexplicable.

"Yeah, well, maybe if she hadn't she'd still be—!"

"Brayden, shut the *fuck* up!" East's voice is raw and furious, so unlike him, so unlike the guy Leo found in the theater's AV room, bundled into a pink hoodie, crumpled up in a chair.

"—she'd still be alive!" Brayden has spittle in the corner of his mouth now, his cheeks and neck mottled with bright pink spots.

Leo's mother's skin had looked the same way at the funeral.

Brayden's almost chest to chest with East now, and Leo sees a tiny flinch cross East's face. "Maybe if she hadn't been in *your* car, if *you* weren't driving, maybe then she'd be—!"

East swings first and then it's a mess of arms and legs flailing, Dylan and Kai jumping in at the same time as Brayden's friends, and all Leo hears are grunts and cries and, somewhere deep down in there, a horrible wail of grief.

She doesn't know whose it is. It might be hers. She'll never know.

Watching the fight is like that old experiment they did in elementary school, pouring metal shavings on a magnet and watching them gather in thick piles at opposite poles. Suddenly it's like every guy at the party is suddenly in the melee, swinging sloppily as their backward baseball hats fly off, East and Brayden still grunting in the middle.

Six months before she died, Nina took a self-defense class with some friends at the local community center and came home ready to fight anyone and everyone.

"Look," she said to Leo, who was sitting cross-legged on her bed with Denver's head on her knee. "You want to throw them off-balance, right?" She squatted down like she was about to take someone down at the waist. "Like this, okay?"

Leo nodded. She still wasn't allowed to stay out past 11:00 p.m. on the weekends and even if she could, there was nothing to do in their town except sit around at Starbucks and wait for the employees to finally shoo them away. The idea of having to tackle someone before they attacked her was both mystifying and slightly thrilling.

"Also," Nina huffed as she stood back up. "You want to aim for the kidneys. Punch, hit, kick, whatever."

"Okay," Leo said, and tried to remember where the kidneys were. Were they near the appendix? Which side was her appendix on again?

"They're in the lower back," Nina said before Leo could even ask. "Right here. Make 'em pee blood if they try to hurt you, okay, Leo?"

And now the fight's getting near her and it hurts in a very different way than she could have ever imagined. The boys are scuffling like puppies in a cage, the high-pitched squeaks of their sneakers contrasting against the low grunts and swears, and through her fog of alcohol and confusion, Leo sees a girl next to her, holding a new, unopened can of beer.

The fight shifts so that Brayden's T-shirt-clad back is to her, so she can see his hands on East, the way he's squeezing so tight that the skin around his hand is bone-white, and Leo feels that surge of anger swell in her chest, a rage so strong that it presses under her skin, makes her feel like the Hulk, like nothing could ever contain her grief. These stupid boys are here—alive and breathing, their pulses racing and blood flowing—and her sister is dead.

Make 'em pee blood if they try to hurt you, okay, Leo?

And fucking hell, does Leo *hurt*.

She snatches the beer from the girl, who protests with a "Hey!" but sounds more confused than upset. Leo ignores her, pulls her arm back, feels her anger gather right at her shoulder, and hurls the full can straight into the fight.

It hits Brayden square in the back.

"Fuck!" Brayden screeches, and he lets go of East long enough for East to scramble away. It's like the whole crowd is breathing as one, chests heaving, and Leo gasps along with them, surprised at herself. She doesn't even kill *spiders*.

Brayden swears again, his hand going to his back, right where the beer can made contact. Behind him, East's eyes are wild, looking toward Leo like he might need to spirit her away. "Who the fuck are *you*?" Brayden spits.

Leo is suddenly very aware that every single pair of eyes at the party is on her.

"I'm her sister," she tells him, and forces her voice not to wobble on the last word.

Brayden's shoulders go down as his eyes go wide. "Leo?" he asks.

She startles. She can't help it, can't stand that there's someone in the world who knew her sister but didn't know her. It makes Nina feel too alien, too full of secrets, like there are too many pieces that Leo will never be able to fit together to make Nina whole again.

And there's East, standing next to him, holding his own memories, the ones that Leo should have but doesn't, and she finds herself wishing that she had another beer, or a brick, or anything heavy that she could hurl at him, too. The anger is so bright and sharp that it would be almost frightening if it didn't overpower every other emotion swirling in her chest.

"Get the fuck out of here, Brayden." East manages to find his voice. His shirt is ripped at the shoulder and there's a scratch on his cheek. "Leave her alone."

Leo shoots a glare in his direction. "I can speak for myself, thanks."

Brayden huffs out a laugh and rubs at his jaw. "You," he says to Leo, "are fucking crazy."

Leo thinks he sounds almost . . . *admiring*?, but East is suddenly back in front of her. "Hey!" he yells. "Don't say crazy! It's sexist!"

Leo bites back a reluctant smile. She's not going to give him credit for anything right now.

"Just go home, Brayden!" East yells again. "Get out of here!"

Brayden stays where he is, his chest heaving, his breath coming out in tiny puffs of air.

Leo is the one who turns and walks away.

She can hear East yelling after her, followed by some muttered comment from Brayden, but she walks through the sliding door and into the house, which is empty and messy.

"Leo!" East yells again, and then he's there, taking her by the arm. He's not grabbing her or hurting her, but she yanks it back from him.

"Do not touch me!" she yells back. "You don't get to do that!"

"Okay, I'm sorry." He holds up his hands. "Just . . . don't leave. I'm sorry."

Leo can't decide if she wishes she had had more to drink, or if she wishes she were stone-cold sober. She's somewhere in the middle, her words slurred only a little, her feet constantly moving so that she doesn't topple over.

"No," she says, then takes a step back and holds out a finger to him. "*No*. You do not get to apologize to me for something that you could fix if you wanted to."

East frowns in confusion, then glances back over his shoulder. Against the harsh Christmas tree lights and the iridescent blue pool, he looks older, tired. Leo wonders if she looks the same way, her entire body sagging with grief, pulling her down toward the earth.

"Leo," he says again. "I'm sorry. Brayden's just, he got under my—"

"They dated?" Leo asks, and East nods. "She never told me that. You knew?"

"I mean, a *lot* of people knew," East starts to say, but Leo holds up her finger again.

"Stop," she says. "What else do you know about her, East, hmm?"

"What are you—?"

"You remember." Leo's voice is shaking now. So are her knees. "You *remember* everything from that night, don't you?"

"I don't want to talk about that night, Leo." East's voice is harsh and final. "Not right now, not tonight. Not with . . ." He gestures behind them toward the partygoers, most of whom are too busy focusing on Brayden to see the real drama unfolding in front of them.

"I don't care," she says.

"You're drunk."

"So what? Like that means that what I'm feeling isn't true?"

Despite her warnings, Leo now takes a step toward him. "Tell me. I need to know."

East bites his lip and shakes his head.

"You told me about your and Nina's first kiss, for fuck's sake!" She's angry, not playing fair, and she can tell by the way his head snaps up that she's pushed too far.

"East." Leo feels the tears rising up and is too tired to push them down. "East, please. Please. I'm never going to have any more memories of her and I can't . . . I need to know what all of them are. I need to know what you remember." The alcohol has made her chest feel like it's cracking open, aching and bleeding all over the asphalt, an arm dangling from a gurney.

East shakes his head again, then starts to get his car keys out of his pocket. "We need to get out of here," he says. "I'll drive you home, let me just get Kai and—"

"East!" she screams, and it's as if the entire party turns and looks at them in one swift motion. "Tell me! What happened? I have to know, *please*!"

East's jaw tightens, his mouth smooths into a straight line, and he takes two steps forward so that they're right next to each other, so no one else can hear what he's about to say.

"You want to know what my memories are?" he says, only he sounds broken instead of angry. "Fine, I'll tell you. They're *mine*, Leo. Those memories are mine, they're not yours, and they're *personal*. I know you like to think that you're the only one who loved her, but I loved her, too. You're not the only one who doesn't get more time with her. And I'm going to keep some things for myself. Just because you're her sister doesn't mean you get to have every part of her."

The word "selfish" blazes across Leo's brain, but she's not sure if she's thinking of East or of herself. She's embarrassed and furious and frustrated and tipsy, so she does the only thing she can do in a strange house.

She turns on her heel and starts walking toward the front door. As she puts her hand on the doorknob, Madison comes rushing down the stairs, her halo askew, her hair mussed. There's a boy at the top of the stairs but Leo doesn't care to figure out who it is. She's met enough people tonight.

"What happened?" Madison asks breathlessly. "What did I miss?"

DECEMBER 6
111 DAYS AFTER THE ACCIDENT

"HOW'S THE MEAT loaf?" Stephanie asks as Leo pushes it around on her plate.

"It's great," she says with a smile, and it is, but the smile is so forced that it hurts her face. Stephanie's a great cook (way better than Leo's mom if she's being deeply honest here) but there's a tension at the table that wasn't there the last time she came over for dinner.

Christmas is approaching like a train without brakes, Leo thinks, and it's coming for all of them.

"It's really good," she adds, then takes another bite for good measure. The turkey meat loaf is a new recipe for their Friday night dinners, as was the meal last week, and the week before that. Leo's noticed that Stephanie hasn't cooked a single meal that Nina had eaten, and certainly not one that she enjoyed. She's not sure if that's a coincidence, and she's not sure she wants to find out, either.

Across from her, her dad's shoveling in the meat loaf like he's about to go on a hunger strike and is trying to prep beforehand. He's a nervous eater, always has been. So was Nina. Leo and her mom are the ones who pick at food whenever something's wrong. They've both lost weight since August.

"Um, Dad?" Leo says, setting down her fork. She can't eat anymore. Her dad will probably polish it off when he does the dishes later. Leo and Nina used to clean up when they came over, but now her dad insists that she sit with Stephanie, that he's certainly capable of loading a dishwasher and scrubbing a pan. Leo misses being in the kitchen, though, moving in perfect rhythm with Nina as they put away leftovers and loaded the dishwasher. She misses the physical motions of her sister and the way she could anticipate them, both of them so used to one another's presence that they could move perfectly around one another.

There are so many empty spaces to fill, Leo thinks, that sometimes it's hard to find the solid ground.

And she's about to create another hole.

"What's up, sweetie?" her dad says now, glancing at Stephanie before he looks at her. Leo's gotten used to that move from him, the quick "oh shit, maybe we broke Leo" look.

"Um." Leo wipes her mouth, pushes her plate away, knowing full well that Stephanie won't say a word about her mostly full plate. She's too nice for that. "I know that it's your turn for Christmas this year."

Her dad leans back. Stephanie leans forward. Leo doesn't move.

"And I know that this year is, just, yeah, really weird and hard and all of that, but I was wondering if I could do Christmas with

Mom this year. Or, at least," she rushes on, "Christmas Eve and morning, and then maybe come over here on Christmas afternoon, maybe? Because I don't think I should leave Mom totally alone this year, and not that you should be alone either, but at least you and Stephanie have each other, and Aunt Kelly and Uncle David are going to Vermont because I guess Gertie wants to drop out of college? And yeah, it's just that thinking about Mom being alone——"

"Leo. Honey." Stephanie leans forward more and puts her hand over Leo's. It's cold but still feels warm somehow. "Of course. We understand."

Leo's dad looks like he's less understanding, his mouth in a thin line, and Leo wonders if he's going to call her mom and fight it. But then his face softens and he nods. "Of course, Lee."

Leo still feels terrible, like no matter what she does this Christmas Eve, it's going to be weird and wrong. Every year, Aunt Kelly sends her and Nina clothes for Christmas that were never quite right. Too big, too small, too itchy, and one memorable year, too orange. She tried, of course, and they always sent a thank-you note afterward, but that's how Leo feels now, like her efforts to please were going to fail, and the harder she tried, the worse it would be.

"It's really okay, Leo," her dad says again, and Leo believes him a little bit more this time. His mouth is less thin, in any case. "We can do Christmas afternoon, that's fine. Really," he adds when Leo doesn't respond. "I know that this year . . ." He clears his throat and Leo catches the quick wobble in his chin as Stephanie reaches for his hand, the silent fulcrum between Leo and her dad. "It's going to be a tough one. We can't get around that."

"Yeah," Leo says, because what else is there to say?

"Um," her dad says, and he never says "um," and Leo sits up straighter. So does Stephanie.

Oh shit.

Oh shit.

"Stephanie and I," her dad begins, "have something we want to talk to you about."

Leo wishes her big sister was sitting next to her.

"We found out," Stephanie says slowly, looking back and forth between them like she's waiting for someone to interrupt. And Nina probably would have, is the thing. They all have habits that still revolve around her.

"That I am pregnant."

The air leaves Leo in a whoosh. It's like every emotion is crashing through her, rendering her motionless, and apparently her dad and Stephanie take that as a bad sign because they both looked worried.

"I know," is all Leo can say at first. "Gertie told me."

"*Gertie* told you?" They both echo each other.

Leo nods, still absorbing the news. *Fucking Gertie*, she thinks.

"How does Gertie even know?" Stephanie asks. "You're the first person we told!"

Leo starts to answer, but her dad cuts her off. "We'll address that part later."

"We just didn't want to tell anyone until we were sure," Stephanie says, and now it's her mouth that looks thin, and Leo realizes that the possibility of another loss is on the horizon, and it might be the thing that shatters them all. She wasn't even sure how she felt about it, not since Gertie first brought it up at Thanksgiving, had even decided she didn't *want* to know how she felt since it probably wasn't even true, but now that it's on the table, something pulls at Leo's gut the way it hasn't since that August night.

"When are you—when is it supposed . . . ?"

"May," they both say at the same time.

Leo nods. Her brain hasn't allowed her to think past Christmas, much less into a new year, her first without Nina, and this news doesn't do much to change that.

"It was a surprise," Stephanie tells her. "But we're excited and hopeful and sad, too, that Nina can't be here to share this."

Both Leo and her dad look away, her dad thumbing at his eyes again and Leo focusing on a crumb on the floor. "Is this a new rug?" she asks.

"Yes," Stephanie says without missing a beat. "A wholesaler sent it for a promo post."

"It's nice." When Leo has collected herself, she looks up again. "I'm happy for you," she says, and she is, but she's also sad and scared and tired, and everything's so tangled up inside her that she can't sort it out, and so it sits.

"However you feel is truly fine," Stephanie reassures her, and it sounds like something she read in a book, or in an online article that a friend texted to her.

"Okay," Leo says, and she tries to smile.

That night, Stephanie says she's tired and goes upstairs to lie down while Leo and her dad tackle the kitchen. They work in silence for a while, the only noise coming from the small transistor radio that plays the local jazz station. That radio used to be in their house back when her parents were still married, and it's odd to see it in a new kitchen but still playing the same sounds. Nina would always try to change the station to something more current, would always complain that this was "music for old people, Dad, why are you trying to age yourself?"

"I like this song," Leo says as she dries a pot, watching the warm water evaporate in a spiral.

"Do you?" her dad asks with a wink. "Or are you just saying that?"

"No, I do," she says, and she does.

"It's Jimmy Forrest," he says. "You know, every time I turn on this old guy"—he gestures to the radio—"I keep waiting for a new station to come on. Nina would always change it, you know. I'd be expecting Bill Evans and would get Bieber instead."

Leo rolls her eyes at the reference, but she warms a little knowing that her dad is trying to be dorky.

"Hey," he says, then bumps his elbow against hers. "How are you doing with all of this?"

"Fine," she says, and she's grateful when her dad doesn't push it. She suspects he knows what she's really trying to say, how the word "fine" stands in place of "I have no idea and I need to figure it out first before I talk about it with you." He's a good dad that way. Nina was the one who would announce her feelings to the world, the human equivalent of a Times Square billboard. Her dad was good at navigating that, too, but it's different with Leo.

"I know it's a lot," he says, and Leo turns away to put the pot in the cabinet. She can't look at him while he talks or she'll dissolve on the floor right then and there. "But I'll tell your mom tomorrow. I don't want you to have to—"

"Oh my God, Dad, no." Leo shuts the cabinet with more force than is necessary for something that holds dishes from IKEA. "You cannot tell Mom, she will *freak* out."

Her dad frowns a little. "Lee, this isn't exactly going to be a secret for the rest of her life."

"I'll tell her," Leo says, then shakes her head when her dad starts to interrupt her. "No, I'm serious. I know how to talk to her. You always get her riled up and then she doesn't hear anything."

Her dad opens his mouth, closes it for a few seconds, then opens it. "Are you sure?" he finally says.

"Definitely," Leo says.

"Okay. But I would like to go on the record and say that I am very happy to talk to your mom if you don't want to."

"Let the record show," Leo replies.

"How's she doing anyway?" he asks in that faux-casual way that makes Leo know that he's been trying to figure out how to ask that question for the past two hours.

Leo just shrugs and starts to wipe down the counter in circles. Apparently it becomes noticeable because her dad reaches out and takes the sponge away from her. "Leo, sweetie, look at me."

Leo looks up but not at him. She can't make eye contact because she knows it will shatter her and she needs to keep it together for everyone else's sake.

She's the only one who's left.

"Leo," her dad says again. "This baby, no matter what happens, they're not a substitute for Nina, okay? No one, nothing, could ever . . ."

Leo's just nodding and looking at the radio, can feel her own mouth trembling as her dad's voice shakes.

"Just tell me you know that," he murmurs.

She keeps nodding, and when her dad finally grabs her and pulls her in for a hug, she presses her face against his shirt and closes her eyes.

That way, it's easier to pretend that they both aren't crying.

DECEMBER 2
107 DAYS AFTER THE ACCIDENT

"THERE'S NO WAY."

Leo winces against the sunlight as she paces in front of East, literally paces back and forth across the worn grass in front of their school. She's holding the bathroom pass from her English class, which happens to be a cinnamon whisk broom, even though she has zero intention of going to the bathroom.

East, on the other hand, is holding nothing. She had texted him at the start of the day with an all caps *I NEED TO TALK TO YOU* and he had written back *OKAY WOW THIRD PERIOD ALL CAPS HUH.*

"There's no way," Leo says again, even though East hasn't said anything. He's watching her go back and forth, and then finally tilts his head up.

"What is that thing? A broom? It smells *amazing*. It smells like Christmas."

He reaches for it and Leo hands it over. "Can you please focus for a minute?" she says.

"Leo, all you've said is 'There's no way,' and you've said it about forty-five times since I got here, so I'm not exactly sure what you want me to focus on besides this thing." He waves the broom around, then takes another sniff. "Oh my God, can you just buy these things in stores?"

"East!"

"The future is *now*."

"East! I think Stephanie's pregnant."

That gets his attention. "Your stepmom?"

Leo nods, her eyes wide.

"Did she tell you this?"

"No, I was . . . it's a long story, but my cousin Gertie told me."

East raises an eyebrow. "Look, no offense to your family, but based on what Nina used to tell me, Gertie is not exactly a reliable source."

Leo screeches in frustration, not sure whether she should agree with East or defend her cousin. Across the way, two students rehearsing for the spring play (*Romeo and Juliet*, how original) look up, alarmed.

"Okay, just—here, sit down before the whole school thinks you're the one about to give birth." East tugs at her hand and she falls into the grass in front of him.

"There's no way, though, right? *Right?*"

East pauses before saying, "There are actually a lot of ways Stephanie could be—"

"East!"

He smirks. "Leo, when two people love each other very much—"

"Uh-uh, no. No. Not going down that path, thank you so much."
Leo drops her head into her hands and takes a deep breath. She
hadn't slept at all the night before, dreaming of Nina, of how she
laughed and talked and walked, but she could never see her sister's
face. Leo woke up sweating around 2:00 a.m. and never fell back
to sleep after that, too frightened by what her brain both could and
could not imagine.

"If she's pregnant, I'll . . . I don't even know."

"React like you're reacting now?"

Leo shoots him a withering look and East finally sets aside the
broom, but not before giving it a gentle pat. "Okay, so your stepmom
might be pregnant. That's . . . a development."

"They haven't said anything to me about it," Leo says. "So do I
say something? Do I tell my mom? Oh my God, my *mom*. She's going
to lose it."

"Leo? It's not like this is the worst news in the world."

Leo looks at him. "Are you serious? This is going to *break* my
mom. She's barely functioning right now and if she finds out that my
dad is about to have another kid?" Leo feels the bile rise in the back
of her throat and swallows it down. It feels like the world is spin-
ning way too fast, and she doesn't know if it's worse to be afraid and
alone in your bed at night, or afraid and in front of someone else in
the middle of the day.

"What do you mean, barely functioning?"

Leo waves her hand in front of her. "She's calling in sick to work
a lot, she's not really eating. She's sleeping in Nina's bed every night.

But if she finds out about this, oh my God."

"Did you tell your dad about her?" East asks.

"*No*, East!" Leo cries. "I didn't because, in case you forgot, I just found out that his wife might be pregnant!" She jumps to her feet and starts pacing again. "He's a little busy right now!"

"I don't think your dad is too busy for you," East starts to say, but Leo's not listening to him.

"Should I just ask him? Is that bad? I'm going to ask him."

"Leo, can you please stop pacing?" East puts his hands to his temples. "Seriously, you're giving me vertigo."

"You can't give someone vertigo, it's not a communicable—"

"Leo." East raises an eyebrow. "Sit."

She sits. "What should I do?"

East just looks at her. "Why are you asking me? I have no idea!"

"But you're smart!" Leo flashes back to her last night with Nina, what Nina had said about his smile.

"Yeah, sure, thanks, but I don't know what the rules are about pregnant—"

"Oh my God, *pregnant*."

"—stepmoms. I just have my dad and to the best of my knowledge, this hasn't happened to him. But," he adds before Leo starts to speak again, "I'm pretty sure you're not supposed to ask. I think you have to wait for someone to tell you first."

Leo blinks. "So your advice is to *wait*? That's *it*?"

East shrugs his shoulders and holds up his hands. "I told you, I have no idea. This is free advice and you get what you pay for here."

Leo sighs and falls back onto the grass, looking up at the euca-lyptus trees that softly drift back and forth under the cloudless blue sky. She resents how peaceful they look. She would give anything to live somewhere with dreary weather, with rain and thunderstorms and winds that lashed at the houses. She wants the outside to feel like her insides, torn up and gray and distressed.

They sit in silence for a few minutes, the only sounds being the freshmen rehearsing *Romeo and Juliet*. Romeo is dramatically gasping on the ground. "Geez, spoiler alert," East mutters, but Leo thinks he's just trying to make her laugh, and it doesn't work.

"Hey," he finally says, tapping her with the cinnamon broom. He's right, it does smell amazing, but Leo doesn't feel like admitting to anything right now. "You still down there?"

Leo rolls over onto her stomach. She's fairly certain there are leaves in her hair but when she tries to comb them out with her fin-gers, they crumble. Great.

"How can you always be so calm?" she says to him. "Always. I'm freaking out over here and you're more concerned about a cinnamon broom."

"How am I always so calm?" he repeats, and the storm that Leo was craving suddenly flashes in his eyes, dark and gray. "Leo." He huffs out a breath, then sets down the broom and rests his arms on his knees, looking out toward the parking lot, toward nothing at all.

Leo waits for the clouds to pass, and when they don't, she starts to say, "I'm sorry, that's not what I meant—" before East cuts her off.

"I'm not calm," he finally says, his voice tight. "This is the opposite of calm, okay? If I stop to think, if I stop for even a second and think about her and everything that she doesn't, that she's not . . ." East blinks fast against the salt water that rises like the tide. "Leo, I will fucking fall apart. You know this. You've *seen* it." He clears his throat and says, "Do you really think this is easy for me?"

"No, no, I would never—" In the background, Romeo is dying, falling to the ground with quite a dramatic groan. Leo hates this play so much.

"Maybe it just *looks* like I don't care. Maybe it's different for me. You have no idea. So I'm just going to keep moving and working and skating until it doesn't feel like I'm going to fucking *shatter* all over the place if I even take a deep breath." He's standing up as he talks, brushing dirt off his ripped jeans before grabbing his backpack. "I gotta go, I've already ditched econ too many times this semester."

Leo sits in silence as he walks off. She has that terrible feeling that she's hurt someone that's already been hurt too many times, and the trees rustle overhead as she hears the students continue to rehearse.

"Stay, then! I'll go alone!" one of them shouts. "Fear comes upon me! O! Much I fear some ill unlucky thing!"

Leo picks up the broom and runs her hand over it again and again, waiting for the bell to ring, wondering how she managed to get it so very wrong.

NOVEMBER 28
103 DAYS AFTER THE ACCIDENT

I'M GOING TO need this carmelized onion dip injected directly into my veins," Gertie mutters as she passes by Leo on her way to the Thansgiving appetizer table. Leo's gripping her own empty plate, trying to decide if she wants some scaly-looking carrot sticks and ranch dressing, or if she should attempt a deviled egg.

"You need this," Gertie continues, and makes Leo's choice for her as she slops a spoonful of onion dip down onto her plate, then adds a handful of ruffled potato chips. It's almost a relief to have someone else make a decision for her, one less thing she has to think about today, this day of thanks when Leo feels anything but thankful.

She and her mom moved through the house that morning in silence, showering and getting dressed, gingerly going through the motions as if a single misstep would snap them both, the grief finally seeping out through the broken pieces. Leo turned on the television to see the Thanksgiving Day parade, watched about five minutes, and turned it off again. Her mom changed clothes three times, each time emerging from the bedroom with her face a little bit more swollen than it had been with the previous outfit.

Leo respectfully pretended not to notice. It was easier that way.

Aunt Kelly hosted Thanksgiving every year since she had a bigger dining room, but the house still felt crowded and tight with people. The cousins were all there, and Uncle David and his mom, whom everyone called Mimi. She had dementia and they sprung her from the nursing home for a few hours at Thanksgiving and Christmas. Leo could see her sitting across the room on the love seat, carefully attended to by David's sister. Leo could never remember his sister's name and had given up trying long ago. "Oh, look, it's Whatsherface," Nina used to whisper to her as they stalked the appetizer table together. It always made Leo laugh.

Leo's dad and Stephanie are there, too. After the divorce, they had to reshuffle the holidays and settled on them coming to Thanksgiving for drinks and appetizers before going to Stephanie's dad's house for dinner. (Stephanie had long ago stopped seeing her mom on the holidays, saying that it saved her thousands in therapy bills every year.) Leo and Nina alternated Christmas mornings between their parents each year.

It was her dad's year this year.

Leo couldn't think about that quite yet.

Instead, she lets Gertie lead her by the arm out to the patio, lets her put her into a chair and pass her a Diet Coke. "Don't want a repeat of last time, right?" Gertie says with a wink as she plops down next to Leo, and Leo's stomach flips a little.

She hasn't seen Gertie since Nina's funeral. She looks older even though it's only been a few months, her hair longer with a purple streak in front, her nails painted black but chipped up at the top.

"She acts like she's this world-weary sage who's seen it all," Nina used to fume after their family get-togethers, "but she grew up in the fucking suburbs and went to private school. Her parents are still *married*."

"I'd kill for a cigarette," Gertie sighs now, and Leo hides a smile, imagining Nina's exasperated reaction to that comment.

"How's college?" Leo asks now, picking up a chip and then setting it down. The salt and grease stick to her fingers and she reaches for a cocktail napkin that has a picture of a turkey on it.

"Overrated," Gertie replies with an eyeroll. She had gotten into Columbia but decided to go to Middlebury instead. Nina had lost her shit over that one, screaming "Does she even ski???" when she heard the news.

"I'll be so glad when this semester is over." Gertie sighs now, blowing her bangs away from her forehead.

"Didn't you just start?" Leo asks.

"Don't remind me." She reaches for her own onion dip as she pushes Leo's plate closer to her. "You need to eat something or else my mom will see and then force you to eat a bunch. It's so fucked up, I know, but just trust me on this."

The salt actually tastes good on Leo's tongue, settles her stomach a little. She cranes her neck back to the living room to look for her mom, but all she sees is her dad and Stephanie each holding a glass of wine and talking to Leo's uncle David. Stephanie glances up to see Leo and gives her a little smile and half wave, raising one eyebrow in a silent question that Leo recognizes as *You good?*

She just nods and gives Stephanie a small thumbs-up. She's oddly reassured by them being there this year. Usually, Nina and Leo would do a complicated waltz that involved the two of them swinging back and forth between their parents, entertaining both parties while keeping them safely separated, but Leo doesn't have it in her this year. She's not in the mood to dance without a partner.

"Stephanie's nice," Gertie observes as she helps herself to some of Leo's onion dip, and Leo pushes the plate toward her, nervous for a reason that she doesn't quite understand.

"She is," Leo says. "We got—I got lucky in the stepmom lottery."

Gertie gestures toward Stephanie with a potato chip. "You know she's pregnant, right?"

Leo chokes on her Diet Coke.

When she can talk again, Gertie is looking at her almost sympathetically. "Please tell me I'm not the first person to tell you this," she says. "Leo. It's so *obvious*."

"No it isn't!" Leo cries, then lowers her voice. "What are you talking about? She's, like, forty-four years old!"

Gertie grins. "That doesn't exactly make her a fossil." She gestures at Leo again with a new potato chip. "You have some internalized misogyny to deal with, is all I'm saying."

Leo ignores that one for the time being. "Wait, can we go back a few steps? It's *not* true, but why would you even say that?"

Gertie raises her eyes toward Stephanie. "She's been holding that glass of wine this whole time and still hasn't had a single sip."

"You don't know that."

Gertie shrugs. "Well, we'll find out in a few months, won't we. But I'm telling you now."

Leo looks back at them again, and this time her dad waves at her. Just past them, she can see her mom standing next to Kelly in the kitchen, and Leo has a sudden, horrible, rushing realization that she'll never again stand next to Nina in the kitchen, that Nina will never grow up and have her own Thanksgiving and Leo won't stand next to her at the stove and share a private joke or laugh about their dumb kids or share a secret cigarette outside after dinner, the way Kelly and her mom do every year.

"Hey." Gertie reaches over and puts her hand on Leo's knee. "You good?"

"Um, no, not really," Leo says, and realizes it's the first time she's been honest in a while. She wonders if Gertie will end up being the person that Nina should have been, her partner in crime as they careen toward adulthood, and the thought makes her feel hollow and lonesome.

"Well, why would you be?" Gertie says, her voice uncharacteristically thoughtful and quiet. "Jesus, after what you've been through. This all has to just suck."

Leo pauses. "It does," she says with a laugh. "It just fucking sucks and I'm so tired of pretending that it doesn't."

"What, eating my mom's onion dip while surrounded by a bunch of well-meaning family members doesn't magically solve all of your problems?" Gertie has a soft gleam in her eye, and for just a second, Leo could swear that she was looking at Nina.

"Not yet," is all she says though, then reaches for her soda again and tucks her legs up so that she can rest her chin on her knees. Gertie doesn't say anything this time, just lets the silence hang as she crunches down on another chip.

Her dad and Stephanie leave as soon as Aunt Kelly pulls the turkey out of the oven, their usual cue. Stephanie hugs Leo extra tight and Leo tries not to think about what Gertie had said earlier, tries not to wonder if Stephanie feels wider or rounder than the last time she hugged Leo. Next to them, her dad and mom exchange goodbyes that sound more civil than they did in previous years, and even give each other a brief hug. Leo finds herself instinctively looking for Nina so they can widen their eyes at each other, maybe so Nina can say "Okay, quit it, you two lovebirds" or maybe "Get a room" or something equally inappropriate and funny.

It's amazing to Leo how she can fill in Nina's words for her.

They all sit at the table, Leo in between her mom and Gertie toward the end. The tension is palpable, everyone very obviously not commenting on the fact that there's one less chair than there was the year before. Leo's uncle David says a very brief grace, something so generic that Leo has to wonder if he Googled "quick, inoffensive Thanksgiving prayer" or something.

She wouldn't blame him if he did.

There's silence after that because everyone knows what comes next: They say what they're thankful for. "Well," Aunt Kelly starts to say.

"Kell," Leo's mom says quietly, putting her hand on her sister's arm. "It's okay. It's fine."

"You sure?" Aunt Kelly murmurs, and Leo's mom nods and takes a sip of water. "Okay, then," she says brightly, as if nobody else at the table had heard their exchange. "Let's start with Dave and work our way around, yes?"

Uncle David clears his throat and Leo kind of suspects that he and Aunt Kelly will be having A Discussion later, but he's thankful for his health and his job, Gertie's brother Thomas is grateful for school and his truck, Kelly is thankful for their home and family and for managing to grab the last can of cranberry sauce at the store that morning, ha ha ha.

And then it's her mom's turn.

The silence almost hurts Leo's ears as they all wait patiently and politely for Leo's mom to say something. She opens her mouth, closes it again, then sets her napkin on the table and says, "Excuse me" as she stands up and walks away from the table, gaining speed as she goes. Leo starts to stand up, too, feels like she can't let her mom wander off alone, but Aunt Kelly is already on her feet and waving at Leo to sit down. "Sit, sit," she says. "I'll go. Everyone, please start, we'll be right back."

Leo sits down awkwardly, realizing that it's her turn even though the game is over now. "I'm thankful for Nina," she says quietly, and everyone at the table pauses for just a few seconds. "Can you please pass the salad?"

Her cousin Thomas can't seem to get it to her fast enough.

Next to her, Gertie takes her hand and squeezes it hard, holds on to it for a long time. Leo doesn't mind.

When her mom and Kelly finally come back, nobody mentions the fact that they both smell like cigarettes.

It's an early night, to everyone's relief.

Uncle David's sister has gone out to turn on the car and get the heat running so Mimi doesn't freeze on the way back to her convalescent home. Gertie and Thomas are arguing about something upstairs, their voices floating down on a cloud of frustration, making Leo feel nostalgic for the days when she could get annoyed with Nina. Her mom and Kelly and David are talking in the kitchen, and it's just Leo and Mimi in the living room, both of them wrapped in their coats and ready to go.

"So tell me," Mimi says, turning toward Leo, who feels a brief stab of panic when she realizes she's the only one in the room. Mimi's so old that it scares her a little. She feels really bad about that, but it's true. "Where's your sister this year?"

It takes Leo a few seconds to get through the confusion, to realize that Mimi has no memory of Nina's death and her question is genuine.

Nobody is around. No one will know.

"She's with her boyfriend's family this Thanksgiving," Leo says with a smile. "She was really excited to spend the day with them."

"Oh, wonderful!" Mimi says, and she looks so happy that it eases Leo's guilt a little. "Is he a good one?"

Leo forces her chin not to wobble. "Not as good as her, but he's pretty great."

Mimi leans forward a little. "That's typical," she says, which makes Leo laugh instead of cry. "Well, you tell her that we missed her this year. You tell her that for me, all right?"

Leo presses her lips between her teeth, lets herself have these brief few seconds where Nina is still alive in the world, radiant and happy at East's dining room table. "I'm thankful for mashed potatoes!" she'd probably say, charming them just because she knew she could. Nina and East making out in the backyard afterward, Nina coming home smelling like cold night air and someone else's cooking, Nina coming *home*.

"I'll tell her," Leo says as soon as she can find her voice again. "I absolutely will."

The car ride home is quiet, both Leo and her mom too exhausted to talk.

Once she's home and Denver's been fed and petted and belly-rubbed and ear-scratched, she goes upstairs to her room and texts East.

Leo:

Did you have a good Thanksgiving?

He responds a few minutes later, a selfie of himself and his dad and brother on the couch watching football. They're both asleep and East looks annoyed and amused. *Tryptophan strikes again*, he texts. *You?*

It was good, she lies. *Ate too much. My uncle's mom has dementia and asked where Nina was.*

East's response is slower than before, the three dots popping up and then disappearing several times. *What'd you say?*

> Leo:
> I said she was with you.

East:
Sounds good to me.

> Leo:
> Go Bears.

East:
That's not even one of the
teams that's playing.

> Leo:
> I stand by what I said.

East sends a cry-laughing emoji then, writes back *Happy Thanksgiving Leo.*

She sends a yellow heart in response, puts down her phone, and feels, for the first time that night, grateful.

THE GOOD NEWS is that Leo's mom is out of her bed when she gets home from school.

The bad news is that she's back in Nina's bed instead.

"Mom?" Leo whispers from the doorway. Nina's old swim meet ribbons are still on the wall above the bed, faded from the sun. "Mom. We need food."

Her mom rolls over so she's looking at the ceiling. "There's money in the drawer downstairs," she says. "Or just take my credit card out of my wallet. Thanks, sweetie, I love you."

At the store, Leo wanders the aisles aimlessly, listening to Nina's playlists on her phone to drown out the tinny Muzak playing over the grocery store's speakers. Nina always made good playlists and would force Leo to listen to them. "There's more to music than *boy bands*," Nina would say, and then would play a Nina Simone song followed by some '90s band that was apparently important to know, even though they sounded like all the other classic bands that Nina made her listen to.

Which is why Leo feels a delicious thrill when an old One Direction song pops up on this playlist. *Nina's dirty little secret*, she thinks. She grins and turns it up, then turns the corner and bumps directly into Stephanie.

"Oh! Leo!" she gasps, moving her cart out of the way. "Sweetie, hi! How are you?"

Leo pulls her earbuds out of her ears just as Zayn hits a high note. "Hi!" she says.

As soon as she turns eighteen years old, Leo is moving to the biggest city in the world so she doesn't have to keep bumping into people she knows.

"What are you doing?" Stephanie says. She looks flustered as she pushes her cart behind her, like she needs to make room for someone in the aisle even though it's just her and Leo.

Leo gestures to her own basket. "Shopping?" she says.

"Well, duh, of course." Stephanie laughs. "Let me go get a bigger cart, okay? We can shop together. It'll be fun."

It will not be fun, but Leo doesn't have the heart or energy to say that.

Stephanie returns a minute later with a cart that has a peculiar rattling sound to it. "Seems like this guy only wants to turn left," she says with a laugh. "I always pick the worst carts and the slowest lanes."

"No biggie," Leo says, then empties her basket into the cart. So far, she's bought rocky road ice cream, Keebler crackers (those elves really know how to produce a baked good), strawberry yogurt, and oranges. She and her mom haven't had a real meal in a long time. It's like they're both recovering from the flu and can only handle bland snack foods.

Stephanie, of course, notices. "So how's your mom doing?" she asks as they walk toward the produce section. "Your dad tried to call her the other day but she didn't answer."

"She's okay," Leo says automatically. "You know."

Stephanie nods like she could ever know. "I'm sure. What about you? How's school?"

"I kind of need to talk about anything except school right now," Leo tells her.

"That great, huh?"

"Imagine three hundred people your age staring at you all day, wondering if you're going to have some sort of emotional breakdown in US History."

"Well, that would be awful," Stephanie says. "What about leafy greens? Can you talk about those? I could talk about them all day, personally speaking. Can't shut up about curly kale."

Leo smiles despite herself. "I'm a spinach girl myself."

"Great! Let's head over there." She attempts to steer the cart to the left but it goes right. "Guess we'll just follow this guy instead."

Stephanie puts the spinach in the cart, along with milk and eggs and two boxes of Cheerios because she knows those are Leo's favorites. She also leaves everything else, which is nice of her, and pays for it all at the register. "No, no, I have cash——" Leo starts to say, but Stephanie waves her away as she swipes her card.

Leo loads the groceries and her bike into Stephanie's SUV as Stephanie talks about a dresser she's hoping to win on eBay. "I have a client who would love it, but it's pricey so they'll probably balk. Everyone wants their house to look like a magazine, but they don't want to pay for it." Stephanie rolls her eyes, then waits until Leo ducks out of the way before slamming the trunk shut.

She keeps talking the whole way home, and Leo settles into the white noise of her words, grateful that she can drift away in the passenger seat and not say anything other than "yes" and "uh-huh" every so often. She keeps thinking of the slope of her mom's body in Nina's bed, the brief startling moment of *She's back!!* every time Leo sees her form there.

"—but it's faux bamboo so, you know, we'll see how that goes," Stephanie's still saying as she pulls up to their house. Leo wishes she had remembered to turn off the porch light from the night before. Someone should also mow the grass at some point.

"You need help bringing everything in?" Stephanie asks, but Leo's shaking her head before she can even finish asking the question.

"No, I've got it. I'll just get my bike out first and then the bags. It's fine, I can handle it."

"Yeah, I know you can, sweetie," Stephanie says, and there's something in her voice that makes Leo wants to bury her face in her shoulder and cry for a long, long time, just like she wishes she could do with her mom.

Instead, she pulls her bike out and says goodbye to Stephanie before reaching for her bags. One of Stephanie's grocery bags has tipped dangerously to the side and Leo rights it just as one of their neighbors drives past and honks hello.

Leo looks up and waves, shoves the bag into place without looking, then shuts the trunk.

She never even sees the boxed pregnancy test.

OCTOBER 29
73 DAYS AFTER THE ACCIDENT

"HEY, HAVE YOU seen East?"

Leo shuts her locker in time to see Kai leaning a few lockers away. He's got a flannel shirt pulled on over a white T-shirt and his hair is in his eyes, which look concerned. She wonders if he knows what day it is, if that's why he's looking for East.

"Um, no," she says.

The hallway is filled with kids rapidly trying to leave the building, trying to get out of the cinder blocked walls. Some kids are talking about costumes, but Leo has no plans to wear one. Nina had warned her about that last year as she got ready for her friend's Halloween party, Leo leaning up the bathroom's doorjamb and watching her sister carefully apply eyeliner. "Nobody wears a costume to school on Halloween anymore," Nina had scoffed when Leo asked about it. "This isn't the kindergarten parade, Lee. Sorry, but I don't make the rules here."

Kai grumbles, then pushes his hair so it can flop back into his eyes again. "We were supposed to go shoot at lunch today but he didn't show up and he's not answering his texts."

Leo looks down at her own phone, even though the only person who's been texting her lately is Madison, who's never met an emoji she didn't love. There's nothing from East, of course.

"I don't know, maybe he's in the computer lab, editing?"

Kai shakes his head. "Checked there."

"Maybe he ditched?"

"Maybe." Kai clears his throat a little. "So how are you? I mean, you know, not like, how *are* you, just . . . you know."

Leo does not, in fact, know, but she smiles anyway. "Fine. How about you? Have you been back up to the fire roads?" She's learned how to flip the question. Grief can be quite a teacher, it turns out.

"Yeah, totally. You should come back up with us next time. It was fun having you there."

Leo remembers that afternoon, the way the tension had melted under the rosy pink light of the setting sun, the laughter of teenage boys, as goofy as they were talented. "Yeah," she says, "that would be cool."

"Cool." Kai smiles. "So, yeah, if you see East, tell him to return my texts."

"I will," she says, then turns and goes to class before he can ask her anything else.

But his comments nudge at her all through the fifty-three-minute period. Where *is* East?

Once class is over, she gathers up what she needs from her locker and goes looking for him. He's not in the lab editing, like Kai had said, and he's not talking with the guidance counselor (whose office

Leo observes from a distance after their whole kerfuffle) about college applications, and he's not down by the track where all the soccer kids are running back and forth.

Nina had played soccer for a few years when she was younger. Leo has a memory of going to games: the smell of grass, big matching hair bows, hoping that whoever the snack parent was had brought a few extra juice boxes and granola bars for the tagalong younger siblings.

She climbs back up the hill to campus and passes the theater, then doubles back. The theater is dark after the fall play, there's probably no one in there right now.

Leo goes inside.

Two of the stage lights are on, as are the lights in the AV room upstairs. The theater used to be run-down and shabby until Lila McMillan started going to their school. Her dad, Mac McMillan, was a local celebrity who owned a car dealership, but used to have bigger dreams of being a major film star. Instead, he funded their theater and now it had fancy things like a control room and upholstered seats that tilted back.

Leo creeps in, her backpack over one shoulder as she peeks around. There's a figure hunched over a computer in the AV room, a boy with a pink hoodie, the hood slack against his back.

Leo doesn't have to see his face to know who it is.

She knocks quietly on the door, giving him a few seconds before she lets herself in.

"Hey," East says, surprised and trying to act like he's not. "What are you doing here?"

"Kai was looking for you earlier," Leo says. "Can I . . . ?"

"Oh yeah. Yeah, sure." East reaches out to pull his own backpack off the chair and Leo sits down gingerly. "Sorry, I meant to answer those guys. I was just working on the, um, the fire roads stuff that we shot."

Leo nods. "You should really text Kai. He was worried."

East pulls out his phone, taps out a quick message. "I'm still alive, you dickhead," he narrates as he types. "Some of us are trying to get into college." Then he sets his phone down. "You know Kai likes you, right?"

Leo rolls her eyes. The idea of someone liking her sounds absolutely exhausting. "Great. Anyway," she says as East laughs. "Why are you hiding in the theater?"

"I don't know, it's just quiet, I guess." East gestures to the desktop. "Mr. Barnes lets me use the monitor sometimes when I'm editing. And sometimes it's just . . ." His voice trails off and he reaches for the mouse. "You want to see the footage?"

His voice is easy, relaxed, but his face is saying something else, his forehead scrunched and his teeth biting at his lower lip as he starts to open the file before Leo can even answer. His knee is bouncing, too, a habit that normally makes Leo want to scream when strangers do it, but now it feels like a warning sign, a countdown on a ticking time bomb.

Tell him to return my texts, Kai had said. *Texts*. Plural.

"Sure," Leo says instead, and takes her backpack off and sets it next to his on the floor.

The footage is beautiful. It's hard for Leo to believe that the pack of guys on the screen are the same goofballs that she spent the afternoon with, but on the screen and set to music, it's almost poetic, kids flying through the air and landing safely, laughing and high-fiving at their good fortune.

"East," Leo says after a few minutes of silence. "This is incredible. You're going to get in everywhere."

East just shrugs and starts bouncing his other knee. "It's whatever. It still needs to be edited more. I can't get the transition quite right"—he clicks back a few frames and plays it again—"here."

Leo watches but can't tell what's wrong. "It looks good to me?" she says. "But it's not my college application, so."

East makes a noncommittal noise and then plays the frames again. He's chewing on his hoodie string, his eyes focused so intently on the screen that Leo wonders if his eyes hurt, if he can close them at night more easily than she can.

"East," she says before she even knows what she wants to say after that.

"Hmm?" He doesn't look up.

"Why aren't you answering Kai's texts?"

"Because . . ." East clicks back again, edits out a tiny sliver, then adds it back. "I've been busy."

The room feels very small now, much more so than when Leo first started talking. She wishes she had a hoodie string to chew on, too. "Oh."

"These applications, Leo, they're brutal. Do you know how

many actually talented people are trying to get into these programs? And look at this." He gestures toward the screen as Kai grins into the camera, breathless and joyful with the ocean behind him. "This is the most generic shit. Anyone could do this."

"No, they can't," Leo says immediately because it's true. She thinks of what Kai said to her that afternoon up on the fire roads, about how good East is. "You make it look right," she says now. "No one can see it like that."

East grumbles and starts to close out of the footage. "Let's get out—" he starts to say, but Leo gasps as she catches a glimpse of her sister's face on the screen. "Fuck, sorry." East moves fast, opens the skateboarding footage back up, and Leo feels the quick rush of heartbreak and adrenaline, seeing Nina and then having her disappear again.

"No, it's fine," she says quickly. "It's fine, East, really . . ."

"Fuck, I am *so* sorry, Leo, I know that it's her—"

"East." Her voice is quiet enough that it makes him stop talking. "It's okay."

The air between them is heavy, dense, weighted down with everything they can't say. Leo stands up because she doesn't know what else to do, but she knows she has to do something. His lower lip is trembling, even as he's still chewing on the hoodie string, and Leo walks over to his chair just as he spins so his back is to her and he pulls his hoodie up.

"You should probably go," he says, but Leo's spent too many nights alone in her room to leave East by himself now. Instead, she walks over and bends down, wrapping her arm around his front so that she can hold on to his shoulder, then reaches over with her free hand to the mouse and silently reopens the footage of Nina.

It's awful and wonderful to see her again. It's the video that they were supposed to show at the pep rally, the one that no one ever saw. "Stop it," Nina's saying with a laugh, waving her hand at the camera. "Why do you have to film everything? You need to live in the moment, *Easton*."

"I am!" he says from behind the camera. "I just like to remember things!"

Leo can feel East shudder and she tightens her arm around him, resting her cheek against the top of his hood as he begins to cry silently. Nina's voice rings out around them, laughing as she starts to run away, scaring off a pack of sandpipers that scatter across the sand.

Leo doesn't say anything as East quietly sobs. There's nothing to say. She knows why he's hiding in a second floor production room in a darkened theater. She understands why you sometimes have to feel small and safe before you can open up the photos, hear the words, feel the memories. When it all hits, you need to know that you're contained so that the pieces can't fly away into thin air, that you'll be able to find all of them so you can put yourself back together again, so no one can know how close you came to falling apart.

Leo presses her mouth to the top of East's head, watches as her sister gets smaller and smaller.

The video stops long before East is done crying and Leo looks at the last shot, of Nina running down the beach, wearing, Leo suddenly realizes, the same hoodie that East is wearing now, the same hoodie he always wears. She hugs him a little tighter then, hoping that her sister is somewhere in there, too, holding them both close.

East finally pulls away with a sob and a sigh, running his hand over his face and wiping at his eyes. Leo would tell him not to be embarrassed if she wasn't already sure that would just embarrass him, so she stands back and leans against the desk, letting him pull himself together, wiping at his face with his wrist cuffs. "Thanks," he mutters, clearing his throat. "Nobody else seems to realize what today is, you know?"

"I know," she replies.

"And I'm sorry I didn't, like, text you either."

"What would you even have said?" Leo shrugs. "There's nothing to say."

East glances up at her then, his eyes red and raw, and she holds his gaze. Grief is a language they don't have to speak. It communicates just fine on its own.

"You want a ride home?" he asks her.

"Sure." Leo grabs her bag, ignores the wet patch of tears on her shoulder as she slings it on.

He holds her hand the whole way to the car.

IT'S THE NIGHTS, Leo thinks.

It's the nights that are the worst.

She had thought school would be the hard part, everyone looking at her and wondering how she's doing, wondering what to say, if it's the wrong thing, deciding not to say anything at all. But school has turned out to be easy, like the monkey bars she and Nina used to compete on at the playground. One hand over the other, bar after bar, back and forth. It's a routine that lets Leo go through the motions, keeps her feet moving, her hands reaching for books, pens, for her sister before she realizes that Nina's not there waiting for her on the other side.

It's a routine, one that she needs. She knows how to do school. But at night, it's just space and darkness and too much time until the sun rises up again. At night, Leo wakes and her brain scans across her thoughts, looking for the most disruptive ones, bringing them to the surface with a hiss of *What if . . . ?* and *But maybe . . . ?*

The problem with the worst thing happening to you, Leo thinks, is that it makes every other scary thought not just possible but suddenly, menacingly probable, and her brain knows this, presents them all at her feet at two o'clock in the morning when there's nothing and no one for her to reach for in the darkness.

Her mom could die. Her dad could die. Something could happen to Stephanie, or maybe all three of them? What if they're in a car together without Leo and she's left all alone?

Maybe *that's* the worst part, Leo thinks as she rolls onto her back and puts her hand over her pounding chest. That nobody can tell her that it's okay, that it's not possible, because it *is* possible, and eventually, she will be alone. Nina was supposed to be by her side forever and now she's not. Leo never thought of her sister as being finite, that there would be a limit on how many minutes she got to have with her, or that the very last ones would be a mystery to Leo, lost in the gray murky matter of her traumatized brain. It feels like a book that has the last pages ripped out, an ending that feels so central to every other part of the story, leaving Leo frantically flipping through her memories, trying to fill in the last few missing pieces.

When Leo cries, it's with quiet sobs that rack her bones, her face buried in her pillow so she doesn't disturb her mom, her mom who's gone from sleeping in Nina's bed to not sleeping at all, wandering downstairs in the kitchen at three in the morning. Leo can hear her washing clean dishes, wiping down a spotless countertop, and the background noise should be soothing. It's not. It frightens her the way the idea of ghosts used to frighten her when she was little, someone empty floating around downstairs, looking right through her, lost and drifting.

The books East mentioned had started to arrive. Aunt Kelly had sent several, and a few more arrived from well-meaning friends. Both Leo and her mom had left them by the stairs, gathering dust and dog hair as they moved around them, bypassing grief with every step. They all had pictures of somewhat sad, resigned-looking people on the covers, usually outside surrounded by trees. One had even shown up for Leo, *A Teen's Guide to Grief*, which had a drawing of a girl who looked nothing like Leo on the cover.

Leo flipped through it, saw a worksheet, and immediately took the book out to the recycling bin. The others are still there, though, haunting the downstairs the same way her mom does now, looming quietly with loss and fear tucked carefully into their spines.

Leo rolls over again, this time on her side, and feels the sadness move with her like water in a vessel, adjusting to its new shape and filling all of the empty spaces. She could text East, she knows, or probably even Madison, but what can she say? *I'm sad and I miss my sister.* What would that do? Remind East of his loss, or make Madison remember everything she went through with her dad's cancer treatments? Why should she wake them up, drag them into this dark place with her? It's selfish, she thinks, and closes her eyes as the tide rises up again.

The problem with not having anyone to talk to in the middle of the night is that Leo used to have that person. And now she's gone. Leo knows exactly what she's missing.

She could call her dad, she supposes, but he and Stephanie are probably asleep. And she could talk to her mom, especially since she's not sleeping anyway, but it's different now.

Leo can see how her mom moves through the world, sagged and

limp and resigned, and she doesn't want to add to the stoop in her shoulders, the lines under her eyes. The irony is that she's the only person who could probably understand how Leo feels, what it feels like to go through the house without the one person who's supposed to be there. There's no one bickering in the bathroom, calling shotgun in the car, no fights to settle or sides to take. It's just Leo now. The fact that Leo's still there reminds everyone else that Nina isn't. She's a constant reminder of what her parents have lost, not what they still have.

Leo takes a shallow breath, tries for a deeper one, fails.

It's 2:09 a.m. on October 29.

Officially Nina's birthday.

She would have been eighteen today, a technical adult who still wore a unicorn onesie and talked to Denver in a baby voice and sometimes watched her favorite childhood cartoons on Netflix when she was stressed or sad. There would have been a cake, a quiet party with family, a raucous party with friends. There would have been joy. There would have been life. And instead here's Leo under her covers, watching the top sheet rise and fall with her breath, faster and faster as she begins to feel the weight of Nina's absence, the black hole of everything that should have been and was instead sucked away in a flash.

Nina had loved Halloween, or as she called it, "second birthday," and was the one who usually rallied for elaborate decorations and the kind of pumpkin carvings that go viral on Instagram. She may not have dressed up anymore, but she was the one who bought Denver his first Halloween costume, a caterpillar complete with antennae and legs, which the corgi wore with a desperate, pleading look in his eyes. She gave the same gusto to all the holidays, but Halloween was special. It was hers.

This year, Leo thinks, Nina's birthday seemed like the sound of a bullet being fired out of a gun, warning them of the inevitable, excruciating pain that was about to tear them all apart over and over again for the next two months: the holiday season.

Leo feels the anxiety burn in her chest, roil her stomach, and she tries to breathe again. It hurts.

Only five more hours until the sun comes up again.

What else can she do but wait for the light?

OCTOBER 15
59 DAYS AFTER THE ACCIDENT

"HEY. LEO."

Leo glances up from her lunch, which consists of crackers, carrots, and turkey pepperoni, all things that she had to dig out of the back of the refrigerator that morning, sopping wet hair dripping down her shirt and wearing two socks that she later realized were different shades of blue.

Her mom hadn't gotten out of bed all day Sunday, had called in sick to work on Monday. Leo had opened her door a crack on Monday after school. "Mom?" she had whispered, but her mom hadn't moved, and Leo hoped she was just sleeping. They needed more groceries, though, and the kitchen faucet had started to drip in a way that seemed designed to drive both Denver and Leo up a wall.

"Oh," Leo says now, squinting up at the person standing over her. The sun is super bright— one last heat wave before their mild autumn finally kicked in. *It's not October until you have a wildfire and a heat wave,* Nina used to say. "Hi, Madison."

Madison gestured to all of the empty space around Leo. "Can I sit?"

Leo really needs to find a more crowded place to eat lunch. Safety in numbers and all that. But what she says is, "Of course, yeah," and moves her crackers closer to her.

Madison sits down, her hands looped underneath her backpack straps. "I just wanted to see how you were doing after, you know, last Saturday."

Leo nods like this is the first time she's heard about Saturday. "Oh yeah, I'm doing so much better," she says. "I think it was just this thing I ate. Made me a little woozy."

"I texted you on Saturday night," Madison says, and Leo feels like she's inadvertently just kicked a puppy. She knows what's coming next.

"But I didn't hear back from you. I was kind of worried."

Leo is officially the worst person in the world. She'll have to clear space on her bookshelf for her enormous "You're a Complete Jerk!" trophy. "Oh, I'm sorry. I was with my mom on Sunday and things were a little . . ." She trails off so Madison can fill in the blanks however she'd like.

But Madison just tilts her head a little, like Denver when he hears the treat bag open. "Yeah, okay. I just wanted you to know that if it was something more than that, I get it." Her eyes go wide and round as she says, "I *truly* get it."

Leo stays silent, tucks her hair behind her ear, and decides to drop out of school so she never again has to have a conversation as awkward as this one. It's a rash decision, she knows, but ultimately for the best.

Luckily, Madison can't hear her desperate internal monologue.

"I used to get these really bad anxiety attacks back in middle school," she says. Her hands are still tucked into her straps, like she's hanging on to a jet pack instead of a backpack, and Leo wonders if Madison would like to blast out of this conversation as much as she would.

"My dad, he got really sick a while ago. He's okay now, he's doing a lot better, but it was rough. I guess I forgot what it feels like to go through it, you know? Like, that feeling of being around people when you just want to be alone."

Leo's heart is threatening to leap out of her chest and she feels suddenly, horribly exposed. But all she says is, "Totally. Yeah, I know."

"Anyway!" Madison shrugs as she stands up, once again the perky person that Leo's come to know. "Just wanted to say that. Maybe we can hang out again soon? Just you and me. We don't have to be with Sophie and Olivia if that's easier for you, or we can go somewhere quieter."

"Okay," Leo says, only she actually means it this time. "That'd be fun."

"Cool!" Madison bounces on her toes. "I'll text you!"

"Cool."

To her surprise, Leo feels a little lonelier once Madison leaves.

AFTER HE'S DONE shooting video footage on Saturday afternoon, East decides that he wants to stay up on the hill to get the sunset. ("Ambience," Aidan says with an approving nod. "*Nice.*") Leo decides to stay up there with him, not quite ready to go back down to earth yet and also not sure how else she can get home since the other three only have their skateboards with them.

It's quiet and Leo and East sit side by side, cross-legged on the paved road, the breeze kicking up as the sun starts to disappear into the ocean. East has his camera set up on a tiny tripod next to him. "Looks like a little pet," Leo says with a smile, gesturing toward it. "Like a loyal camera dog."

"How *is* Denver, anyway?" East asks. He's got his hoodie pulled tight over his head so all Leo can see is a shock of hair, the outline of his nose, the point of his chin.

"He's fine," Leo says. "He finally started sleeping in my room at night."

East nods without looking over. "That's good."

"Yeah, I guess." There's so much space between their small words. Leo doesn't tell him how dark Nina's room always looks now, how it seems muted and dusty, like an old museum wing. She doesn't tell him how her mom is still sleeping in Nina's bed most nights, Nina's old baby blanket tucked up under her head. "He's a dog. It's hard. He doesn't really understand."

"Yeah. Poor dude."

"Did you . . . ?" Leo starts to ask, then plucks a few long strands of grass that are growing out of the pavement and starts to shred them between her fingers. "Did you bring her up here a lot?"

East nods again, and turns his head enough so that Leo can see the set of his jaw. Her dad sometimes looks the same way, like he's grinding his teeth so that he can keep his mouth closed, so that he doesn't start screaming a scream that might never end.

"We, uh, yeah. I did. A bunch of times. She and Dave the goat became pretty close once she wore down his grumpy exterior."

Leo grins and pulls out a few more blades of grass. "I don't know if you're kidding or not," she tells him. "But either way, I believe you."

East laughs this time, then pulls his hoodie further down over his face and looks back at the setting sun. "We had our first kiss here, actually."

"Really?" Leo asks before she can stop herself. East was the first person that Nina had ever truly been googly-eyed over, it's not a surprise that they had kissed. But it still feels intimate to hear him say it, like she's reading Nina's diary or something.

"Really," East replies, then gestures down the road a little. "Right up there. You can see the ocean better from there. I thought it'd be all romantic and shit." He huffs out a laugh that doesn't sound funny. "It was."

"Were those the pictures that you were going to put in the slide-show?"

"Yeah, from that afternoon." East is quiet for a minute before he speaks again, and now his voice is lower, more reverent. "She used to always make me tell her all the reasons I loved her. At the time, I thought she was just being goofy, you know, or teasing me. But now I wish I had told her more."

Leo looks out at the sun and blinks away the tears. "What were they?" she finally asks when she can speak again.

East groans and rubs his hand over his eyes. "This is so embar-rassing, Leo."

"Well, you started it!" Leo laughs, hears the wetness in her voice. "It's not my fault! You set the trap for yourself."

"*So* embarrassing, oh my God." East makes a growling sound and then sits up straight. "Fine, fine. She, um, she would do this little nose wrinkle thing when she was happy sometimes. This—"

But Leo's already wrinkling her nose with a smile. "Like this?"

"Yes," he says, and Leo can see both the relief and the pain in his eyes. "Exactly like that."

"I remember that," Leo says. "I forgot about that. She would also do this little shimmy thing when she ate something she really liked—" And then both she and East are wiggling their shoulders up and down and laughing, a perfect imitation of the person they both loved more than anything in the world. "Yep. Classic Nina."

Leo thinks for a minute, then looks up at East with a sly smile. "She could also be a huge asshole, though."

East bursts out laughing so hard that he falls back on the pavement, putting his hands over his face. "Her road rage!"

"Oh my God!" Leo cries, and now she's laughing too. "She literally broke our mom's car horn, she honked it so much. It, like, *gave up*. And she got hangry a lot, too."

"Believe me, I know," East says. "I once suggested that maybe she should have a snack—"

"Big mistake," Leo tells him.

"The biggest." East sits up a little, then rests back on his hands. "She even once told our freshman Spanish teacher that he was sexist. They got into this huge fight about verb conjugation—"

"Oh, God, that's so her," Leo says.

"I know, right? But then it turned into this whole *thing* and she was firing off all these quotes about how equality is an economic privilege and I was such a dumb kid, I had no idea what she was talking about but . . ." East mimes his eyes exploding with love, like a cartoon character who's seen the love of his life for the first time. "I was just so knocked out. I would have followed her into any classroom after that. It took another three years before I got up the nerve to talk to her, though.

"And then just a million other things. The way she loved Denver. The way she loved you. All of it. When my mom died, one of my dumbass neighbors, they sent us this card that talked about how only the best people leave the world early because they're too good to be here for long. And back then, I was like, 'What the fuck,' but after Nina, you know." He takes a deep breath, lets it out slowly. "When she died, the other part of me thought, 'Well, yeah, duh.'"

"The cards are the worst, aren't they," Leo says. She still remembers all of them from the days after the accident, the days before the funeral, a blur of saccharine greetings in faux-elegant fonts.

"No, the cards aren't the worst," East says with a chuckle. "The *books* are the worst. Has anyone given you one yet?"

Leo thinks for a minute. There are unopened packages still sitting in their front entry, their origins a mystery. "Maybe?" she says. "My mom's not really keeping up with the mail right now."

"Well, just wait because they're coming. After my mom died, one of my dad's friend's wife sent my brother and me this book about grief called *Let's Be Grief Friends*."

"Ouch," Leo says with a sympathetic wince.

"Just warning you. They're out there and they're coming to your door. Give it another month." East sighs and then sits forward, helping himself to his own blades of grass. "People want you to rush through grief so that *they* can feel better. Don't let them do that to you, okay?"

Leo nods, imagines herself armed at the front door with a heavy spatula, wearing a metal colander on her head, batting away every misguided effort, every grief-riddled book, every calligraphed card.

"So," East says. "You want to tell me why you were hiding in a Starbucks bathroom today?"

"Not really," Leo says, but East keeps looking at her until she finally gives in. "I went shopping with Madison and Olivia and Sophie—"

"Oh God. Did you tell Dylan that Sophie was there?"

"Not on purpose, but yeah. That's a fucked-up situation, right?"

"Extremely. But go on. You were shopping with the Powerpuff Girls . . ."

Leo laughs, her voice echoing into the canyon below. "Shut up, they're nice."

"What? So are the Powerpuff Girls." East has a gleam in his eye, though, and Leo gently socks him in the shoulder.

"Any*way*," she says. "I was with them and I just started to feel, I don't know, trapped. Like I didn't know how to be around people anymore? Does that make sense?"

East nods sympathetically. "Of course," he says, and the teasing is gone from his voice.

"And it was like everyone knows that Nina's dead, but no one talks about it, no one says a word, which makes me feel like *I* can't say anything about it, and I'm out here pretending like everything's fine but everyone's *looking* at me and I feel like I have to be both the Before Me and the After Me, you know? But I don't even know how to be the Now Me. I'm sorry, this is so stupid."

"It's not stupid, Leo," East says. "I totally get it. I get it."

Leo sighs, shifts a hand through her hair and wishes she had brought a heavier sweater with her. She hadn't known the day was going to end with her on top of a mountain. Life just keeps surprising her that way.

"I guess I just thought that Nina and I were supposed to do all these things together, right? Like, grow up, get married, have kids, be best friends, all of that. There was this future there and now it's just . . . gone."

The sun sets behind the water, a sliver of pink giving in to the blue waters.

"But the worst part"—Leo can hear the wobble in her voice and she bites it back—"is that the past is gone, too. Like all those things you were talking about, they're gone. Nina and I had all of these in-jokes, all of these past fights and secrets, and now I don't have them with anyone anymore. I don't have a sister. *I'm* not a sister anymore."

East is nodding next to her, his arms draped over his knees, and he's quiet as she quickly wipes at her eyes. "Sorry," she says.

"If you apologize again, I'm going to sic Dave the goat on you."

This makes her laugh, at least, and she dabs at her eyes again. "Not Dave," she says.

"You're still a sister, Leo," East tells her. "You are. Even if she's not here."

But Leo shakes her head. "Not really, though. I know what you're saying, but not anymore. My mom and dad, they're still parents, Stephanie's still a stepmom, but me . . ." She shrugs. "Not really."

East is quiet for a minute as the winds pick up. "You know," he finally says. "After my mom died, I thought that it was going to be like she was never there at all. That now I just had a dad and a brother and that was it. But what I started to realize was that even though she was gone, I never felt less loved. Does that make sense?"

Leo nods. "I still feel like I can talk to Nina all the time."

"Exactly," East says. "Love doesn't just disappear. It doesn't work like that. People go but there's something bigger that stays behind." Then he pauses and says, "I learned that from *Let's Be Grief Friends*."

He can't keep a straight face, though, and Leo starts to laugh despite herself, despite the tears stuck in her throat and the ache in the base of her rib cage. "Shut up!" she says. "You're terrible."

East is laughing, too. "No, it was some expensive therapist that my dad made my brother and me go see until insurance stopped covering our visits. But still! It's something to keep in mind. And also, *Grief Friends* made an excellent doorstop so it wasn't entirely useless."

"Always a bright side," Leo says.

They sit for a few minutes in silence, waiting for the last strands of pink light to fade into blues and purples. "I don't think I ever said this," Leo finally speaks up, her voice almost lost in the wind. "But I'm really sorry that your girlfriend died."

East huffs out a breath, then looks toward the sky. "Thank you," he says. "I'm sorry your sister died."

"Thanks," she murmurs.

"You ready to go?" he asks.

"Not really."

"Me either."

They stay until the sky is deep purple, until the moon starts to appear over the ocean, until the sun has left them and moved on to light someone else's sky.

Afterward, East drops Leo off at her house and she lets herself inside. The TV is humming again, this time with a show about baking and camaraderie. Her mom is bathed in the blue light, but at least the kitchen lights and a tripod lamp are all blazing. Leo's learned to judge the evening by how many lights are on. The nights where she comes downstairs to find her mom bathed in just the blue light of the TV? Those nights feel the heaviest.

"Hey," her mom says with a weary smile. "How were the girls?"

"They're fine," Leo says.

"Did you have fun?"

Leo shrugs and sets her purse down on the entry table. "It was okay. How was your time out with Aunt Kelly?"

This time, it's her mom's turn to shrug. "It was okay." She holds her arm out to Leo. "C'mon. They're making croissants."

Leo curls up next to her. "I saw East at Starbucks," she says.

There's only a brief second of tension. "Oh, good," her mom says. "How is he?"

"He's okay, I think." Leo cranes her head to look up at her mom. "Did you know his mom died a long time ago?"

"Yes, I remember. I think East was around eight or nine. Brain tumor. It was so sad. She was a beautiful photographer, very talented."

Leo nods and settles back in against her mom's side. They watch another few minutes of the show. Someone's pastry is too wet, another person's dough isn't rising, and the frustration is palpable. "Mom?" Leo says.

"Hmm?"

"Can you, like, ground me so I don't have to go to the mall again with everyone?"

Her mom reaches for the remote and pauses the show on her first try. "Why? Did something happen?"

"No," Leo lies. "I just don't really know how to be around people anymore, that's all."

Her mom hugs her closer, rests her head on top of Leo's hair. "I know what you mean," she says quietly. "When I was out with Kelly, all I could think was, I'd rather be home." She's quiet for a minute before she adds, "I don't know what's worse. When people know about Nina or when they don't know."

Leo scoots down so she can put her head in her mom's lap. "Can you start it again? I need to know what happens to Peter's croissants."

Her mom smiles and playfully flicks her forehead before resting her hand on Leo's shoulder. "Consider yourself grounded," she says, and presses play once again.

OCTOBER 12, 5:04 P.M.
56 DAYS AFTER THE ACCIDENT

KAI, AIDAN, AND Dylan lead the way up to the fire roads, cutting through the park and up into the grassy hills that seemed to catch fire every ten to fifteen years or so. "The golden hour!" Kai cries, raising his board over his head before getting a running start, dropping it, and coasting down the paved road.

From where Leo stands, it looks like he's about to sail right into the sun.

Dylan, the one who had been blatantly flirting with the barista, sidles up next to her. "Yeah, Kai's *definitely* showing off for you," he says, running a hand through his hair. Nina used to always say, "You can't throw a rock in our school without hitting some guy's floppy hair," and well, her theory still holds up.

Leo feels obligated to say something like, "Shut up, no, he's not," but Dylan groans suddenly and pulls his phone out of his pocket, grimacing at the screen.

"Sophie?" Aidan asks.

"Sophie," he replies.

"*Sophie?*" Leo repeats. "You're *Sophie's* boyfriend?"

Dylan looks suspicious, which Leo is pretty sure is not how anybody should look when asked if they're someone's boyfriend. "Um, yeah?"

"Oh!" she says, and tries not to sound so strangled. "Cool. That's cool. She seems . . . cool."

"Yeah, if she'd stop texting me every ten minutes." Dylan rolls his eyes.

"Have you tried texting her back? Maybe?" Leo feels a new stab of sympathy for Sophie.

Aidan just laughs and then drops his board on the ground. "Trust me," he laughs as he starts to run. "Don't get involved."

"Oh, man, fuck you," Dylan says, but he's grinning as he follows Aidan down the hill. Leo pulls her phone out of her pocket and texts her mom.

Decided to have dinner with Madison and everyone. Still at the mall. Will be home later. Then she adds a heart emoji and a smiling emoji, which she's discovered is the best way to make all of her parents think she's doing okay.

Leo knows that Nina had been up here before. She wonders if she saw things the way Leo's seeing them right now, if the world had felt as limitless and possible to her as it seems to feel to the four boys now barreling down the hill, whooping and shouting. East sails behind them, his camera attached to a gimbal that he holds over his head.

It's like everyone else just jumped off the high dive and Leo's still dipping her toe in the shallow end, testing the waters.

It's not a great feeling.

"Okay, hi, sorry," East says after a few minutes, jogging back up the hill with his board in his hand. He's breathless and happy, though, and Leo realizes he hasn't looked like that since the night of the accident.

"You don't have to babysit me, you know," Leo says, gesturing toward him with what she realizes is his drink. "Oh. This is, um, yours. Sorry."

"Keep it. And I'm not babysitting you. You're going to be my assistant." He points at her to follow him down the hill.

"Pretty sure people get paid to assist," she teases, even as she dutifully follows him.

"Pretty sure they get paid to babysit, too," he replies without looking back at her.

Leo shuts up after that.

East sets her up so that she's standing in the wild grass that lines both sides of the road, then hands her the camera and gimbal and motions to her to squat down. "You're filming their feet," he tells her.

"Filming their . . . *feet*," she repeats. "Is this how you wooed Nina?" She realizes too late that maybe she's overstepped, that maybe she's not close enough with East to say those kinds of things, but he just grins.

"No. I tried but she was shit at it. I tried to set her up here once and she wandered off down the hill and found a bunch of goats eating all the grass. She named four of them by the time I found her."

Leo laughs and then watches as East kneels down to focus the camera. "Okay, your job is to make sure it doesn't fall over. Can you handle it?"

The truth is she's pretty sure that's *all* she can handle right now. Her episode at Starbucks has left her feeling exhausted, like she's been running for miles without taking a single step. But all she says is, "Depends on the goat situation. Are they friendly or—?"

"I'm sure they're harmless." He pauses before adding, "Except for Dave, of course."

Before Leo can ask for more information, East is grabbing his bag and board and running back to catch up with his friends. "Let's fucking goooo!" he cries. "We're gonna miss the golden hour and then I won't get into college so I can get a job and support your lazy asses!"

Leo pulls her sweater tighter around her and keeps an eye out for Dave.

It's hypnotic, watching these guys bomb down the hill, and Leo looks at the camera's viewfinder as they zip by again and again, a blur of old skateboards, beat-up hightop Converse, dirty checkered Vans. East is all business, following behind them with another camera as the sun goes from honeyed yellow to blushing pink, whooping and cheering whenever one of them lands a trick or, more often, crashes into the grass.

Up here in the light, it's easier to breathe.

Leo pulls her knees up to her chest as Kai comes jogging over to her. He's flushed and breathing hard, but smiling, and Leo realizes that she's smiling back without having to even think about it. Baby steps.

"Hey," he says. "Cool if I sit?"

"Totally," she says, then scoots over even though they're on top of a hill and there's literally acres of room.

"He's so good," Kai says as East skates past them again, laughing as Aidan sails into the grass and immediately tumbles forward. "Like, with East, he just makes life look so *good*, you know?"

Leo thinks of the staid yearbook photos that had played over and over at Nina's memorial service at school, all of East's magic missing from the presentation, Nina looking nothing like the sister Leo knew. "I know," she says.

"It's good to see him smiling, too," Kai continues. "For a while, he was really . . ." He shakes his head and looks away, and Leo watches the ripple effect of her sister's death flash across his face.

"Broken?" she offers. She remembers how she felt the night they found out Nina had died, like she had been scattered to the sky.

"No," Kai says. "Worse. It was like he wasn't *anything*."

Leo glances over at East, who's giving her a thumbs-up as if it's a question. She returns it and he nods before going back to work.

"You were Nina's sister, right?" Kai asks in a way that tells Leo he already knows the answer, makes her think that he's just looking for an inroad to talk to her.

"Yeah," she says, then checks the camera again even though she has no idea what she's checking for.

"Yeah," Kai replies, and then they sit in silence for another minute before he blurts out, "I'm really sorry, by the way. Nina was, like, so cool. I hope it's okay if I say that."

"It's okay," Leo says, and feels her body go to war. Her heart is thrilled by the kindness, the recognition of her sister, but her brain throbs at the past tense, the *were* and the *was*. "She's, uh, she was really special, I agree."

Kai nods, his face somber and respectful. Leo thinks of the kids fidgeting and giggling in the bleachers at school during Nina's memorial. "So how'd you get roped into being East's assistant, anyway?"

"Oh, you know." Leo rests back on her hands and feels the setting sun on her skin. "I was just in the wrong place at the wrong time."

Kai laughs, then rests his elbows on his knees. "Come on, Aid!" he yells as his friend heads toward them. Aidan's arms are out at his sides and his board curves back and forth like a snake on the road. From a distance, he looks graceful, almost balletic.

Leo sits back and wonders what it would feel like to do that, to move through the air and look like you're flying instead of falling.

OCTOBER 12, 2:32 P.M.
56 DAYS AFTER THE ACCIDENT

LEO'S MOM DROPS her off on Saturday afternoon at 2:30 at the shopping center, a big outdoor structure with huge dining patios, cobblestone walkways, a streetcar, and fountains that danced to music every thirty minutes. Nina always rolled her eyes at it, called it "suburban and generic," but Leo had noticed that she still went there with her friends at least twice a month, even once a week during the holidays.

"Just promise you'll call me if you need me to come pick you up," Leo's mom says as they pull up to the drop-off area, which is packed with a bunch of other parents also dropping off their offspring who are too young to drive themselves. Nobody makes eye contact when they're getting picked up or dropped off. It's especially awful if there's a carload of kids from your school driving past, sans parents. It's the drop-off corner of shame and everyone knows it.

"Oh my God, I'll be fine," Leo says to her mom, and tries not to think about how Nina used to always drive her there, honking at least three times on the way. How far the mighty fall. "Seriously. I'm *fine*. Stop worrying."

"Okay, okay," her mom says. She's wearing lipstick today, which is good. She's supposed to meet Aunt Kelly for coffee, which Leo suspects is really a drink at happy hour. Her mom doesn't even drink coffee, but Leo doesn't call her out on it. She's just glad they're both leaving the house. Weekends had started to feel suffocating without the familiar rhythms of work and school, two tender survivors bouncing around in a house that felt both too big and too small.

"Tell Aunt Kelly hi," Leo says as she climbs out of the car, studiously avoiding eye contract with three kids scrambling out of the Lexus hybrid SUV behind them. "Be safe and have *fun*!" the mom yells as they leave and Leo blushes for them.

It could always be worse, she figures.

"I will," her mom says. "Madison's mom is picking you up, right?"

Leo sighs and starts to shut the door. "Yes, but I don't know when, I'll text you. *Bye*."

"Bye!"

Madison and her friends are waiting by the fountain, which is doing a sultry little dance to Frank Sinatra's "Luck Be a Lady." "Oh my God, hi!" Madison says when she sees Leo, then runs up to hug her. "Hi, sorry, I'm a hugger." She giggles as she pulls away, but Leo doesn't mind. It's not the worst thing in the world to be hugged, after all.

She waves to Sophie and Olivia, then lets the three of them decide where they should go first. They're all talking excitedly, like they've done this forever, and Leo has the sinking realization that they *have* done this forever, that this is a dance she doesn't know, a script she hasn't read.

Next to them, the music stops and the fountains fall with a resounding, loud smack, spraying all of them with mist. "Ugh, my hair," Olivia says.

It's two hours, Leo thinks to herself. *They're nice. How bad could it be?*

Within fifteen minutes of meeting up with Madison, Sophie, and Olivia, Leo realizes that this has been a very bad idea.

Being around people is exhausting. Keeping up with these girls is exhausting. Walking and breathing and blinking and laughing makes Leo feel like her soul is being yanked out of her body. They go into three separate stores to try on clothes and Leo's the first to disappear into the dressing rooms, even though she doesn't have money to buy anything, just so she can stand and breathe and close her eyes in desperate, silent solitude.

In between stores, they try to figure out what to text to Sophie's boyfriend, who's ignoring her texts. "He's such a jerk," Sophie fumes, then refreshes her messages once again.

"How long have you been dating?" Leo asks, grateful to have something to say for once. "Like, two weeks, I guess?" Sophie shrugs. "It's whatever. It's fine," she adds in a tone that makes it clear that it's very much not fine at all.

Behind her, Madison rolls her eyes at Leo as if to say, *Can you believe this?* then smiles. She's a very smiley person, Leo has realized over the afternoon, which makes her feel like she has to smile a lot, too, but now her face is hurting and she's starting to feel a little sweaty under her sweater.

"Guys, my mom is going to be here in, like, fifteen minutes," Madison announces as Olivia takes a selfie in front of the store, glances at the screen, frowns, deletes it, and tries again. "Do you want Starbucks before we have to go?"

There's a resounding chorus of yeses, Leo included, so they go across the shopping center to the café, which has a line. At first, Leo is just relieved to be somewhere that looks and smells familiar, but the crowd is oppressive and tight, and her friends chattering away next to her create a white noise that quickly becomes unbearable.

Leo feels it happen all at once, the way her head feels both heavy and floaty at the same time, leaving her looking down at her own body like it's not even hers, something both frightening and oddly calming. But she can feel her pulse pushing the blood through her veins at a hyper-fast rate, pounding like a bass drum, making her ribs go tight, almost squeezing the breath out of her. Even her skin feels like it's not there anymore, that there's nothing to hold her all together, and she thinks that if she doesn't get out of there fast, everyone will be able to see just how shattered she truly is, how she's all grief and no healing, a puppet whose strings are about to snap, leaving her in splinters on the ground.

She turns on her heel, smells her shampoo as her hair hits her in the face. It's Nina's shampoo, actually, and now the smell makes her want to throw up.

"Hey, what are you going to get—where are you going?"

Madison says, but Leo doesn't even turn around.

"Bathroom," she says. "Get me whatever you want, it's fine. I don't care." She has to force the words out of her mouth, her tongue going fuzzy and soft against her teeth, and Leo blindly grabs on to the door handle and shoves her way into the blissfully empty space.

The only thing she feels like she can do is put her head between her knees, so she sits down on the closed toilet and does exactly that.

This is the moment, Leo realizes, where Nina would plant herself in front of her sister and say, *Stop spiraling.* Leo could always imagine every single terrible thing that could possibly happen (except for, of course, the most terrible thing that did happen), while Nina always managed to see sunny skies and clear sailing. "Everything works out," she said once, when Leo had been hand-wringing about the gymnastics module in eighth grade PE. And while it hadn't quite worked out—Leo had sprained her ankle while doing a backward roll, which the PE teacher later said was almost anatomically impossible, and *yet*—Nina had been right. It hadn't mattered. Leo had lost three nights' sleep for nothing.

It had happened again the night before Leo's first day of freshman year. The idea of navigating a new building, new people, new teachers, and new emotions left her frozen on her bed, Nina knocking on her door and flitting in before Leo could even tell her to come in or stay out. She had seen Leo's chest rising fast, her hands gripping the blankets, and Nina had sized up the situation, shut the bedroom door behind her, and walked over to put her warm hands on Leo's cold shoulders.

"Breathe," she had said. "Stop spiraling. You're fine. I'm here."

Leo remembers. Leo breathes and wishes she could feel her big sister's hands again, weighing her down before she can float away.

She takes another breath, breathes again. She does that for a very long time. A few people knock on the Starbucks bathroom door, but she ignores them, instead threading her fingers at the nape of her neck and pushing her head further down. The floating feeling goes away after a few minutes, but her pulse is still strong and fast, her words still stuck in her throat. The hum of the Starbucks slowly surrounds her as her sister's voice dies away and she breathes in and out to the sound of steam, whipped cream canisters, the call of customers' names and orders.

Stop spiraling.

Once she can stand, she goes over to the sink and washes her hands twice before wetting a paper towel and putting it against her cheeks and forehead. The girl in the mirror looks like a fish out of water, gasping with shock and pale with fright, and Leo turns away. She can't stand to see herself right now.

There's another knock at the door and Leo's ready to answer it, but then Madison's soft voice rings through the door. "Leo? Are you okay?"

"I'm fine," Leo calls back, but it's hard and her throat hurts. "I just . . . I think I ate something weird?"

In the embarrassment hierarchy, Leo's pretty sure that having a new friend check up on you in a public bathroom is way worse than being dropped off by your parents. She's really knocking it out of the park today.

"Are you sure?" Madison's voice sounds very unsure. "My mom's here, do you want to . . . ? Do you need anything?"

There's no way Leo is going to try to explain any of this to Madison, Madison who's the human equivalent of cotton candy and marshmallows and those cute little Sanrio characters that everyone liked back in fourth grade. She would never understand.

"No, it's okay, I already texted my mom," Leo lies. "She's going to come pick me up. Thanks, though."

"Okay, well. Text me later, yeah?"

"Sure!" Leo calls. "Thanks!"

She can obviously never talk to Madison again for the rest of her natural life. This friendship is officially dead.

Leo waits another ten minutes, then washes her hands again and smooths her hair down so that it doesn't look so wild before she leaves the bathroom. She really doesn't want to text her mom and explain everything, and texting her dad would also mean texting Stephanie, and Leo just can't deal with them, with their earnestness, right now.

She resigns herself to walking home and hoping that Aunt Kelly has kept her mom out for an extra drink when she hears him say her name.

"Leo!" East says. "Hey, what's up?"

He's with a few friends, all of them standing around the order counter waiting for their drinks. Leo recognizes them vaguely from school but doesn't know any of their names. One of them is blatantly flirting with the barista, smiling with all of his teeth, holding a skateboard in his hand.

Leo looks at East and hopes he can see from the look on her face that she's not fit for human contact at this moment in time. She hopes he just leaves her alone and goes back to his friends.

She gets 50 percent of her wish.

"Whoa," he says softly. "You're, like, *white*."

"Order for, um, Beast?" the barista shouts. Next to him, East's friends start to snicker and he rolls his eyes. "Very funny," he says. "Idiots." He takes his drink with one hand and Leo with the other, and then hustles her over toward the condiment bar. It's a lot less crowded in the café now. Leo wonders how long she was in the bathroom.

"Are you okay?" he asks her, taking the top off his drink, then refastening it. Leo realizes that he's pretending to add things to it just so he can talk to her more privately, and it makes that already fragile thing in her chest start to shake apart again.

"East, I just . . . I can't really talk right now. Like, I physically *cannot* . . ."

He's watching her the way Nina used to watch Denver whenever she thought he was about to throw up, wary and concerned at the same time. "Okay," he says softly. "Are you about to lose it? Do you need to go in the bathroom or something?"

"I never want to go in that bathroom again," Leo chokes out. "I just need . . ." She has no idea what she needs.

"Okay," East says again, and he puts his drink in her hand. It's wonderfully cold against her skin and her ribs loosen a bit. "Drink this." He waits until she takes two long sips. It's sweet and bitter at the same time. Definitely not an iced caramel macchiato with extra caramel, extra whip.

"You want to hang out with us?" he asks. "We're going up to the fire roads, I'm going to film these dumbasses"—he gestures over his shoulder at the three guys now gathering up their drinks—"skating for my college applications."

Leo nods and sips again from the drink. As long as she doesn't have to think, she doesn't care where she goes. She starts to pass the beverage back to East but he refuses. "No way," he mutters under his breath. "You still look like a fucking ghost. It's freaking me out.

"Hey," he adds in a normal voice, nodding to his friends. "Leo's going to hang with us, okay? Her ride bailed on her."

"Cool," Smiley Dude says and the other two nod. They look harmless and goofy and Leo knows they won't demand anything from her.

"Let's do this," East says. "We're gonna lose all the good light and I won't get in anywhere."

The three guys skate ahead toward the parking lot as East and Leo walk behind them. Leo's still holding his drink but no one's noticed or mentioned it. "Thanks," she whispers after a minute and East just squeezes her arm in response, a silent acceptance that Leo doesn't realize how bad she needs until it's hers.

OCTOBER 10
54 DAYS AFTER THE ACCIDENT

UP IN HER bedroom on Thursday night, Leo can hear her mom talking on the phone downstairs. She rarely talks on the phone anymore, usually just to Leo's aunt Kelly, low tones and quiet voices, sometimes a small laugh that dissipates into the air like vapor. But she sounds annoyed now, her voice spiking sharply every so often, and that's how Leo knows that her mom is talking to her dad.

It's how they used to argue before they got divorced, clenched teeth behind closed doors, muffled mutterings downstairs late at night while Nina and Leo lay together in Nina's bed. Nina had been ten years old, Leo eight, and Nina had put glow-in-the-dark stars on her ceiling, moving them into the shapes of constellations.

"You know they're getting divorced, right?" Nina had said to Leo while they looked up at a glowing, green Big Dipper.

"Duh," Leo replied, but she hadn't known and the news made the room spin, sending the stars into a whirl.

"It's so obvious," Nina whispered, even as she reached down and took Leo's hand, squeezing hard. "My friend Kara's mom and dad got divorced and her dad moved to Virginia and started a whole new family."

"Wow," Leo said. She felt like crying then, but didn't want to be the little sister who was both ignorant *and* emotional. Nina seemed to coast through big life events like she was on roller skates and Leo had learned early on that she had better hang on for dear life if she didn't want to get left behind.

"Dad's not going to do that," Nina said. "But still."

"Yeah," Leo said, just as the cheap adhesive on one of the stars that made up Orion's Belt gave out, and the star plummeted to the carpet.

"A falling star!" Nina cried, laughing in delight. "Did you see it?"

"Girls!" their mom yelled up the stairs. "You're supposed to be sleeping!"

Leo wriggled closer to Nina as she giggled behind her hands, whispering, "Do you think they'd make us choose where to live, though?" That had happened to a character in a book she had read once. Only once.

"Doesn't matter," Nina had replied. "I'd choose you."

Now, upstairs and alone in her own room, Leo scrolls through her phone and listens to her mom's side of the conversation. She's not sure, but she has a suspicious feeling that it's about what happened between her and the guidance counselor. She's 75 percent sure that she's heard the word "Marshall" at least twice.

Denver's in her room with her. It's been a slow migration for him, moving from Nina's room to Nina's doorway, then to the hallway, then Leo's doorway, and finally to Leo's bed. He has a special blanket that she very carefully spreads over the end of her bed every night. The rest of her room is a wreck, but Denver's blanket is always neatly folded, a small offering of stability in the chaos. When Leo can't sleep, she crawls down to him and whispers in his ear to both of them. "She's not coming back." Denver never stirs or opens his eyes, his breathing still deep even when she presses her face against his fur and feels it get wet with tears.

It's the only time that Leo can bear to tell him the truth.

He's asleep now, his head on his paws, and when Leo's mom finally knocks on her door, he raises an eyebrow but doesn't move otherwise. It takes a lot to get Denver to move off a bed, which is why he and Nina had been such a good fit. With her, there was always a lot happening and it never seemed to faze him.

"Yeah?" Leo calls, but her mom still waits a second before coming into the room, as if Leo has some super-secret activities happening in there and not a snoring corgi and a phone that never buzzes or dings.

"Hi," she says. "Can I come in?"

"I mean, you're halfway here, might as well complete the task."

Her mom smiles a little, which makes Leo feel a bit warmer, and she sits down beside her and Denver on the bed. Denver rolls over slightly and sighs as if exasperated with humans in general.

Leo can relate.

"I was just talking to your dad," her mom says.

"I could tell," Leo says.

Her mom pauses, then decides to let it pass. "Well, we were talking because we both got a call from your guidance counselor today. She's a little concerned about you."

"Well, I'm a little concerned about *her*," Leo says.

"Leo." Her mom has that quiet, annoyed clip that it had downstairs on the phone with Leo's dad a few minutes ago.

Leo rolls her eyes a little. "She wants me to talk to her about my feelings, and I said no thank you. Politely." Leo pointedly does not look at her mom when she says that last part. "I don't even know her. I mean, would you have wanted to talk to a guidance counselor about *your* feelings when you were my age?"

"No way," Leo's mom says and the tension has melted into fondness, the same way she used to look at Nina whenever she was having a tantrum about something. For just a second, Leo feels like nothing has changed, that their mom is rolling her eyes at Leo as if to say, *It's you and me versus the drama, right?* but then her mom goes to brush Leo's hair out of her eyes and it's gone. The sadness is back on her face and Leo's shoulders sag.

"She did say something interesting, though. She said you wrote a speech for Nina's memorial service at school last month. She said it was beautiful."

Leo squirms away, not liking this feeling of adults sifting through her life like vultures pecking at a dead animal. "That was nice of her."

"Can I read it?"

"I can't stop you."

"Leo, if you don't want me to, that's okay. I don't . . ." Her mom pauses, takes a breath. "I know that you and Nina had something very special. It's okay if you don't want to share everything with me."

"It's fine," Leo says, before she has a chance to think about how maybe it isn't. "I'll AirDrop it to you. But only you. Don't send it to Kelly or anyone."

"I would never." Her mom moves her hand down to Denver's furry tummy and Denver makes himself available. "So, do you have any plans this weekend with your friends? Anything fun?"

It's amazing to Leo how parents can believe they're being so subtle. Absolutely amazing.

"I think so, yeah," she says. "Maybe with this girl Madison? We had English together last year."

"Oh, that's great!" her mom says, in a way that makes Leo feel equally sad and guilty, like her mom didn't really think that she had plans at all, and isn't this such a happy surprise! "Well, if you need a ride or anything." She goes to stand up, then kisses the top of Leo's head before planting one on Denver's for good measure.

"Hey, Mom?"

"Yeah?"

"Are *you* doing okay?"

Her mom pauses in the doorway, her back turned, and Leo can see the smallest of shudders run down her spine. It's scary how they can go from being her parents to being just people who are hurting and how Leo has the power to flip that switch with one question, one split second.

"Don't worry about me, babe," she says, turning around half-way. "I'm hanging in there. Lights out by eleven, yeah?"

Leo nods, then waits until the door clicks shut before reaching for her phone.

She's going to need to make some plans by Saturday.

Leo and Madison had sat next to each other during middle school homeroom, but had sort of separated at the beginning of ninth grade. She had waved hi to Leo a few times in the hallway so far this year, hugging her books close to her chest but still smiling. Leo had smiled and waved back like everything was normal.

OMG LEO!!!!! Hiiiiii! Madison texts back almost an hour later. It's technically lights out but Leo's fine with her phone under the covers. *How are you?*

How the hell is Leo supposed to reply to *that*.

I'm OK, she writes back, but then the phone just feels leaden in her hand. She types out a few emojis, responds with the right ("right") words for a bit, and then says, *Hey do you want to hang out this weekend maybe?*

It's so awful, so pathetic. Leo's cheeks color with shame even though she's in the dark by herself.

The three typing bubbles stay up for a pretty long time, then disappear, then come back. *Sure!! Maybe we can hang with Sophia and Olivia too??? They're cool I promise.*

Ah, so she was gathering reinforcements. Leo understands. She would have done the same thing. Game recognizes game.

Totally!

Cool! Maybe coffee or a movie? We can talk tomorrow at school.

Awesome, that's great! Leo wonders when she started sounding like a cheerleader who's unaware that her team is losing.

After a few more minutes, she tucks her phone back under her pillow and looks out her window.

From her room, she can almost see the constellations, spiraling around and around and around.

OCTOBER 7
51 DAYS AFTER THE ACCIDENT

DURING HER LUNCH period, Leo feels a tap on her shoulder and looks up to see the school's guidance counselor, Mrs. Marshall.

Nina hadn't exactly liked Mrs. Marshall. "If the color beige was a person," she would say whenever their parents suggested that she talk to her about her upcoming college applications or possible scholarships. "I can figure it out myself, thanks."

Leo thinks of this now as she looks up at Mrs. Marshall, who is, in fact, wearing a beige sweater and oatmeal-colored linen pants. Nina could be harsh sometimes, but she was rarely wrong.

"Hi, Leo," she says now, smiling warmly in a way that makes Leo feel weary instead of soothed. Adults have been smiling at her like that for over a month now, teeth bared as they attempt to console her, to rationalize the horrible thing that's happened, to somehow make it better.

There was no making it better.

"I was wondering if you wanted to stop by my office sometime this afternoon," Mrs. Marshall says. Her hair is shoulder-length and brown, her glasses are tortoiseshell. "I just wanted to chat with you for a few moments."

Leo sighs inwardly. This was another common occurrence. All of her teachers had called her up to their desks after class to ask how she was doing, like there was any way Leo could even answer that question. But she had smiled and nodded and assured them that she was doing okay, that she didn't wake up soaked in sweat in the middle of the night, hearing the crunch of metal and a boy crying. Her sister may have been dead, gone violently and way too soon, but she could totally write an essay about *The Scarlet Letter* by next week, no problem!

The only good experience had been with her math teacher, Mrs. Pfaff, but then Leo got a D on a quiz the following week and that soured her a little on the whole thing.

Mrs. Marshall smiles down at her. Leo sort of wishes one of her teeth was crooked but they're not.

Leo can hear Nina now. *Veneers.*

"Sure," Leo says. "I have bio afterward but—"

"I'll write you a note," Mrs. Marshall says, then smiles again.

Leo nods. "Okay. See you then."

It would have been a lot easier to say no, she thinks later, if she hadn't been eating lunch alone.

It's not that Leo wants to eat lunch alone. It's just that it kind of . . . keeps happening.

At first she stayed busy in the school library, pretending like she was working on a project that required her to be in the stacks every day at lunchtime. But then the school librarian, Mrs. Stewart, started talking to her about her own sister, who wasn't dead but had married a pothead who *never* worked and had basically ruined *both* of their lives and wasn't it *terrible* when things like that happened, and Leo had looked her right in the eye and said, "It's not the same."

She's not sure who was more surprised, Mrs. Stewart or herself. The librarian had immediately begun stuttering apologies, sputtering about how "No, of *course*," and "It's very different, I was just . . ." And Leo said, "No, *totally*, it's fine," even though it wasn't fine, and she hated that she was trying to make someone feel better when she herself happened to be falling apart. It made her head hurt.

The ache spread to her stomach, and when East had seen her in the parking lot after school, he had tilted his head to the side. "You okay?"

"Yeah," Leo told him. "I just ate something weird at lunch."

Still, she dutifully goes into Mrs. Marshall's office that afternoon, just as a girl wearing a Harvard sweatshirt comes out, frantically tapping on her phone. Leo's pretty sure she can hear easy listening music, like the kind in dentist offices, playing softly inside.

What's beiger than beige? Nina would have said at this point.

"Hi, Leo," Mrs. Marshall says, and Leo has to admit, her office is pretty soothing. There are still cinder block walls and that harsh strip of fluorescent light, but it's a far cry from the riotous, primary-colored hallways of their high school. There's even a lamp that Stephanie would no doubt approve of. Leo thinks it might be from Target.

"Thanks so much for coming in on such short notice," Mrs. Marshall says, like Leo has a bustling social calendar. She gestures to a chair and Leo sits gingerly, like something's about to jump out and scare her. "I just wanted to chat for a few minutes. No pop quizzes, I promise!" She laughs a little, so Leo laughs, too. Guidance counselor humor! High-*larious*!

"So," Mrs. Marshall says, leaning forward and folding her hands into her lap. "How are you doing, Leo? I know it's been, what, almost two months now since Nina—"

"I'm okay," Leo interrupts. She's got this script down now, like she's a character in a play and not a person in her own life. Sister of a Dead Girl. Hit your marks, say your lines. "You know, it's been really hard but we're getting through it. My mom and dad and I, I mean. And Stephanie, my stepmom. She's really great." That was another thing Leo had learned to add after she said the word "stepmom," reassuring them that Stephanie was indeed a perfectly normal person and not some Disney villain. "You know, it's . . ." Leo lets the sentence hang there, lets everyone else fill in the blanks in a way that makes them comfortable.

"Well, that's good," Mrs. Marshall says with apparently no sense of irony. Behind her, there's a comic poster that says "The Five Stages of Grief: AP Style" and shows a bunch of students worrying about the AP exam scores. Leo has the sudden urge to rip it off the wall and run it through the scary-looking paper shredder that sits in the school's front office.

"I wanted to tell you," Mrs. Marshall continues, "first of all, that

I really liked your speech." There's a little bit of a squint in her eye, though, like she and Leo are suddenly sharing this big secret, and Leo's spine goes straight.

"Also, I wanted to chat with you because some of your teachers have said that you don't really seem to be present in their classrooms."

It hits like a lightning bolt in Leo's stomach, searing and sharp and filling her with white-hot heat. A saxophone solo starts to softly wail in the background. "Okay," she says. She's glad she hasn't taken her backpack off yet.

"Leo," Mrs. Marshall says again. "I promise, you're not in trouble or anything like that—"

Boom! The accompanying thunder settles into her lower back and legs.

"I just wanted to make sure that you have everything you need to move forward after what's happened to your sister, and if you need—"

"I don't need anything," Leo says.

"I understand that. I also want you to know that you can always be honest with me—"

And just like that, Leo realizes what she's experiencing.

It's anger.

And honestly? It feels fucking *great*.

"You know what?" Leo says, and is surprised by how quiet her voice sounds. "Maybe the reason I'm not really 'present'"—she makes finger quotes around the word—"is because Mr. Colleran only chooses dead white guys for his reading list, and I'm just really bored. Did anyone really think of that? That maybe it has nothing to do with my sister?

"And also, I don't really care if I'm in trouble. My sister is dead, what else do you think you all can do to me here? Assign me to detention? *Please*." Leo laughs but hears her sister's soft cackle instead. "And she is indeed dead. Everyone says Nina's *gone*, like she just vaporized off the planet, or that we *lost* her like she's accidentally misplaced, but she's *dead*! Why am I the only one who can say that word?

"And you know what else? You *earn* honesty! You've literally never talked to me until today and now you want me to, I don't know, tell you everything about how I feel? Like that's so easy to do?"

"Leo—"

"You want to know what I need? My sister back, that's what I need. And until 'raising someone from the dead' or 'building a time machine' falls under your job training skills program, I don't need your help! Okay?"

Mrs. Marshall looks blank, not angry, which is almost worse. "Okay," she finally says, and Leo feels her chest rise and fall, feels herself breathing hard and fast like she's been running.

"You said I could have a note for bio," she says. "I'd like that now, please." Mrs. Marshall silently writes one and tears it off the pad, then hands it to her. Leo takes it without saying thank you, which is the rudest she's been to an adult in, like, ever, then hitches her backpack up on her shoulders and leaves the room.

There's still forty-three minutes before the last bell rings.

Fuck it. She's going to Starbucks.

How had she never noticed before that Starbucks had an entire menu hanging on the wall of their store? Was this new?

Leo stands in line, her backpack making her shadow on the café's floor look like a turtle and not a high school sophomore who had just yelled at her guidance counselor. She wonders what the repercussions are for something like that. Nina would have known the answer to that question. She probably hadn't ever yelled at the guidance counselor, though. Leo never thought that she would outpace her sister in terms of inappropriate behavior, but here she is, screaming at authority figures and ditching class with a pass held tightly in her fist.

Nothing, it turns out, is going according to plan so far this school year.

The Starbucks is fairly empty: two moms chatting to each other while their babies nap in strollers, several people typing away at laptops, a man checking his phone while he waits for his drink. Leo's only ever been in this Starbucks a few times since sophomores aren't allowed to leave campus for lunch. In fact, all of the times she had been here had been with Nina.

You should get a scone, they're really good. But not a currant scone, God no. Why would anyone do that to a perfectly good scone. Get the one with the maple frosting, it's the best.

And Leo had, because she had always done what Nina told her to do. She had been right about everything, including the one with the maple frosting, and Leo is suddenly rocked by the knowledge that Nina will never, ever again tell her what to do.

"Welcome to Starbucks, what can I get started for—oh!"

Leo blinks herself back into reality as the Starbucks employee stares at her. "Oh," she says again. "You're . . . you were Nina's sister."

Leo should have just gone to her bio class.

"Yes," she says instead. "I'm . . . yeah. That's me." She almost makes some sort of sarcastic joke about how having a dead sibling means you get a free drink, but the young woman's face looks so soft and sad that the words die on Leo's tongue.

"Wait, can you just hang on a minute?" She holds up a finger as she starts to scurry away from the register, and Leo glances apologetically at the person who's in line behind her. They're looking at their phone, though, scrolling quickly through something, so she turns back and waits.

The woman comes back less than a minute later, holding a sage green envelope. By this point, Leo can recognize a sympathy card from ten feet away in the dark, and she feels her stomach swoop and sink at the same time.

Definitely should have just gone to bio.

"Um, this is from all of us here?" the woman says, like she just decided that and it's not an actual fact. "Nina was, like, one of our favorite customers. She'd always be nice and tip in cash. She came in almost every morning."

The year before, Nina had started high school at 7:00 a.m., Leo at 8:15 a.m. She hadn't known this about Nina, and the knowledge now makes her feel a bit lonely for her sister, coming in for coffee by herself morning after morning. "Oh," Leo just says instead. "Wow. Thank you. This is so nice of you. I'll make sure my parents see it."

The woman—her name tag says Jennifer—just nods. "We all knew her order, too. Venti iced caramel—"

"—macchiato with extra caramel, extra whip," Leo finishes, then laughs. Jennifer laughs, too, both of them delighting in the fact that they knew this about Nina. Leo hasn't realized how desperate she was for a connection, how much she needed to hear someone say something banal about her sister, a small fact instead of a big eulogy.

"Actually," Leo says, "I'll order that drink, please."

"Coming up," Jennifer says.

She doesn't let Leo pay.

Leo takes her time wandering back to campus, setting foot on the grass just as the bell rings, and she heads toward East's locker. The drink is so sugary that it makes her teeth feel sandy, but she sips at it anyway. "Hey," East says when he sees her. He's shoving books into his locker while pulling others out, his hoodie slung over his arm like he's just pulled it off. "Where'd you get that?" He points at her drink.

"I yelled at the guidance counselor and then ditched bio and went to get a drink." Leo holds up the green envelope. "They gave me a sympathy card. Nina was their favorite customer."

East laughs a little as he slams his locker. "I thought you were just going to say, 'I went to Starbucks,' but sure, that works."

Leo holds it out to him. "Want a sip?"

"Is that a venti iced caramel macchiato, extra caramel, extra whip?"

Leo sips at it again. "Yes," she says. "I can confirm."

East takes it from her and sips without even wiping off the straw. It makes Leo feel warm toward him, like they're actually friends now. "This is a good one," he says, and Leo realizes that he'd probably sipped from Nina's drink more than a few times.

"So you really yelled at the guidance counselor?" he asks as they walk. "Mrs. Marshall is like a cream puff."

"I don't think I yelled," Leo says. "It's more like I spoke low and quiet. Like a serial killer."

"Oh, that's much better," East says. "Damn, this drink is good. I can see why she ordered it all the time."

Leo feels the grit scratch on her teeth, the sugar, or something, burning in her bloodstream, and carefully carries her green envelope home.

SEPTEMBER 20
34 DAYS AFTER THE ACCIDENT

THE LAST TIME Leo felt her knees shake like this, it was in the emergency room.

She's in the gym now, though, waiting for the pep rally to start. It smells like gyms always do, like deli meat and dirty socks and sweat and floor lacquer. It's not her most favorite combination of scents, that's for sure, especially when she already feels like she might throw up from nerves.

She emailed her speech to the principal a few days earlier and got back a "Leo, this is beautiful" response that talked about how lucky their student body was that they would get to hear about Nina in this way.

Leo read the email, deleted it, then heard her mom come in through the garage door. She listened for the familiar pattern of steps, but they were jumbled and broken up now, not sounding like they used to.

When Leo went downstairs, her mom was unloading a bag of groceries. (Leo checked later to make sure that she got everything they needed. Sometimes things were missing and Leo had to supplement on her way home from school.) "Hey," Leo said gently. She wondered if she should mention what she saw that afternoon, then decided against it.

"Hey," her mom said. "You were with East?" She pointed to the notepad where Leo had jotted down her hasty note.

"Oh yeah. Just a school thing." Leo wiped her suddenly sweaty hands on the back of her jeans. "Speaking of. Remember how I told you about the pep rally thing? It's tomorrow."

Her mom paused mid-stride, one hand holding a six-pack of sparkling water. They still had a ton left over from the funeral. "Tomorrow?" she repeated.

"Is that okay?" Leo asked. It's not like she could change the date, of course, but it still felt like she should ask.

Her mom nodded, but her eyes were blank. "That's fine."

"Are you sure?"

"Of course, sweetie." Her mom smiled then, but it wasn't quite right. Still, Leo smiled back.

Backstage—or "backstage," as Leo thinks of it, since it's really just a heavy, dusty curtain that's separating her from the students starting to stream into the gym, she wonders if maybe she shouldn't have said anything to her parents. But then what if they ran into someone else's parents and they mentioned Leo's speech, and then her parents would think that she was hiding things from them and wouldn't they be disappointed, especially after Nina—

Stop spiraling, Nina whispers to her, and Leo tries to catch the memory before it flits away.

Her knees wobble as the principal, Ms. Henks, comes out and tells everyone to simmer down, reminds them of good citizenship and listening, and then immediately gets everyone riled back up by yelling into the mic, "Is everyone ready for a great year???!!!"

Leo's only been through one full year of high school, but she's sat through enough pep rallies to know that at least half of the cheers out there are sarcastic. No one's happy to be back at school. They never are.

The good news is that Leo's knees stop wobbling, but now her hands are shaking.

She doesn't want to do this.

"Leo!" someone whispers behind her, and Leo turns to see her freshman year English teacher, Mrs. Pollock. As usual, wearing her trademark thin silver whistle around her neck. She has that chipper, severe personality of someone who knows they're going to be perpetually disappointed but still decides to give it their best anyway.

"Leo, I read your essay. Ms. Henks forwarded it to me. I hope you don't mind."

Leo minds. She minds a *lot*, but instead she just nods. "No, no it's fine."

"It was a beautiful piece." She reaches out and gives Leo a sharp pat on the shoulder. "How come you never wrote like that when I had you in *my* class?" Then she winks and heads back out toward the gym, where two of her students are trying to arm wrestle in their seats and failing miserably.

Leo goes cold.

Ms. Henks goes through the announcements—water polo team tryouts, an upcoming car wash benefitting the JV cheerleading team (Leo can hear the very practiced cheers at that one), a meeting in the guidance counselor's office to discuss college scholarship opportunities—and then her tone turns somber as she says, "As you know, several weeks ago, we lost one of our own."

Their own. Leo bristles, feels the hair on her neck stand up.

"Nina Stott was supposed to be a senior today—"

Where is East? Leo's standing up now, holding her printed speech in her hands, waiting for her cue to walk out from behind the curtain and on to the makeshift stage, which is really just a riser. Maybe he's with the tech guys, getting ready to cue up his montage, making sure everything's working properly.

Stop spiraling.

"—her sister Leo, a sophomore, would like to say a few words that she's written about her sister, so please join me in giving her a very warm Viking welcome!"

Leo steps out to applause that sounds polite, at best. Ms. Henks gives her a big hug and Leo returns it with the arm that's not holding her speech, and then she goes to the mic and looks out at the crowd.

Her dad and Stephanie are down near the front. Her dad looks shattered but still manages to give a thumbs-up, and Stephanie is wiping at her eyes with a tissue. Across the room, her mom is sitting with her aunt Kelly, who has her arm around her mom's shoulders. It looks as if she's holding her up like a puppet.

The rest of the audience is, well . . .

Two boys are blowing snot rockets into another kid's hair, giggling to themselves and looking innocent whenever he turns around with a frown. There's a junior braiding her friend's hair, chewing contraband gum and looking bored. Another kid is reading a textbook, and the girl in front of him has her chin propped up in her hand as she glances down at her phone.

Leo realizes that she's made a terrible mistake. None of these people care about Nina, not like she does, and her face burns as she thinks of her speech, how heartfelt it is, how emotional she got while writing it.

She is so, so stupid.

"Nina was my sister," she says into the mic, surprised by how loud her voice sounds. "I loved her a lot. She meant the world to me and my family. We lost her in a horrible accident and nothing will ever be the same."

Down below, Ms. Henks is frowning a little, double-checking her copy of the speech. Leo doesn't even bother to look toward Mrs. Pollock and her dumb whistle.

"Please don't drink and drive. Get your friends a safe ride home. Thank you."

They applaud again, even more muted this time, and Leo hurries backstage and presses her cold hands to her hot face. "Thank you so much, Leo," Ms. Henks says. She clearly wasn't ready to be back on the stage this soon and fumbles a bit through her papers. "And now we have a special video presentation from Easton—"

There he is. Leo sees him on the other side of the stage, his arms crossed in front of him as he looks out toward the audience. He's wearing a dark navy hoodie that looks black in the dim light, the drawstrings pulled tight so that they dangle down, and Leo hurries around the curtain and goes to his side.

East looks down at her. It's clear he heard every word she said. "They don't deserve her," she whispers. "They don't deserve any part of her."

He smirks a little, then reaches out and puts his arm around her. To anyone else, it would just look like her sister's boyfriend comforting or consoling her, but as the video presentation begins, Leo understands: it's a moment of solidarity.

On the screen, images of Nina start to flash. All of them are from previous yearbooks: Nina in freshman cheerleading, Nina at an MUN conference, Nina in the middle of a mock trial session, Nina on Crazy Hair Day. Leo watches as the flat, static images cycle through again and again, all of them set to a Maroon 5 song that drones on for way too long. Out in the audience, Leo can see Poppy and a few girls with their arms around each other, swaying to the mid-tempo beat of the song.

When Leo looks back at East, he just shrugs. "I told Ms. Henks this morning that I couldn't get it done in time. I guess the yearbook guys threw this together." He pauses for a second before adding, "You're right. They don't deserve her."

Leo starts to laugh despite herself, hiding her smile behind her hand so no one thinks she's laughing at her dead sister's photo montage. "Nina would have fucking hated this!" she giggles, and now East is nodding in agreement and trying not to laugh, too. He tightens his arm around Leo's shoulders, though, and for one brief, glorious second, Leo can sense her sister right next to them, and everything feels exactly the way it should.

SEPTEMBER 17
31 DAYS AFTER THE ACCIDENT

LEO SPENDS ALL of the next week working on what she's going to say at the rally.

It was pretty well known in her family that she was the writer and Nina was the talker. When Nina once got grounded at ten years old for not cleaning her room, she ranted and raved for over two hours about how her room was *her* room and she should be allowed to keep it however she wanted. And when Leo was grounded two years later for the exact same offense, she submitted a neatly written and numbered list of reasons why the punishment was unfair, slipping it under her mom's bedroom door.

Still, though, writing *about* Nina was something else entirely, and Leo works and types and edits and deletes, trying to make the words on the page match the vision in her head of her sister, even as her sister eludes her, slipping around sentences and disappearing onto the next page, always just out of reach.

"What are you working on?" her mom asks her as she types away at their kitchen table, and Leo thinks, *Oops*.

"Um, they asked me to talk about Nina at the back-to-school pep rally on Friday?" Leo says, like it's just a suggestion and not a thing that's actually happening. "I told Dad about it," she adds.

Her mom nods slowly, and Leo can't tell if she's sad, pissed, or just numb still.

"You should come, probably," she says. "If you want. East is going to make a video . . . thing."

"Okay," her mom says, but then she puts two dishes from the sink into the dishwasher before wandering back upstairs, Denver at her heels, and an hour later when Leo goes up to her room, she finds them both in Nina's room, Denver with his head on his paws and her mom sitting at Nina's desk, gently running her hand over the wooden edge. Leo almost asks if she's okay, but she already knows the answer, so she quietly turns and sneaks back to her own room.

The night before the rally, she's a wreck.

Why does this even matter so much? It's not like this is the thing that's going to bring Nina back to life, after all, or somehow undo all of the damage that's happened over the past month. Even the realization that it's been a month—more than thirty days since her sister went somewhere that Leo couldn't follow—sends Leo reeling, bending over at the waist and pressing her hands to her mouth, as if time has punched her straight in the stomach, reminding her not only of her memories but of the black hole where the memories should be, the last and most important ones, seemingly lost forever.

She has a couple of friends she could call, of course, kids from her freshman classes that used to sit near her, but she hadn't kept in touch with them over the summer and now that Nina's gone, the chasm between them is even wider. Leo wonders if they're afraid of her, afraid of what has happened to her, like death is something you could catch or inherit.

There is one person, though, who will get it. Leo texts him.

Hey, she types. She uses her own phone now, not Nina's.

Hey. East's response comes back almost immediately. *What's up?*

I'm working on that essay about Nina for tomorrow. Can I send it to you?

Ha, I'm working on the video stuff. Want to come over? We can collaborate. He adds a little nerd emoji at the end and Leo laughs despite herself.

Sure, she says. *I'll be there in a bit.*

He sends her a thumbs-up and Leo leaves a note for her mom, who's at the grocery store, then hops on her bike. East only lives about ten minutes away, and when she knocks on the door, his dad opens up. He looks better than when Leo saw him at the funeral, and when he sees her, he smiles and Leo has to fight the urge to hug him around his waist.

"Hey, Leo," he says. "Easton said you'd be stopping by. He's up in his room, working on something. How are you? How are your mom and dad doing?"

Leo can tell that he doesn't need an honest answer, but at the same time, this isn't a situation where "Oh, we're fine!" would sound at all accurate. She's learned a lot over the past month about how to answer the most innocuous questions, that's for sure.

Instead, she just shrugs, and he nods at this and lets her upstairs. East's dad probably understands better than anyone, she realizes as she climbs the stairs, why the vague answer is sometimes the best one. "How are you?" she asks then, mostly because it feels rude not to.

"We're okay," he says. "East's been working so hard on his college application portfolios. I think that's what he's doing now, probably. I always tell him, his mom would be so proud to see his work," he adds with a small smile, and Leo can't help but think that his dad's eyes look a little sad, even as he's smiling, like he can somehow buoy East up with all of his kind words, keep him from drowning in everything else.

When Leo gets upstairs, East is sitting at his desk, a huge computer monitor in front of him and oversized headphones wrapped around his neck. "Hey," he says when he sees her. "I was listening, I didn't hear. Did my dad let you in?"

"Yeah," Leo says. This is the first time she's ever been in a boy's bedroom (aside from her cousin Thomas but he definitely does *not* count), and she looks around, trying to figure out where to sit, where to stand, where to put her bag. The thought that Nina was once in East's room, maybe even in East's bed, makes it worse.

"You can throw that anywhere," East tells her, gesturing toward the room in general. The window looks out to the trees in the backyard, making the room feel more like a tree house, and Leo gingerly sets her bag down by the bed. *East makes his bed*, she thinks to herself, and feels a little pleased by this piece of information. She doesn't know why.

"So how's it going?" Leo asks him as she sits on the edge of the mattress.

"It's, um, brutal and awful and also really good to see her face again. What about you?"

"Same," she says. "It's like I can't make it be like *her*, you know?" She bites down on a ragged cuticle, ignoring Nina's voice in her head that tells her how gross it is to chew on her own finger. "I keep trying, but it isn't *enough*."

East's walls are lined with framed, very professional-looking black-and-white photos. "Did your mom take these?" Leo asks, standing up to look at one of East and his older brother, fingers in their mouths, making ridiculous faces, silly in a way that they would never be again. There's a signature at the bottom of each one in tiny script: *Sloane Easton*.

East nods. "Yeah, this is all her. Sort of like an inspiration wall, I guess." He sits back in his chair. "You want to read to me what you've got?"

Leo pauses, then smiles a little, embarrassed. "Can I just email it to you so you can read it to yourself instead?"

"Nope." East grins at her. "Think of it as practice for tomorrow."

Leo rolls her eyes, mostly because she knows he's right, then pulls her computer out. "Seriously," she says. "You have to tell me if it's terrible."

"I will definitely let you know if it's terrible, don't worry."

"Or too long."

"Got it."

"Or too short."

"Leo."

"Or if you think Nina would hate it."

East laughs at that. "You think *you* wouldn't already know that?"

He has a point.

Leo sits up a little straighter, putting her shoulders back the way her mom is always telling her to do, and then she says more than she has in the past thirty-three days.

"A lot of you knew my sister Nina. That was probably because she always made sure that you knew her, that you knew what she was doing, where she was going, what she liked and hated. Nina wasn't shy about any of that, about being herself.

"But I think my favorite thing about my sister was that just by being herself, she made you feel like *you* could be *yourself*. Nina was like a prism, each person's light reflecting through her, showing you every single thing that made you special. She even made me, her annoying little sister, feel special.

"I think the biggest compliment I can pay her is that she was our dog Denver's favorite person. She was *my* favorite person. The night she died, she told me that we were going to make this year count. I think she was mostly being sarcastic, trying to make me laugh, but she wasn't wrong. Only this year isn't going to count like I thought it was. This was supposed to be the last year that I ever went to school with my sister, ever lived with her in the same house, and I guess I wasn't ready to let go of that yet. I didn't know that it was all going to be taken away from me like this.

"Nina died in a terrible accident, but I hope that more than anything, we can remember how she lived. Nina was the compass in our family, the rudder, the North Star. She set the course, stayed the path, forged forever forward. I know we'll somehow manage to find our way back without her, but the shore won't ever be the same. Nothing will ever be the same again, except for the fact that I still love her, and I always will."

When she's done, Leo realizes that her hands are shaking. Worse, though, is the stricken look on East's face. "What?" she asks. "Is it that bad?"

East blinks fast, then clears his throat. "No," he says. "No, Leo, it's wonderful. Fuck." He quickly runs his sleeve over his eyes, then glances out the window. Leo stays quiet, letting him collect himself, but her cheeks burn hot with the compliment.

"The thing about the prism, that was her. That was totally her." East's voice is more stable when he speaks again. "*Fuck*."

"Thanks," she says, because she knows the swear is really a compliment. "Okay, your turn."

East barks out a laugh, then turns around in his chair to face away from her. "No way, not after that."

"That's not fair!" Leo says, and *oof*, does she sound like a little sister right now. But she still stands up and turns his chair back around. "I'm going to see it tomorrow anyway."

East runs his hands over his face and makes a sound that's half groan, half growl. "*Ugggh*, it's going to be embarrassing."

"No, it's not," Leo promises. "It's fine. I have faith in you. Nina said that you were a really good photographer. Better than *yearbook*, even."

East laughs behind his hands, then pushes his fingers through his hair and sighs as he enlarges the video screen so that it fills the entire monitor. "If it sucks—"

"I will tell you," Leo says. "Now hit play."

East reaches for the keyboard, but then glances over his shoulder at her, and his face is suddenly serious. "Are you sure you're ready? To see her, I mean?"

Leo nods. She still sees Nina all the time, but it's only the same memory: sitting on the edge of the diving board, smiling and laughing. That's all Leo ever sees.

"Okay," East says, then starts the video.

And oh, Leo has forgotten how beautiful Nina is. A gentle plinking, plunking song starts over the video as Nina smiles into the camera, posing a little. She's at the beach, the golden sunset falling around her, her grin not moving. Finally, East laughs from behind the camera. "It's a video," he tells her.

"Oh!" Nina cries, then bursts into giggles, putting her hand out in front of her as she pretends to push him away. The video fades into another one, Nina running behind East's skateboard up on the fire roads behind their neighborhood, like she's chasing after something just out of reach, and as the images flash across the screen, Leo realizes that she may have been able to write a love letter to her sister, but East knew how to film one.

Leo makes a quiet sound when the next image of Nina studying flashes up on the screen, the same huge headphones that are around his neck now over her ears. She's still and intense and Leo puts her hand on East's shoulder, overcome with such emotion that her stomach twists. He puts his hand over hers, squeezing hard, and they watch in silence until it fades to black, until Nina is gone once again.

Leo takes a beat, gathers her breath and her words. "East, it's beautiful. That's not even a good enough word."

East is still looking at the computer, his hand still on Leo's, but it doesn't feel weird or uncomfortable. It feels like an anchor, a port in a storm that's shared with the only other person who knows how hard the rain can fall. "Thanks," he says after a minute.

"Seriously, it's just . . . it's her, it's perfect."

East nods, then shifts his gaze out the window. "Well, it's a good thing we both didn't suck," he says. "Because Nina would probably kill us if we made her look bad."

Leo laughs at this, a sort of barking, honky noise that only happens when she's truly amused. Nina used to try to make her laugh when she was a baby because she was so delighted by Leo's strange little giggle. "She probably would," she agrees, and it feels so good to think about Nina seeking revenge that she almost forgets that Nina is no longer there with them.

Almost.

She stays a little longer in East's room, making him play the video again and then studying the framed photos on his wall a little more, realizing that she's looking at a different kind of memorial.

"After she died," East says, gesturing up toward the photos, "my dad got all of her film rolls printed. He said we should see everything that she saw so that we wouldn't forget her."

Leo reaches up and touches the sharp edge of a frame. East's dad looks so much younger captured in time. "Does it work?" she asks softly.

"Sometimes," he murmurs. "I wish I had more of her, though. She was always behind the camera." He pauses before adding, "Sometimes I can't remember her face. I just remember the photos."

When his dad comes upstairs and says that it's time for dinner, both he and East are very polite and ask if she wants to stay.

"Oh, no, I can't," she says. "I have to get back, my mom is probably waiting for me."

She feels warm on the way home, like she stayed out in the sun too long, and she takes the long way on her bike, weaving through the neighborhood rather than taking the main streets. When she's almost four blocks away from home, she sees a car that looks like her mom's, and when she gets closer, she realizes that it *is* her mom's.

And then she sees her mom sitting behind the wheel, her hands pressed to her eyes, her shoulders trembling with sobs. She looks small in the seat, ragged and frail, and Leo stops her bike and watches her for almost a minute. She wants to go to her, yank open the door and put her arms around her mom the way Stephanie had done for her the night of the funeral, but she realizes that if her mom is getting in the car and driving away from their house just so she can cry, maybe Leo's not supposed to know about it.

She turns her bike around and heads home.

The lights are off and she turns them all on as she makes her way upstairs. Denver's in Nina's room as usual, his head popping up once he sees Leo, and Leo sinks down next to him and hugs him, pressing her face against his neck and breathing in that familiar, comforting smell of her dirty dog.

Denver lets her.

When her phone rings, Leo knows that it's her dad. Nobody else calls her.

"Hey, sweetie," her dad says. "Big day tomorrow! How are you doing?"

Leo thinks of Nina's laugh, the trees outside East's window, her mom's secret, silent tears. She thinks of what East said, about forgetting his mom's face. She can't imagine that happening with Nina. That would never happen. Nina was too vibrant, too alive. How could Leo ever forget something like that, someone like *her*?

"Hey, Dad," she replies. "I'm fine."

SEPTEMBER 13
27 DAYS AFTER THE ACCIDENT

LEO'S DAD CHECKS in on her every day, calling and FaceTiming while Stephanie shouts hello and waves from the background. They have Leo over for dinner one Friday night soon after school starts, spaghetti and meatballs that Leo pushes around on the plate because the red sauce reminds her too much of blood, of Nina's wet hair, the stain on her shirt, of the gash across East's face.

"I can make you something else, honey," Stephanie offers. Their dining room looks like it's straight out of a sponsored Instagram post, and it probably is.

It takes all of Leo's power not to shove the plate away, to scream *How can anyone just sit and eat like everything is normal???*

But she doesn't. She doesn't want to hurt her dad's or Stephanie's feelings. She knows they must be aching inside, too. Why would Leo ever make it worse? Plus she's still embarrassed by what had happened at the funeral, of what she had said to Stephanie.

When she glances up at her, though, Stephanie just smiles reassuringly and says, "You let me know if you change your mind."

"This is fine, thank you," Leo replies.

"So how's school?" her dad asks.

"It was okay." Leo uses her fork to cut the meatballs into even smaller bites that she won't eat.

It was a half-truth: things had been okay but also like East had warned her, a lot of parts just sucked. All the other kids had stared at her in the hallway, of course, maybe waiting for her to suddenly burst into tears or something? Leo had no idea.

The teachers had apparently all signed a condolence card to her family that Leo jammed into her locker, unopened. And when she went to Calculus I, her teacher Mrs. Pfaff ("I give three Fs for every A, just like my name!") kept her after class and pressed a cold metal figure into Leo's hands. "Someone gave me this many years ago after my mother died," she said to Leo, and it was suddenly way too strange to be standing that close to her math teacher, even worse than the time she and Nina were standing in line at CVS buying tampons and saw their vice-principal directly behind them, also buying tampons, and Nina raised up her box and said, "Heavy flows, *represent!*"

"This brought me a lot of comfort," Mrs. Pfaff said to Leo, then patted her hand.

Leo glanced down at the object: a brass infinity symbol, worn and tarnished over time.

She at least made it to the bathroom before anyone could see her cry.

Leo doesn't tell her dad and Stephanie any of this, though, just that yes, school was okay and yes, people were nice to her, and then they make painful small talk about everything except the fact that they're three people at a table that seats four. Afterward Leo says, "I'll help clean up," and her dad replies, "Actually, let's go for a drive, get some ice cream."

They wind up sitting in the parking lot of Dairy Queen, the neon lights bouncing off the hood of her dad's car as they eat their respective Blizzards: M&M's for her dad, strawberry cheesecake for Leo. She thought about getting Nina's order in honor of her—Reese's Peanut Butter Cups—but it felt wrong somehow, almost disrespectful.

"So," her dad says, and Leo wonders if the sudden sharp pain in her head was an ice cream headache or something else. "How you doing, kiddo?"

Leo shrugs. "Not sure how I'm supposed to answer that."

"Let's try another one, then. How's your old mom?"

"Not sure how I'm supposed to answer that one, either."

Her dad is quiet, letting the answer hang there before he says quietly, "I'm worried about both of you."

He doesn't have to say it. Leo's worried about them, too. Her mom had taken a leave of absence from work, shuffling around in black sweatpants and watching HGTV for hours at a time, home makeover shows that seemed to fix everything that was wrong in less than an hour. Her hair was slack around her face, her eyes sunken and tired. Sometimes Leo would sit next to her and watch TV, and sometimes she would put her arm around Leo and sometimes she wouldn't.

Leo didn't know which option was worse.

"Mom's just sad," Leo says to her dad. "That's all. It won't always be like this."

Her dad nods in a way that clearly means, *I disagree with you but I am being an active listener right now, the way that one podcast about how to raise teenagers told me to.* Then he takes another bite of his Blizzard before saying, "I was wondering if maybe you'd want to talk to someone besides your old dad."

Leo bites back her annoyance at her dad's nonchalance. *Just tell me what you want me to do*, she wants to say. *Be the fucking parent!*

Instead she says, "I talk to people," which is only a little bit of a lie.

"Oh yeah?" Her dad sounds bemused. "Who? Mr. Socks?"

Leo rolls her eyes, feeling oddly defensive of a stuffed bear. "They asked me to talk about Nina at the welcome back pep rally next week. I can talk to a bunch of people all at once."

Her dad's eyebrows raise slightly. "They did? Who's they?"

"The principal," Leo says. She had actually pulled Leo aside in the hallway that morning, explaining how they wanted to do a tribute to Nina. "She was beloved at this school," Ms. Henks said, and Leo had to look away when her eyes appeared wet, almost embarrassed by the fact that the principal was about to cry in front of her.

"We've also asked East if he could do a video tribute," Ms. Henks had added, like the addition of East would sweeten the deal, or maybe just make her look like a jerk if she was the only one who said no.

"What did you say?" Leo's dad asks her now.

"I said I'd do it." She's starting to suspect that she'll never be able to eat a strawberry cheesecake Blizzard again, not without remembering this conversation.

"Well, that's great, kiddo, but I meant like, actually *talk* to someone."

"I do talk to someone," she tells him. "East. I talk to East."

As soon as the words are out of her mouth, she can hear Nina's voice in her ear: *Leo? You're an idiot.*

"You *do*?" Now her dad's genuinely surprised. "When do you talk to East?"

Leo buys some time by taking a big spoonful of Blizzard. "The other night, before school started. Why, are you mad about that?"

"No, no, not at all, I just didn't realize that you and he were—"

"It's not like that!" Leo feels herself start to flush, remembers the new-smelling cotton of East's shirt. After the funeral, she had thrown her dress away. She wonders if East did the same thing with his shirt, the one she had cried all over. "Oh my God, *Dad*. It's not *even* like that. He's a friend, he's, he was Nina's—"

"Lee, that's not what I was saying." Whenever her dad sounded like this, it would send Nina into a patronized frenzy, but it works on Leo and she feels her embarrassment ebb away. "I just didn't know that you were in contact with him, that's all. It's fine, I'm glad you two can talk."

Leo is, too. *You're the only one who gets it.*

"Well, in case you need to talk to more people than just East and Mr. Socks, let me know, okay?" He takes a deep breath before saying, "The other thing is, Stephanie and I were wondering if maybe you'd like to come live with—"

"*No*," Leo says, surprised at her own vehemence. "No, I need to stay at Mom's."

"Lee, sweetheart—"

"It's not just Mom, Dad. It's . . ." Leo hesitates just as the ice cream starts to melt over the side of the cup and onto her hand. She watches as it runs down, trying to find the words she needs. This was the part Nina had been good at, always having the right phrase at the right time. Leo hadn't even started talking until she was two years old, and why not? Four-year-old Nina had done all the talking for her.

"Nina's not in your house," she says quietly. "She's in Mom's. I need to be where she is. Was. Whatever."

Her dad's eyes grow sad and heavy, just like her mom's did whenever the chipper couple on HGTV showed the eager family their brand-new home, and Leo immediately feels bad. "Sorry," she says. "I, uh, I'm getting ice cream all over the seat."

"No, no, it's fine, it's fine," her dad says, but he still passes her a napkin. "And I understand, I really do."

Two cars and a minivan drive past them on their way to the drive-through before her dad speaks again. "I just . . ." He clears his throat and Leo glances at him out of the corner of her eye, like it would be too much to look at him directly. If he says he's lonely, that he needs her, Leo thinks she'll collapse from the weight of his sadness. She needs the glasses like they had had during the last solar eclipse, something to shield her from the blinding pain of someone else's white-hot grief.

"I just don't want you to think"—he clears his throat again—"that I'm not grieving, too. I think about Nina every minute of every day. Sometimes I even think I *hear* her, you know?"

Leo nods. She does know.

"You know, when she was born, I thought to myself, I can't believe I'm lucky enough to have her, and now I know that I *was* lucky because I can't believe I got to have her for as long as I did." A tear runs down his cheek and Leo passes her sticky napkin back to him. They should have gotten more.

"It's okay, Dad," Leo says softly. "We're all just grieving differently. Nobody's doing it wrong."

Her dad looks over at her like she's suddenly spoken Latin, and then laughs and reaches forward to gather her in a hug. "When did you get smarter than me?" he whispers into her hair. It was something that he used to say to Nina whenever she managed to outmaneuver him in a debate over bedtimes, car keys, new clothes, but it still feels familiar and warm to Leo.

In the cup holder, the Blizzard drips onto the floor of the car. The stain will be there until the car is too old to drive anymore.

When Leo gets home that night, her mom is on the couch watching TV. She's changed into a different pair of sweatpants, but when Leo curls up next to her, she can tell that her hair is still unwashed.

"How were Dad and Steph?" her mom asks her, not taking her eyes off the TV.

"They're good. I brought home some leftovers if you want them."

"Sure, thanks."

"Spaghetti and meatballs."

"Great."

Leo draws her knees up to her chest. The whole house is dark, save for the blue light of the flat-screen TV. On the screen, a blindfolded couple are holding hands outside of their renovated home, squealing with anticipatory glee.

"Dad thinks I should talk to someone," Leo says softly.

"Huh." They wait for the big reveal before her mom says, "And what do you think?"

Leo rests her head on her mom's shoulder and waits for her to put a hand on her leg, an arm around her shoulders. When it doesn't happen, Leo shifts slightly. "There's really not a lot to talk about, I guess."

Her mom just nods, the motion moving Leo's head back and forth as if in agreement. On screen, the couple are screaming and hugging everyone. "I don't like that paint color," Leo says.

"Same. Hey." And then her mom is squeezing her knee and Leo feels something unfurl in her chest. "Have you seen Nina's phone? I can't find it anywhere."

"Not in a while," Leo says, which isn't technically a lie.

"I know I should cancel her plan," her mom continues in a quieter voice, and Leo's pretty sure she's not talking to Leo anymore. "But I just can't. I can't do anything with any of her stuff."

Leo curls up tighter against her mom. "What kind of flowers are those? The ones by the front door. They're pretty."

"Those are perennials," her mom replies, and her voice is tight as she adds, "That means they bloom forever."

SEPTEMBER 4
18 DAYS AFTER THE ACCIDENT

AFTER THE HORRIFYING call, Leo spirited Nina's phone away and tucked it into the bottom drawer of her nightstand next to a hand-written note from her grandma, a single dried-out rose from the bouquet her dad and Stephanie gave her when Leo graduated from eighth grade, and her childhood teddy bear, Mr. Socks, who was too embarrassing to leave out on the bed and too precious to give away.

The phone fit there nicely and lit up every so often with social media notifications, although once the funeral was over, after Nina's ashes were spread out over the Pacific Ocean, after the casseroles and flowers and cards stopped arriving, the notifications were less and less frequent. At first, Leo clicked on them with sweaty fin-gertips, her heart racing as if she was going to see her sister alive again, smiling and waving on the small screen, but it was mostly just people tagging Nina in choreographed lip synchs and heartfelt notes that came in just under 280 characters. One girl, Poppy, kept tag-ging Nina in her own selfies, eyes big and woeful as if to say, *Can you see how much I'm mourning?*

Leo blocked Poppy on every platform and doesn't even feel bad about it.

It's like she didn't have room for *any* emotions anymore. It was weird but also strangely uplifting? Like no one expected her to care? Nobody demanded that she brush her teeth, change her clothes, make her bed. It's like she was preserved in amber, unable to change or grow ever again, and that this was her life from now on, suspended in time just like Nina's had been.

But on the night before school starts, Nina gets a text message. The *ping! ping!* is so familiar that Leo checks her phone first, but when it's blank, she looks toward the nightstand and then dives across the bed so she can open the drawer.

The first seconds are always the worst: it feels like Nina's still there, waiting for a text, refreshing her social media feeds, coming into Leo's room and demanding to know why Leo has her phone. Leo still hasn't looked through her photo albums yet. It still feels too wrong, too raw, like she's violating Nina's privacy, but here she is, 7:30 at night, entering the passcode she already knows by heart: Denver's birthday.

The message is from East.

East:
I miss you so much, Neens.

It's the nickname that gets Leo. Nobody was ever allowed to call Nina "Neens," not even their parents, and now Leo wonders if

maybe she had been saving that privilege for someone else, someone special. Three dots float below the message before another one
appears.

East:
This is stupid.

Before she can stop herself, Leo's thumbs are flying across the
keyboard.

Leo:
Hi. It's Leo.

His response comes back fast: Leo????????

Leo:
I kept Nina's phone. Sorry.

East:
It's OK. I just saw the dots and thought . . . never mind.

Leo:
I know. I'm sorry.

East:
It's fine.

Leo holds the phone and watches as the text bubble pops up for
a minute before East writes back. She hasn't talked to him since the
night of the funeral. She had found his suit jacket in her backyard

the morning after, had brought it inside and hung it up in the very back of her closet so she wouldn't have to look at it.

The phone pings. *You want to go for a walk?*

Yes, she types, even before she checks in with her mom or asks if it's okay. Her mom is downstairs in the kitchen—Leo can hear her shuffling around down there, opening cabinets and then closing them without taking anything out—and suddenly their house feels too small for both of them.

East:
Fifteen minutes? The park?

Leo gives the message a thumbs-up and then hops off her bed. "Hey, Mom?" she calls. "I'm taking Denver for a walk!"

Denver leaps up at this declaration, which kind of breaks Leo's heart. He hasn't been getting his normal walks lately—that had been Nina's job.

"Sorry for neglecting you, buddy," she says as she slips his leash on, then grabs her house keys. Her mom still hasn't responded, so she ducks into the kitchen, feeling Denver try to pull her toward the front door. He's short, but his neck strength is impressive.

"Mom?" Leo says.

"Oh!" her mom says, jumping a little. "You scared me." She's holding a box of water crackers, probably left over from the funeral, and wearing her bathrobe.

"I'm going to take Denver for a walk, okay?"

Leo waits for her mom to say no, that she has her first day of school tomorrow and needs to go to bed early, or get her bag together, or make sure that her first-day clothes are cleaned and ready, but her mom just nods and puts the crackers back in the wrong cabinet. Denver is pulling so hard at the leash that when Leo turns back toward the front door, he face-plants but recovers nicely.

The park is a ten-minute walk away, but it takes fifteen since Denver has to inspect every single lawn, fire hydrant, and rain gutter along the way. By the time they get to the park, East is at the far edge, away from the playground and closer to the walkways, slowing rolling back and forth on a skateboard. When he sees Leo, he raises a hand in a wave, but breaks out into a huge grin when he sees Denver.

"Hey, pally!" he says, bending down to rub the corgi's ears. "Hey, buddy, I missed you! C'mere, c'mere." And as Denver immediately rolls over for a belly rub, it occurs to Leo that maybe Nina's nightly walks with the dog had been mutually beneficial.

East is still making dog sounds, Denver is eating it up, and Leo feels like the third wheel, which isn't something that she ever thought she'd feel by being around her *dog*, but okay. At least East appreciates how great Denver is.

"Hey," East says, glancing up at her. "Hi. Sorry, it's just been a while since I've seen this guy."

"Well, he insisted on seeing *you*," Leo tells him, and East laughs a little. "He's relentless."

East eventually stands up and brushes corgi hair off his hands and onto his jeans. "Hey," he says again, then brings her in for an awkward one-arm hug. "I'm glad you answered her phone."

"Me too," Leo tells him, and she is. Being outside makes it easier to breathe, the walls of their house not pressing in on her, surrounding her in their sadness. "I'm sorry if I, you know, freaked you out or anything."

East just shakes his head and stands back up on his board. "Probably no more than I freaked you out, so don't worry about it."

Leo and Denver walk alongside East as they make their way around the park. It's usually pretty full on a summer night, kids playing and people picnicking, but it's almost empty tonight, all of the families at home, getting ready for the first day of school. Leo feels an odd twinge as she thinks of her own mom, alone at home.

"Um," she says, clearing her throat a little, and East looks over at her. "I just wanted to say that I'm really sorry about, you know, that night at the funeral, and I totally get it if you—"

"Leo, Leo." East stops skating suddenly, and Denver goes past him and has to double back. "It's cool, it's fine. We're good."

"But I—"

"It's *fine*. I promise. That's not why I wanted to meet up, not even at all."

"Okay," Leo says, but she knows she's going to feel bad about it for a long time, regardless of East's reassurances. "But just for the record, I'm sorry."

"I am, too," he replies.

They keep walking, looping back toward the sandbox, when East asks, "How's your mom doing?"

Leo is silent, not quite sure how to answer, and East fills the blank space with, "Yeah, I thought so."

"There's really nothing I can do except, you know, just be there," Leo adds. "But it's not the same and the house is, like, way too big and way too small, and my mom keeps sleeping in Nina's room and—sorry, that's not what you asked."

"It kind of is, though," East says.

"I guess it's just hard because . . ." Leo traces her finger over the rough cement, feeling it snag her skin over and over again. "It's happening to both of us, you know? It's not like I'm sad and she can help me, or vice versa. It feels like we can't help each other but we live together so we're all we've got. And right now I've got a mom who hasn't showered in five days."

East laughs a little. "Yeah, after my mom died, my dad became this obsessive cleaner. I don't think he had ever even run the vacuum before, but suddenly the house was spotless. It freaked me and my brother out so much." He pauses before saying, "We all grieve differently. Nobody's doing it wrong." Then he cocks his head toward the corner. "You want a Slurpee or something? My treat."

Half an hour later, their mouths stained red (Leo's) and blue (East's), they're sitting outside their high school, both of them perched on the huge cement sign that has the words "Los Encinos High School" etched into it, even though there isn't a single oak tree anywhere on campus.

Denver is asleep in the grass next to the sign, exhausted from the walk. He snores, but only a little.

"So how are *you*?" Leo asks East, using the tiny spoon at the end of the straw to get the last icy bits of her drink. She's been wanting to ask the question for a while, feeling it sit heavy on her tongue.

East just shrugs, though, shaking his cup a little bit. "Honestly? I don't even know."

"Yeah. Same."

"Some minutes it's fine and then I go to text her or I see a photo on my camera or my phone and it's like . . ."

"Like it's happening all over again?" Leo offers, and East looks over at her. In the twilight, she can see why Nina fell so hard for him. It's hard not to talk to someone when their eyes are that kind.

"Exactly," he murmurs. "You too?"

Leo shakes her head. "I actually don't remember anything."

East is silent for a few beats before setting his cup down on the sign. "What do you mean?"

"I remember the party, that part's pretty clear, and I remember sitting outside with Nina"—Leo's voice catches a little at the memory, her sister's arm so warm against hers, and East is quiet as she gathers her thoughts—"and I remember riding with you and singing that song. And that's all. The accident happened but I don't remember any of it."

East's voice is soft, almost reverent as he asks, "What's the first thing you remember about after?"

"Gravel," she admits. "Asphalt. Waking up. A man." Leo gestures to her own shirt, just over her heart. "He had a badge right here and that's how I knew something had happened. Something bad."

East is still staring at her, his blue eyes huge in his face.

"I know, it's really weird," Leo says, and she forces out a little laugh. "My mom said that the doctor at the ER called it dissociative amnesia? Because I didn't hit my head or get a concussion or anything. I just don't . . . remember. It's not my fault, though, the doctor said—"

"No, no, that's not, sorry." East clears his throat, shakes his head. "Sorry, I was just taking it all in, that's all." His voice is more gentle as he says, "Definitely *not* your fault."

"Do *you* remember?" Leo asks him, and East's jaw tightens before he nods. "What do you remember? Like, everything?"

"I'm not," East starts to say, and then he clears his throat a little. "I'm really not ready to talk about that, Leo." He's not making eye contact with her now, and Leo gets the feeling of watching a treasure chest being locked away instead of opened, and she bites back the urge to ask again for those lost minutes of her sister's life.

"If you ever," she says instead, reaching down to rub Denver's soft ear between her fingers. "If you ever want to tell me, I—I want to know." Leo tries to be gentle, tries not to scare him away with her sudden desperation. East still smiles, though, even if it doesn't quite reach his eyes.

Nina always smiled with her full face, her eyes crinkling up when she was truly thrilled, and Leo finds herself missing her sister so hard in that moment that she has to look away from East.

"I asked about you and I'm talking about myself," Leo says. "Rude."

"Not rude. Normal."

East is quiet then, and Leo suddenly feels desperate to fill the silence, to put something over it so that it doesn't hurt as much. "I don't know if this helps or not," she says, "but I think Nina really loved you."

East's jaw grinds a little as he nods and then he's blinking fast. It's gotten late enough that even the purple twilight has melted into the darkness, and against the fluorescent lights of the school, his face looks drawn, tired. "The night before the accident," he says, "I told her I loved her."

"She lost her shoes," Leo says.

"Yes!" East says, and then he laughs, bright and sharp against the quiet hum of suburban traffic. "The sprinklers got us afterward, but at least I managed to say it."

We had to run through the grass, Leo can hear Nina say, her voice happy and soft and so close that it feels almost cruel.

"She loved you, too," Leo tells him. "She didn't tell me that part, but I could tell. I saw it on her face."

East nods, his jaw tightening and relaxing. "I guess that's what I keep thinking about, you know? At least I said it. I least I told her. Because maybe if she was scared or cold or . . . at least she *knew*. And maybe that made her feel a little bit better? I don't know. I sound stupid right now."

Leo doesn't realize that she's crying until she feels a tear drip off her chin, and she's grateful when East looks over and doesn't try to comfort her this time.

"She knew," Leo says, quickly wiping at her face.

East nods, then swipes quickly at his own eyes before sighing heavily. "Tomorrow," he announces, "is going to *suck*."

Leo looks toward their school, the lockers and yellow classroom doors and cinder block walls waiting for the students to arrive. "Yes," she agrees. "Yes, it is."

"You ready to be the sister of the dead girl?"

Leo smiles despite herself. "Never. You ready to be the boyfriend of the dead girl?"

"Nope." East swings himself off the sign, startling Denver to his feet. "I'm glad we hung out, Leo. You're the only one who gets it."

"Me too," Leo says. "It's like I can . . . when we're together it's like . . ."

"Like she's here, too," East finishes.

"Exactly," she whispers.

They make it about half a block home before Denver sits down, refusing to walk another step. When Leo tries to hoist him into her arms, East says, "Wait, no, I've got a better idea," and settles Denver on the skateboard right in front of his feet. He looks so cute that Leo snaps a picture of the two of them on her phone, both of them with their tongues out, East making the "rock on" sign with his hand. "Get ready for the ride of your life, Denv," he tells the dog.

When they get home, Leo's mom is watching TV and Leo gets Denver some fresh cold water and a treat shaped like a tiny toothbrush before heading upstairs to her own room. Nina's room is dark and she thinks about turning on the bedside lamp, but she's afraid of what it will look like when she does that, how empty and lonely it will be.

In her own room, she pulls her phone out of her pocket and sends a text, the picture of East and Denver and the comment *You would have loved this*. Seconds later, Nina's phone pings and Leo smiles a little to herself.

When she sees herself in the mirror, her eyes are crinkled up, just a tiny bit. Just enough.

THE FUNERAL TOOK place eight days after Nina died.

Leo remembered very little about those days, just small images and quick words, as if they were one of East's photographs and not a three-dimensional memory.

She remembered Nina's phone ringing bright and early on Monday morning, less than forty-eight hours after the accident. That's how they kept referring to it, the accident, like it was something that just happened that nobody could control, like a man with five DWIs on his record hadn't plowed his car directly into them, killing Nina.

When the phone rang, both Leo and their mom—her brain always skitters on this part, reminding her that it's just *her* mom now, there's no "their" there—jumped. They were in the kitchen, the morning already sunny and warm, and the ringtone blasted through the room's silence like breaking glass. Leo's dad had gone back home on Sunday, back to Stephanie and his life and his own bed, and it was just the two of them now.

She knew it was stupid, she *knew* this, but when Nina's phone rang, Leo thought, *Maybe that's her!* and she could tell from her mom's face that she thought the exact same thing because they both stood up at the same time, as if to greet Nina together.

When it rang a third time, her mom finally reached out to answer it. "Hello?" she said. Leo could hear the way grief had shredded her voice.

"Hello!" a chipper voice said. "I'm calling from UCLA's student orientation department. I'm returning a, I think a Nina Stott's message about a campus tour?"

The voice was so loud and bright that even without the speakerphone on, Leo still winced. Her mom's face froze, then crumpled just before she set down the phone and put her hands to her eyes. "Hello?" the woman said again, less bright and sure this time, and Leo reached over and held Nina's phone in her hands. It felt weird and wrong.

"Hello," Leo said, only she didn't make it a question. Leo had no room for anyone's answers, not right then. "Thanks for calling back, but Nina died this weekend."

There it was: the first time she had to say those words. She pushed them out with the full strength of her body, watching her mom bend over the kitchen sink with her head in her hands. The UCLA woman was shocked into silence on the other end of the line and Leo kept it that way by ending the call.

She remembered police officers, gently gruff as they sat in the living room and asked Leo questions. They had asked her questions at the hospital, too, at least they said they did, but Leo had no memory of that. She had no memory of anything between riding with Nina and East in the car, and the blue lights, and she told the police this. She knew that the other driver was killed instantly, that he was drunk and had DWIs on his record, but Leo had no emotion left for him, not even anger or grief. She didn't want to give him a single piece of her that could have gone to Nina instead.

"Have—Have you talked to East?" she asked one of the officers. She didn't bother to remember his name. They were all starting to look alike anyway.

"We have," he told her. "Poor kid, he's having a really hard time. One minute he's driving his girlfriend and her kid sister and then the next . . ." He shook his head, then flipped to a new page in his book. "Leo, can I ask, why do you think your sister wasn't wearing a seat belt?"

Click!

The sound. It stuck in her brain, the metal pieces coming apart. But it was only a noise, one she had heard hundreds of times over the years.

Leo shook her head. "I don't know," she said, and the silence hung there for several seconds, as if they were all waiting for her to have an epiphany.

"Thank you for coming over," Leo's mom said before anyone could fill in the blanks. "We'll call if Leo remembers anything else."

"Is it bad that I *don't* remember?" Leo asked her after they left, but her mom just sighed and ran her hand over her daughter's hair.

"Honestly, honey, I wish I could forget everything, too."

It wasn't exactly the most comforting thing to hear, but Leo felt a little better anyway because she knew it's exactly what Nina would have said.

She remembered the first time she hears her mom say "fuck."

"Who's this from?" she said when a huge bouquet showed up at the door, roses and gerbera daisies and irises all tucked into a leaf-lined square vase. It's the sixth arrangement that had arrived that day and the house looked like a florist had a going out of business sale.

"I don't know," Leo said, peering over her mom's shoulder at the note, even though she wasn't expecting much. It was like everyone had received the same grief template: expression of sorrowful emotion, euphemism for death, euphemism for spirituality, euphemism for grief.

Thinking of you during these hard days. Please know we are here for you if you need us.

May your love always outweigh your grief.

The memories will live forever. We share in your sorrow and pain.

Wishing you peace and comfort as you move forward.

This note was no different:

We are so sorry for your loss. Sending prayers and love during this difficult time.

Leo's mom turned the card over, read it, and frowned a little. "Who the *fuck* are the Rusconis?"

Leo shrugged.

The Rusconis' flowers sat on the table for a week before someone—Leo didn't know who—finally threw them away.

Leo remembers the funeral most of all.

It's at a rec center one town over, a room that's beige and plain and perfect for filling with love or grief or whatever emotion can be expressed for a rental fee and within a two-hour time limit. "You have the place from three to five p.m.," a woman tells Leo as she and her parents and her stepmom Stephanie unload from the black town car that someone hired to take them there. "And we just ask that you please take everything out with you when you leave, including the flower arrangements." She smiles at Leo. There's lipstick on her front tooth.

"'Kay," Leo says, and brushes past her to catch up with her family. They look small and incomplete ahead of her, a smile with a lipstick-stained tooth missing.

She sits between her parents, her dad holding both her hand and Stephanie's. Leo feels bad for her mom that no one's holding her hand, but when she tries to take it, her mom just sits there and doesn't move. At the mic, Poppy, a girl Nina had known and secretly loathed, is talking about her.

"She had a smile for everyone," she says, sniffling into a pink tissue. "She was everyone's friend, she was always there for you."

"Oh, *please*," someone behind Leo snorts, and she turns to see her cousin, Gertie, sitting behind her, arms and legs crossed. She winks when Leo sees her and Leo feels some of the tension ease in her chest, even if she also spots dried tears on Gertie's cheeks.

"*Gertrude*," Aunt Kelly whispers now, nudging her, and Leo turns back around to her own mom. It's been a long time since she's seen Gertie. She looks sharper, older. Leo wonders if Nina would have been happy to see her here.

"I love you, Nina," Poppy whimpers, and her sobs make the mic squeal.

Everyone cringes.

The funeral bleeds into the memorial afterward, which is held back at their—*her*—mom's house, family and friends and strangers crammed into their kitchen and living room and pouring out into the backyard. Their yard backs up to a greenbelt, making it look a lot bigger than it actually is, and people take up that space, too. There's music playing and Leo can tell from how old the songs are that her dad probably made the playlist: Tom Petty singing about wildflowers, Bruce Springsteen rasping away about Valentine's Day, the Beatles harmonizing about what's in their lives.

Leo hears it all and realizes that she can never listen to any of these songs again.

Teachers are there, parents and friends and people Leo has never seen in her entire life, her parents' coworkers chatting with their elementary school principal, great-aunts deep in conversation with their next-door neighbors back before her parents got divorced and they had to sell their house and move. It seems everyone who's ever *looked* at Nina has shown up to remember her, and also eat all the food that has somehow appeared on every counter and tabletop in their home.

Everyone's talking but the conversations are hushed, like they're all in church or a museum. Leo hears one around the corner in the kitchen, where she's dutifully straightening cans of soda that don't need to be straightened. "Lily's neighbor was the first officer on the scene," the voice murmurs. Leo doesn't recognize it, but she'll never forget it. "I heard they found all three kids on the pavement. Her sister and the boy, both of them like they were crawling toward her." The voice *tsks*. "Such a shame."

Leo's walking into the living room when she sees East for the first time since the night of the accident, and she stops mid-stride as if she's done something wrong.

He's sitting on their piano bench, the first person to do so in years, and his dad's arm is around his shoulders, hugging him close as another person crouches down in front of them, their hand on East's knee. It's the Spanish teacher at their school, the one who liked Nina even though she couldn't "roll her r's for shit," as she once gleefully announced.

The worst part is that East is sobbing. His hands are grinding into his eyes as Nina's junior year portrait looks down on all of them from the top of the piano, smiling like she knows it's all going to be okay. Their Spanish teacher is talking quietly but East continues to cry and Leo watches from the hallway. Simon or Garfunkel (Leo has no idea which one is which and isn't interested in finding out) starts to sing about a girl who died in August and she takes that as her cue to leave.

She goes outside, sitting just off to the side under a tree whose branches seem to dip and close around her, hiding her within its limbs. She shivers as it gets dark, not because it's cold but because the last time she was outside at night, something very bad happened, and she shivers again when she realizes that.

Leo curls her knees up toward her chest, making herself small so that she can be alone with this feeling. There's no one who could ever understand it.

Except for maybe one person.

"Hey," East says, and Leo sits up at the sound of his voice, just like Denver suddenly appearing whenever someone opens the cheese drawer in the refrigerator.

"Hi," Leo says.

He sits down next to her under the tree, his knees up so his elbows can rest there. His black tie is loose around his neck, the top two buttons on his white dress shirt undone. He looks puffy, exhausted, and Leo's pretty sure she doesn't look much better.

"Where's your camera?" she asks.

"Oh, I, uh, left it at home. Didn't think it would be right, you know, taking pictures right now." He smiles a bit, but it doesn't make anything feel okay, not this time.

"Hard to breathe?" she asks, and he looks over at her.

"What?"

She motions to her own throat, mimes undoing the tie, and he smiles. "Yeah, a little bit. Just had to get out of there for a few minutes, though. Thought I would try to find you. Your mom was looking for you."

"She's not looking for me," Leo says quietly. "She's looking for Nina."

East doesn't say anything for a minute, and Leo shivers a little. "You cold?" he asks, then shrugs out of his suit jacket and gently drapes it across her shoulders before she even answers. Leo's only read about this kind of thing happening in books before, some of her mom's romance novels that she kept in her bedside drawer and that both Leo and Nina had read to each other when they were younger, snickering at the sexy parts while also privately filing that information away for future use.

Leo wonders if East had once put his jacket around Nina, if that's why she had fallen so hard for him.

"Thanks," she says. It smells like fabric and salt, like riding home after a long day at the beach, tired and warm and safe.

Even in the dark, she can see his lip tremble, but when he turns to look at her, it's gone.

"I'm so sorry," he whispers. "Leo, I'm so sorry I let you—"

"No," she says. "No, it's not . . . You were just driving. You didn't do anything."

He's quiet when she says that, his head dropping down for a few seconds before coming back up.

"I can't stop thinking," Leo starts to say, and when she stops, East nudges her with his arm.

"About that night?" he asks. "Me too."

For the first time all day, Leo feels like she can breathe.

"Just . . . Do you think she was scared?" Leo asks, and then she's crying, the tears feeling hot and sharp on her face. "I'm just scared that she was scared, you know? Because I can't . . . I keep think-ing . . . I don't know how . . ."

"Leo," East whispers, and then his arms are around her, pulling her in so she can tuck her head against his shoulder, and Leo feels the burn of her tears against the scratchy cotton of his shirt. East's chest is shaking, too, and the two of them hold on to each other and sob about what they've lost, about who should be there, too.

East is warm, though, and his heartbeat is fast and strong and he's alive, and Leo wraps her arm around his waist, hanging on to this person who loved her sister almost as much as she did. "East," she whispers, and she wants more of that warmth, doesn't want to feel the cold grass anymore, and she turns her head up to him just as he's leaning down toward her, and when they kiss, it's soft and real, a safe place to land.

They don't mean to do it.

It just happens.

"Leo," East says, and then he's pulling away, putting a distance between them that makes her shudder. "I'm sorry, I can't. Shit, sorry. I didn't mean, I don't . . . I made a promise but it's not like that."

"No, no, I know," Leo says, but she's still crying, now stupid and embarrassed, alone outside a houseful of people, wearing the jacket of a boy that she barely knows. And when she goes inside, Nina won't be there to hug her and laugh and tease her for being so ridiculous. It's that loneliness that hurts more than anything, and there's no one—not even her parents—that will ever be able to fill the empty, scraped-out feeling that's spreading through her.

"I'm sorry," East says again.

"Me too," Leo whispers, and then someone's calling East's name, maybe his dad, Leo's not sure, but he gets up and hustles away, leaving Leo alone once more, but not for long.

"Who was that?"

"Jesus!" Leo gasps. "Gertie!"

Gertie just raises an eyebrow, silently repeating her question. She's at least a head and a half taller than Leo, lean and long and dark-haired. If Nina's personality had been champagne, Gertie's is a shot of espresso.

"He's cute," Gertie adds when Leo doesn't say anything.

"That's East," Leo finally tells her. "He's—he was Nina's boyfriend."

Gertie raises an eyebrow and nods like she's made a fascinating discovery. "He was the driver?"

"Yes," Leo whispers.

Gertie sucks her teeth, then clicks her tongue. "Poor kid," she says, then takes Leo by the elbow and pulls her to her feet. "C'mon, let's go find the cousins and get you drunk."

"You cold?" Gertie says, and when Leo doesn't answer, she peels off her cardigan and puts it on her cousin's shoulders. Leo has no idea where East's suit jacket has gone. Gertie's cardigan smells like incense and the faintest hint of spice and cigarettes, not like Nina at all, and Leo only leaves it on because she's too drunk and too polite to take it off.

Leo's never been drunk before, had only had a half glass of

champagne on the past two Christmas mornings, so Gertie takes
the lead and Leo soon finds herself out on the greenbelt with her and
a few other older cousins, Thomas and Madeline and Abigail.

"We're family," Gertie says, leaning toward her, a finger up and
pointing as if it was almost an accusation. "We're here for you, Leo,
you know that?"

Leo hasn't seen Gertie since last Thanksgiving. They went
around the table and said what they were thankful for and Gertie
said "birth control" when it was her turn and Leo's aunt Kelly stayed
pale and thin-lipped for the rest of the meal.

But now Leo just nods.

"Damn straight," Gertie replies, agreeing with Leo's silence.

All of her cousins were either in college or supposed to be in
college, and they mostly talk to each other and not to her. Leo feels
very young and dumb as she sits in a circle with them, as the dew of
the grass starts to seep into the seat of her black dress.

But the white wine eases that feeling after a few sips, and then
she's hugging Gertie's cardigan tighter around her as Thomas hands
her the rest of the bottle with a sharp laugh. "Look at you go," he says
to her, and Leo giggles. It's not the same without Nina, but none of
them are talking about her sister, so she keeps it to herself.

She drinks until she can see the stars in the night sky, silent wit-
nesses to the worst night of her life, and she lies down in the grass
to look up at them. She wonders if they remember what she cannot.
The constellations are moving fast now and Leo puts her hands in
the grass and grips the blades, feels their sharpness on her skin again.

Her cousins are drunk now, too, and they don't notice when tears run from Leo's eyes, across her temples, and into her hair. "She's totally passed out," Madeline snickers. "We did our job too well."

They eventually leave her in the grass. When Leo sits up, the world tilts and spins and it takes a second for her brain to catch up to what she's seeing. Is this what drunk feels like? She'll have to ask Nina. She'll know.

Another second and her brain catches up to what she already knows. She'll never be able to ask Nina anything ever again.

Fuck, she should have never had this much wine. Everything is slipping past her and it reminds her of that night.

"Hey, hey, here," East says, and then he's there, moving next to her, putting his arm around her shoulders. "Steady, easy. Jesus, who the hell gave you this much wine?"

"Gertie," she whispers.

"Wait, was that *Gertrude?*" he asks.

"You heard about her?"

"Just that Nina won the birth order lottery."

"I don't like her sweater. And I lost your jacket."

East doesn't say anything to that, just pulls Leo to her feet with a grunt and a quick grasp of her shoulders so that she doesn't topple over.

"I can't remember," she sobs. "I can't remember the car, or her, and I feel like if I could just . . . maybe she would be . . . I could just . . ."

The emptiness makes her cry harder, and East is crouching

down in front of her, looking so sad and concerned that she both wants to hug him and shove him away.

"Shh, baby," he says, and the ache suddenly turns into an embarrassed fury. How dare he sound paternal? Who does he even think he *is*?

"Get away from me," she says, but East hangs on to her and puts her on a bench before running back to the house. Leo buries her head in her hands and tries to breathe, and when the sound of shoes brushing through wet grass returns, all she can think is, *My mom is going to kill me.*

But it's not her mom. It's Stephanie.

"Leo?" she says, crouching down in front of her. "East said you might need some help."

"I need *Nina*," Leo tells her, her whole mouth twitching as she finally says the truth, and Stephanie reaches up and pushes her hair out of her face.

"Is Gertie somewhat responsible for this?" she asks.

"Little bit."

Stephanie sighs, and Leo politely waits until Stephanie gets her into the house, up the stairs, and into their—*her*—bathroom before she starts to throw up.

It's awful. She blames the wine and she blames Gertie, but most of all, she blames herself.

Stephanie, though. She stays there the whole time, locking the bathroom door and putting cold washcloths on the back of Leo's neck, doing all of the things that her mom should be doing, but Leo can't bear for her mom to see her like this. She can't share her grief because she doesn't think that her mom has room for it, but she doesn't know quite what to do with it either.

Leo doesn't know how she's supposed to hold this all by herself.

Stephanie handles it, though, and after Leo's done throwing up, she gives her a small cup of water and then sits down next to her on the floor. Leo, eyes and makeup runny, looks over at her. "I know she didn't really say it," Leo tells her. "But Nina liked you a lot."

Stephanie's face twitches. "I know," she says. "Believe it or not, Nina wasn't as good at hiding her emotions as you are."

They both laugh then, but Leo realizes that it's all past tense, that Nina will never be here in this room, this house, with them again, and Stephanie reaches for her as she starts to cry.

"I just need five more minutes," Leo sobs. "Just five, please, Stephanie . . . *please* . . ."

"Shh, I know," she whispers, but she doesn't know, not really, and Leo hangs on to her stepmom's arm and pleads with someone, anyone, to give her more time with Nina.

Just give me five more minutes.

When she's finally cried out, Stephanie helps her into bed, taking her shoes off like she's a child before covering her with a blanket and turning off the light.

Leo's asleep before Stephanie even leaves the room.

AUGUST 18, 4:13 A.M.
5 HOURS AND 47 MINUTES AFTER THE ACCIDENT

LEO WAKES UP at 4:00 am the night Nina has died.

All of her bedroom lights are still on and there's grass stuck to her cheek. Outside, the crickets are going, a steady, cheerful chirp that makes Leo want to blowtorch them into oblivion.

Instead, she gets up and picks her way through her messy room and down the hallway. The rest of the house is dark and silent, which feels as scary as it did when she was a little kid, and she makes her way to Nina's room. At first her heart leaps when she sees the small lump under the covers, but the hair is short and blond, not dark and curly. Her mom is in the bed, asleep or passed out, Leo's not sure, nor does she really care.

She tiptoes into the room and goes to the bed, carefully peering over to see her mom fully out, her mouth open, her body limp. She's breathing heavily, though, and Leo crawls up on the empty side of Nina's queen-sized bed. It smells like her, perfume and hair products and detergent and Nina, and Leo scoots closer to her mom.

"Mom?" she whispers, and when she doesn't respond, Leo lies

down on the pillow and reaches for her mom's hand. It's cold and limp and offers zero comfort in the night, but Leo hangs on to her anyway, too afraid of what will happen to her if she lets go.

AUGUST 18, 1:44 A.M.
3 HOURS AND 18 MINUTES AFTER THE ACCIDENT

LEO FOLLOWS HER parents into the house. She doesn't know where Stephanie is.

It's just her and her mom and dad, all of them silent as the garage door squeaks shut behind them. The large hanging mirror reflects all of their faces, numb and shocked and salt-streaked. Leo sees her eyeliner running down her cheeks, pooling at her jawline, and feels like she's been punched.

Denver comes running in to see them, doing his regular ankle sniff to make sure that everyone is there and accounted for, and when he doesn't find the person he's looking for, he sniffs again, and then a third time. "Oh, buddy," their dad says, his voice breaking. "Oh, pally."

They sit at the kitchen table, Nina's backpack on the floor, and it's so normal that it takes Leo a minute to realize that it's *Nina's backpack on the floor.* Her sister's stuff that she touched with her own hands, her handwriting, her hair scrunchies and school ID and lip gloss. Leo has a sudden, almost triumphant thought that Nina's DNA is all over that bag, as if they could put it in a lab and reanimate her, re-create her.

Her brain is slipping back and forth, from past to present, and Leo feels like she's being tossed in the sea.

Her mom sits, then stands up and goes to the refrigerator. She opens the door, stands there, and when she doesn't move after a full minute, Leo watches as her dad goes to her and enfolds his ex-wife in his arms, both of them beginning to sob.

Their parents have barely spoken in seven years other than cursory texts and polite nods at holiday pickups and drop-offs. "Oh, they *haaaate* each other," Nina always said blithely whenever someone asked about their parents' divorce, but watching them hold each other, Leo now realizes that that isn't true. They may not love each other anymore, but they desperately love their girls, and maybe that was the strongest bond they had ever had, the one that could never be decreed by a church or severed by a court.

Wait until I tell Nina about this, she thinks.

But then the thought hits her that Nina is not here, that she will never know about this, and Leo feels herself physically recoil at the thought, grabbing on to the kitchen table so that she doesn't double over and hit the floor with the full weight of her realization. Denver is at her feet now, curled up and calm, and Leo reaches down and touches him with the backs of her fingers, suddenly desperate to feel something alive that isn't also falling apart.

It doesn't upset her at all that her parents don't bring her into their arms with them, even as their tears grow desperate and wretched, bouncing off the cold marble countertops, the warm wooden floors. Leo knows that she's not the one they want to hold in that moment, she's not the daughter they need between them, and she starts to stand up, to leave them alone, when her mom pulls away with a horrific shudder and says, "Baby, baby," as she reaches out for her only living child.

Leo goes to them, lets them gather her up, but she doesn't cry. She needs her parents, yes, but not half as much as they need her. Instead, she focuses her eyes on Nina's backpack, on Denver's soft paws and the dirty dishes stacked near the sink, everything now a symbol of Before, and feels herself disappear.

Their mom falls asleep in Nina's bed that night. Their dad takes her up to Nina's room after she begs, dirty clothes and used glasses littering the floor and nightstand. Leo and her dad stand in the doorway and watch as their mom pulls back the covers and climbs right into Nina's sheets and blankets, still fully dressed. She's taken something that has made her sleepy, but Leo doesn't know what. Nina will know, though. Leo will ask—

Nina's not here.

"What?" their dad says, glancing down at Leo, but she just shakes her head. She feels like if she says anything, if she even opens her mouth, the house will fall down around them.

"I'm going to sleep in the guest room tonight, I think," he says. Leo's mom already has her back to them, her breathing finally even, and Leo just nods.

"Do you need anything?" he asks, and Leo can almost hear the gaping space between what he wants to say and what he knows how to say. It was like that with Nina, too, their dad struggling to figure out how to speak to daughters who are no longer little girls, who can't be appeased by an extra episode of *My Little Pony* or a clandestine ice cream run.

Nina's voice comes back to Leo, as sharp and bright as the lights had been. *These are real problems, Dad!* she had yelled one night after he had made a flippant comment about something environmental, Stephanie covering their dad's hand with hers as if to say, please please shut up. *Your generation didn't do anything so now it's up to us!*

"Sweetheart?" their dad says again, and Leo shakes her head no. There's nothing in the world he can give her right now. "I want you to wake me if you need anything," he says, and Leo believes him and also knows she won't do that.

Her room is dark as the door clicks shut behind her, still the same mess it was before the accident, before the party, before, and Leo sits down on her bed as she snaps on her bedside light. It's all her stuff, her space, but it all feels different now, like a photo image that's been flipped, recognizable but now completely unfamiliar. Her bed is still unmade—

We had to run through the grass.

Suddenly Leo is standing up and flinging the duvet off her bed. Her breath is hard and sharp in her chest, like she can't get enough of it, and when she sees the fitted sheet, she thinks she's the one who's stopped breathing.

Leo falls into the bed with a gasp, then a sob, and she spreads her fingers through the soft cotton and into the grass and mud that are still there. "Nina?" she cries, just in case her sister can hear her, but the silence is her answer and Leo feels her chest rack as she bends her head and inhales the earth.

It smells alive.

THE EMERGENCY ROOM is so bright, the fluorescent lights almost blue in their whiteness, and Leo finds herself thinking that there have been too many lights that night. She squints against them but she feels her head throb, the rhythmic pulse of the pain the only thing that makes sense in that moment.

"Where's my sister?" she asks again. "Where's East?" But the paramedic pushing her gurney through the swinging doors ignores her, just like they did in the ambulance. The siren had been loud and shrieking, its noise reaching down into Leo's chest and rattling it like a cough she couldn't shake, an itch she couldn't scratch.

Nina had left in an ambulance, its siren wailing as it sped away, and Leo had listened so hard after it disappeared, trying to hear her sister in any way that she could. "You'll be okay," the paramedic had said to her as he checked her pulse and oxygen levels, explaining everything that he was doing as he did it, but Leo kept asking for Nina, saying "Where is she? Where is she?" until it became a chant, a prayer.

Leo's only ever seen an emergency room on TV shows before. It's a lot scarier and louder than she thought it would be.

She really, really wants her mom.

People are shouting and running around as a doctor looks at Leo, only they're not shouting for her. They're running past the small room where they've wheeled her in, the squeak of their sneakers on the linoleum floor reminding Leo of Nina's freshman year basketball games, Nina running and grimacing and never looking like herself until the game was over.

Hustle hustle hustle . . .

Female, seventeen . . .

Fuuuuck fuck fuck . . .

Another round of epi . . .

Foxtrot 40 . . .

"Okay, Leo, yes? How are you feeling? You okay, Leo?"

"Nina," she whispers.

Trauma team one, trauma team one . . .

"You got hit pretty hard so we're going to take you down, do a CT scan, just make sure everything is—"

There's a honking sound, a duck or goose bellowing over and over again—

"Leo, Leo, look at me. Can we call your parents? Do you know where your phone is?"

"I—I don't know," she says because she doesn't. She can't even remember her mom's number, the one she's had drilled into her head since she was five years old in case of situations just like this one.

"It's okay," the doctor says again. "We'll get them in here, we'll find them."

"Where's my sister?" she asks again, but then she's gone, being wheeled away just as she hears East's voice screaming out, "*Nina!*" and it makes her start to cry.

She trembles through the entire CT scan even though she's supposed to stay still, her body shivering after it's over and they're wheeling her back up. "It's just shock, sweetheart," a nurse says to her. "It's all right, it's just adrenaline."

"Where's Nina?" she asks.

"You're going to be fine. The scan looks fine."

But it's not fine.

Back in the ER, everything is quiet now, almost holy in its silence.

They release Leo from her neck brace and let her sit up, put a cup of water in her hand, but she just holds it, not sure how to move her hand to her mouth and back down again. Her palms are scraped up, she realizes, and she spots blood on the sleeve of her shirt, the one Nina had let her borrow to wear to the party.

Nina's going to *kill* her for this.

Across the hallway, there's a room with curtains pulled across glass windows and people in blue scrubs are coming out, soaked in blood, sweating, heads down and limbs heavy. "We've got a DB," someone says, but Leo doesn't know what that means.

What she does know, though, with a cold prickle of fear that begins in her spine and trickles down to her toes, is that absolutely no one is looking at her.

"*Nina!!!!*" someone screams, and Leo whirls to see who's calling for her sister, but it's their mom, so undone by fear and terror and confusion that Leo doesn't even recognize the sound of her voice. She's looking at Leo, her face changing as she realizes that she's Leo, not Nina, and Leo glances down at Nina's shirt again.

She wonders if she looks like a ghost.

"Mom!" Leo cries, and then her mom is there, grabbing her up and smelling like home, like Nina, like the place they'll never be able to get back to again. She had thought she wanted her mom, but once she has Leo in her arms, Leo realizes that this isn't the mom she wants. This one is sweating, trembling, crying, scared, and unsure. She wants the mom that would be by her bed when she woke up from a bad dream, the one who sat up with her when she was sick as a child, steady and calm and reassuring.

She doesn't want her mom after all, Leo suddenly realizes. She wants Nina.

"We went to a party!" Leo sobs. "I'm so sorry, Mom, we went to a party! I'm so sorry, I'm so sorry . . ."

The room is quiet around them, the world creating space for something that will forever be too big to hold.

WHAT HAPPENED TO *the party?*

The ground is hard, the gravel sharp under her skin, and Leo wonders what happened to the pool, to Madison and Sophie and everyone else. What about the pool, the cups?

Where is everyone?

There's a light now, a red one, not blue like the pool, and people are talking all around her. All she can see is their shoes, black and sturdy. Sensible.

Her first thought: *Nina will hate these shoes.*

"Hey, sweetheart. You okay? You waking up?"

Leo tries to move, tries to sit up, but hands push her back down. They're gentle but strange and she tries to move them away from her when she feels the hands again. "I don't know you," she tries to say, but there's blood in her mouth and it tastes so awful that she starts to retch.

"Back down, back down, okay," the voice says again. He's talking to her like she's a frightened child, and Leo realizes that's exactly what she is. "Just stay still for me, all right?"

"Nina," she tries to say, but the words are so hard to say that they get stuck in her chest.

There are people shouting, voices that are loud and scared, words that Leo knows but doesn't know.

Passenger space intrusion.

Moribund.

Coding.

She can smell gasoline now, chemical and sharp against the damp night air, and there's a strange car upside down, people gathered around it. Where's East's car? Where's East?

And where is Nina?

"Sister," Leo manages to say this time, but the man isn't listening to her. He's saying things about a c-collar, board, hospital, conscious. Leo feels the words float past her and she's too groggy to grab them, hold them up to her ear like a shell so she can understand what they're saying.

Someone's crying. It sounds like a man, or maybe a boy.

Leo tries to speak again, but then someone's snapping a collar around her neck, slipping a board underneath her, and there's a sharp white light in her eyes, blinding her. "We've got you," the man says, and Leo finally sees an official-looking badge stitched on his shirt, just over his heart.

"Why—?" she starts to say, but then the light is gone and she's going up, she's floating just like the words, and as she goes up, she finally sees Nina.

She's on a gurney and there are tubes and bags and a man on top of her, hitting her in the chest so hard that Leo tries to tell him to stop, that he's hurting her.

But all she can think is that her sister just looks so small, that this must not be her because Nina is so *big* all the time, that she fills whatever space she's in, so this is wrong and that's not Nina, even though Leo can see the small silver ring on her left hand, her wet (wet?) brown hair falling over the edge of the gurney as someone loads her into an ambulance.

The opal birthstone on Nina's ring is shining so bright under the lights.

Leo tries to speak, to shout, but her chest is collapsing and she falls back into the dark, into the stars, pulled down into that comforting place that has no space or sound, just black, and she watches as the red lights fade into nothing, as the man leans over her and says in a tearful, shaking voice, "Don't you go anywhere, you hear me?" and the last thing Leo thinks is that wherever Nina is, that's where she wants to be, too.

AUGUST 17, 10:26 P.M.
THE ACCIDENT

NINA WAS UPSTAIRS getting dressed when she yelled, "East is here, Leo! Can you answer the door?"

"Can you not *shout*?" their mother called back in a voice that wasn't a shout, but wasn't exactly quiet either. Nina huffed back something under her breath that neither of them could hear, which was probably for the best.

Tensions were high in the house that night and it was UCLA's fault.

More accurately, Nina did not book a UCLA campus tour online the way her mother asked her to, and that devolved into an entire argument that unfolded while Nina was carefully applying Leo's eyeliner, Leo trying not to blink as her mother and sister argued over her head about responsibility and overbearing parents and the party they're going to (*"Yes*, it's chaperoned, I can't believe you even have to ask") and where they're going beforehand ("In-N-Out, duh, where else is there to go in this town?").

Leo glanced at the mirror over the entry table as she headed toward the front door, then leaned in for a closer inspection of her eyeliner, accidentally knocking over a framed picture of her and Nina in the process. Her right eye was a tiny bit more uneven than her left eye, but Leo didn't think anyone would notice.

She was pretty sure no one would be looking at her that night.

"I don't know why people can't just pick us up in the driveway like the rest of the modern world," Nina grumbled as she stuffed things into her bag while hurrying downstairs at the same time.

"If someone wants you to ride in their car, they come to the door," their mom said from the kitchen. "Don't let someone beckon you with a car horn. It's rude."

Nina said something under her breath and Leo didn't have to hear it to know that it, also, was rude.

"What was that?" their mom asked.

"Nothing."

"Mmm-hmm."

"But you've met East—" Nina, who never met a fight she didn't like, started to protest, even as Leo opened the door. Nobody was honking the horn or ringing the bell to come see *her*, after all, so she didn't really understand why Nina always got so worked up about it, but she had to admit that her mom had a point.

She opened the door while holding Denver back with her foot. "Don't worry, he'll only attack your ankles," she said to the boy at the door.

"Good thing I've got two of them, then," he said, then grinned. "Hi. I'm East."

It took all of two minutes for Leo to lose Nina at the party.

It was probably for the best because if Nina ever asked, Leo would never admit that, standing in the kitchen of this massive house with a pool and diving board and vintage arcade room, it seemed to her that parties were actually, maybe, sort of, kind of *boring*?

There was a pool with a slide outside, that was pretty nice, and some guys she recognized from school were taking turns flipping themselves off the diving board into it, trying to outdo each other with every go. There were some girls standing off to the side, squealing and giggling whenever they got splashed with water, and Leo found herself half wondering why they didn't just move to the side, and half longing to be the kind of girl that boys wanted to make squeal and giggle.

Inside, there were more people in the living room, including two girls that Leo didn't recognize making out on the couch, and then more people standing in the hallway. Almost everyone seemed to have a red Solo cup, which was the only part of the party that had lived up to the hype so far. In every movie she had seen, there were red Solo cups *everywhere* at parties, and she had a brief, fleeting thought that maybe she'd save one, a small souvenir.

There was just one problem: she didn't have one and wasn't quite sure how, exactly, to *get* one, especially after Nina pushed her through the front door, whispered a dire-sounding "Don't accept a drink from a boy, no matter *what*" warning in her ear, and then disappeared into the house with East.

At least In-N-Out had been fun. It was crowded inside so they sat outside at a table that they snagged because Nina stood there shooting daggers at the people there who had finished eating long ago, all while talking to someone on her phone. And just like she said he would, East paid and brought the food out. All three of them had gotten their fries Animal-style, covered in secret sauce and cheese, but Nina still helped herself to Leo's fries every now and then.

"Okay, here's the rule," Nina said, hoisting her fry in the air to point at both her boyfriend and her sister. "Leo is not—I repeat, not—drinking tonight."

"Wait, what?" Leo cried. "I thought we were going to a party! You made me dress up! You did my *eyeliner*!"

"Are you kidding? If you get drunk or if Mom smells beer on you, I'm a dead person. She'll ground me until I'm thirty-five years old and basically a decrepit crone that lives in the den. Nope, uh-uh, absolutely not."

Leo glanced over at East, who was eating three fries at once and seemed very bemused by Nina's declaration. "Decrepit *crone*," he repeated.

"Would you still date me if I was a decrepit crone?" Nina asked East, carefully picking the tomato out of her burger with her fingernails and placing it in East's paper basket of food.

East pretended to think about it for a minute. "Probably not," he said, which earned him a laugh from Leo and a wadded-up paper napkin from Nina. "Decrepit's pretty bad!" he protested, throwing the napkin back at her. "What if I kiss you and your face falls off or something?"

"I thought true love conquers all," she said.

"Oh, is that what this is?" he asks. "Love?"

There was something private and teasing in his voice, something that Leo didn't recognize, but Nina did, her cheeks flushing and her head suddenly ducking down to bite into her tomato-free burger. East just smiled at her, and Leo had a sudden and horrible realization.

She was the third wheel.

She looked down, focusing on her half-eaten burger. The truth is that she wants to go the party with her sister and East, wants to finally be the person who said that yeah, she was at the party last weekend, why do you ask, but the safe and secure pull of familiarity kept her longing to stay home, to stay in bed or downstairs with her mom, scrolling through YouTube videos or whatever HGTV show her mom always insisted on watching. More and more, Leo had realized that she liked the potential of things, rather than the things themselves. Parties always seemed better when she was imagining them, thinking about all the ways she would be smart and funny and cute. Her imagination lets her succeed in a million different ways that reality often didn't, and why would she want to mess with that?

And at the party, with the small of her back pressing against the cold marble countertop and her arms wrapping around her waist, there were no other wheels at all. The reality was that Leo was alone at this party. She thought she saw Sophie from her English class, and she was sort of sure that Madison, who she recognized from the hallways at school, was in the living room, but she didn't think she knew them well enough to go up to them and just start talking. *Who even does that?* she thought. She wondered if she could track down Nina, but she didn't want to be the annoying little sister who needed her big sister for everything, even though she kind of *did* need her sister right then.

"Here," a voice said, and then East was pushing a red cup into her hand. "Relax," he added as she peered into it, "it's ginger ale. If you're holding a drink that looks like beer, no one's going to try to make you drink a beer. Little party trick. Plus it gives you something to do with your hands."

"I don't know," Leo said. "Nina said not to take drinks from boys."

"Well, Nina's actually downing a shot while standing on the diving board, so I wouldn't worry about her right now. And I'm pretty sure she'll vouch for me." East gestured out the kitchen window toward the pool, where indeed, Nina was doing exactly that. There were a few people around her cheering her on, and she knocked the drink back and raised the glass triumphantly. She looked like a statue, Leo thought, a young warrior frozen in time.

East smiled. "She's crazy."

"Don't say 'crazy,'" Leo told him. The ginger ale was lukewarm and reminded her of when she had food poisoning last year, her mom's cool hand on her forehead, Nina making her a very sincere playlist called "Songs That Won't Make You Hurl a Lot."

"Sorry?" East said.

"It sort of sounds like it's making fun of people with mental health struggles," she said, then sipped at her ginger ale again because this was the longest she'd talked to East in, like, ever, and now that he was standing next to her, Leo thought that he might just be a *smidge* more intimidating than he had been in their math class. "Plus it's sexist. No one ever describes men as 'crazy,' you know?"

Sip.

East stood there for a minute, a slow smile dawning across his face and looking almost . . . nostalgic? Leo didn't know how else to describe it. Just behind his head, Nina whooped and hopped delicately off the diving board onto the cement. "Huh," he said. "I never, uh, thought of it that way before."

Leo shrugged as Nina caught her eye and gave her a questionable thumbs-up sign. Leo gave it back and Nina nodded approvingly and moved on. "It's just a thought," she said, even though it wasn't, it was actually something she *believed*. "Anyway."

"Any*way*," he repeated. "Thanks for the language update. I'll try to remember that."

"Cool." Leo sometimes wondered where her words went in situations like this, if they found a dark hole to hide in and if she could maybe follow them down there sometimes.

"So, you excited for school to start?"

Leo looked up at him and frowned. "Why do you sound like my uncle David trying to talk to me at Thanksgiving?" she asked, and then it dawned on her. "Wait a minute. Did Nina tell you to *babysit* me at this party?"

East froze, then laughed, then froze again.

"Oh my God!" Leo was mortified.

"She didn't exactly use those words," East admitted. "No one said the word 'babysit.'"

"What words did she say, then?" Leo glanced back out the window to look for Nina. She had a different finger she'd like to raise for her sister this time.

"She just told me to look out for you," East said. "And I promised I would."

"Well, she told *me* not to accept any drinks from boys, so I guess only one of us listened to her," Leo muttered. "I'm going to kill her."

"It's not a big deal," East insisted, which, easy for him to say. He wasn't the one being completely infantilized at a party. "I think she just wants us to get along and this is her way of doing that."

Leo just shook her head as she stared down into her cup. She hated to admit it, but East was right about the cup giving her something to do with her hands and she didn't look *totally* out of place at this party anymore. "Oh, Nina," she said, just as her sister danced past the window again, laughing at someone behind her. The pool lights made her look blue and pale.

"Hey!" Nina called, and East looked up, his face relaxing into a smile once he saw her.

"I like *you* a lot!" she yelled at him, then held up her hands in the shape of a heart. East just grinned wider and Leo saw a tiny bit of a flush span out across his cheeks.

"I like *you* a lot, too," he mouthed at her, then glanced back at Leo. "This is, uh, very embarrassing, I just want you to know that."

"Welcome to Nina," Leo said. "She loves a big display of public affection." Even as she said it, though, she thought it wasn't a bad thing. Leo wished she could do that, wear her emotions so wildly on her sleeve for everyone to see, daring them to tell her she was wrong about how she felt instead of always second-guessing herself.

They watched as Nina laughed and headed back toward the pool to someone calling her name. "I'm really going to miss her," Leo sighed.

"What do you mean?"

"When she goes to college next year." She sipped at the ginger ale again, hearing the flash of a song from Nina's sick day playlist even as the music blared at the party. "It'll be weird, you know? Her room will be empty, all her stuff will be gone. My mom is probably going to convert her bedroom into a home office the minute Nina moves out."

"Yeah," East agreed, but then he said, "You know she's freaking out about that, right? College?"

"Um, no." Leo watched as Nina giggled with a newfound friend. "I did *not* know about that."

"She's convinced she's not going to get into UCLA." East sipped at his own drink, watching as Leo watched him. "Sprite," he told her. "Don't worry. Designated driver and all."

"I'm not worried," she said, and she wasn't. She had something bigger on her mind. "Wait, what do you mean, she's worried she's not going to get in? It's all she's talked about for the past three years. It's all my *parents* have talked about for the past three years."

"Yeah, I know, it's just . . ." East looked back out the window toward Nina, almost like she could hear what he was saying. "I think she's just psyching herself out, you know? She's feeling a lot of pressure and it's messing with her head so I think she's just"——he mimed pushing something away from him like it was toxic——"you know?"

"Okay," Leo said, but there was something dark skittering across her brain and she knew this was the thing that would wake her up at two in the morning. Worrying about Nina was always worse than worrying about herself. She'd easily take a college rejection if it meant that Nina would get in.

"It'll be fine," East said, and Leo wasn't quite sure who he was reassuring, Leo or himself. "She's a genius, her GPA has to be like a seven or eight, right?" He smiled down at her, teasing. "She's the only person who actually *wants* to join clubs at school."

"I know, right?" Leo raised her cup and they clinked in a muted plastic toast. "She'll get in, she's fine."

But she still made a mental note to tell her mom about this.

And even though Leo had this new halo of a worry about her head, the party did get better. She laughed to Sophie about how weird their freshman English teacher was, then listened to her complain about some mystery boyfriend for a while. She talked to Madison a little bit and decided she was pretty nice, nice enough that they exchanged numbers, with Madison saying, "I'm totally going to text you!"

Take that, Nina, Leo thought smugly. *I can so make friends.* She couldn't wait to gloat about it once they were back home.

Just as their conversation was ending, Leo glanced out the open front door and saw Nina and East pressed up against each other on the porch, kissing in a way that told Leo that this was different, that whatever this was, it was bigger than Nina and East. His hand was in her hair and her fingers were twisted in the belt loops of his jeans, and Nina was flushed and it was like her spine had gone wobbly, that she was just skin and softness and love, and Leo quickly looked away. It was a public act, but a private moment, and she was both happy and sorry that she saw it.

Later, she wound up outside sitting next to Nina on the diving board, their feet dangling over the pool. Leo thought that Nina was probably the only person she trusted to sit like this with, trusting that she wouldn't shove her into the cold water below or shake the board and just make her think that she'll fall.

Leo didn't mention that she saw her and East kiss.

"Sooo," Nina said, nudging her shoulder against Leo's. "I was right, right?"

Leo just shrugged, mostly because she knew that kind of non-committal response would drive Nina up a wall, and she was right, it does. East was somewhere behind them. Leo could hear the snap and the whir of his camera, an old-fashioned one.

"Ugh, just admit it, he's a good one." Nina nudged her harder and this time Leo pressed back into it and smiled, felt their bones just underneath their skin.

She thought about asking about college, about what else Nina was worried about, what else she was hiding. It was strange to think of Nina being worried about something, like the world was suddenly that much more frightening because now she knew Nina was scared of it, too.

But instead Leo just said, "East's pretty nice. I accepted a drink from him."

"And *only* him." Nina waggled her finger in Leo's face. "He is a good one," she said again, just as two girls ran past them and jumped into the pool, screaming the whole time.

"Whose house is this, anyway?" Leo asked her as they both instinctively cringed away from the splash.

"Michael Rusconi," Nina said.

"Who?"

She shrugged. "I dunno, some kid who just graduated. His parents are apparently at a resort in Puerto Vallarta for their twenty-fifth anniversary, enjoying spa treatments and an all-inclusive food and beverage allowance. I'm jealous. I want to go to Mexico someday."

"Me too," Leo said.

Two more girls ran past them into the pool and Nina watched as they resurfaced. "Well, time to go," she said. "The party always ends once a bunch of people start jumping into the pool."

"Why?" Leo asked, taking her sister's hand as she scooted back on the diving board so she could stand up.

"Because then it's just a bunch of wet people standing around, dripping everywhere." Nina pulled her up, then brushed nonexistent dirt off the back of her denim skirt. "C'mon, let's find East and get out of here."

They just drive around for a while, windows down and warm left-over milkshakes and sodas still in East's car's cup holders. Leo sticks her arm out the window, moving it up and down like a snake against the fast air. She's in the front seat at Nina's insistence, but Nina is right behind her and she does the same with her own arm, the two of them moving in silent synchronicity.

It's moments like this that always make Leo's heart feel suddenly and painfully full. Christmas and birthdays always hold the same promise, but it's not the same as being surprised by normal things, completely average evenings. The orange streetlight spotlights East's car as they drive toward absolutely nothing, and Leo thinks that maybe this is the happiest she has ever been.

"Oh my God, turn it up, turn it up!" Nina says. It's her phone that's synched to the car's Bluetooth, and East hits a button on the steering wheel and fills the car with the beginning of Cyndi Lauper's "Time After Time." "Remember when Mom would play this for us?" Nina says, leaning forward to tap Leo's arm. She's fully back in the car now and the moment is gone.

"Of course I do," Leo says, and she does.

"*Yes!*" Nina cries. "Exactly!" Then she leans toward East, as if he couldn't hear her unless she was close to him. "Our mom would always make us listen to the music she listened to when she was a kid and she played this one song all the time."

"I like this song," East says, then turns it up even louder so that it shakes the seat under Leo, makes her feel like they're at a concert instead of just in a car.

Nina immediately pretends to hold an imaginary microphone, singing into her fist like she's in the middle of a sellout stadium tour, and Leo copies her big sister. Together they belt out the lyrics, pointing at one another when they get to the chorus. Nina grabs her sister's hand and Leo holds on tight and she laughs and sings and fights back tears because of how much she wants to be in this moment forever.

She never wants it to end.

But the song eventually goes into another one, a song that's new and popular but doesn't have that same pull of nostalgia, and East turns it down a little bit. "Okay," Nina says. "It's Leo's turn!"

"Leo's turn!" Leo cries, clapping her hands together.

"Don't worry," Nina tells East. "She's fifteen, she has her permit, plus she drives like a grandma so it's fine."

"Excuse me!" Leo protests.

"I'm quoting Dad. Don't kill the messenger."

"I do *not* drive like a grandma!" Leo protests.

"Fine," East says. "Leo can drive like a grandma for ten feet. But that's it. And we stay out here where there's no traffic. God, you two are a fucking team, you know that?"

Nina just takes a sip of her strawberry milkshake. "We do."

"But first, here are the rules," East says. "Seat belt at all times."

"Got it," Leo says. Nina is too occupied with her shake to answer.

"Both hands on the wheel at all times."

"Where else would they be?"

"No speeding."

"I told you, she drives like a turtle," Nina pipes up from the backseat.

"I'm *cautious*," Leo argues.

"Dad said that it'd be quicker to walk than drive with you."

East looks over at Leo, waiting for confirmation.

"He exaggerates a lot," Leo replies.

Nina snorts out a laugh.

They pull over to the side of the road. It's almost midnight but no one's out on the road, and East and Leo quickly switch places. Overhead, the August night sky glitters, dozens of constellations setting the course, and Leo thinks that some of those stars aren't even there anymore, that their light is still shining even after they're gone.

"Driver controls the music," Leo says as soon as she's buckled in, and both East and Nina complain about it but she's right and so she wins. She's so excited that she doesn't even adjust the seat or mirrors, just leans forward and sits up straighter. Nina cues up another song and Leo feels the rough steering wheel, solid under her hands, as she pulls back onto the road, the music sounding shimmery and sparkly, just like the sky above them.

"Just once around the block," East says, and Leo nods even though she's definitely going to go for at least one extra lap. There's a car up ahead, its headlights just barely visible on the horizon, but that's the only car around so it's fine.

Behind her, Nina is wriggling out of her oversized pink hoodie, tossing it on the car seat next to her and then singing along with the song. Even East is tapping his fingers against the window frame, and Leo feels the wind in her hair, the love in her heart, the possibility of so much pressing so hard against her chest that it feels like she can't breathe.

If this is what happiness feels like, she'll take it.

Leo presses down on the gas and grips the wheel, and with a shout and a laugh, drives them all straight ahead. From the backseat, she can hear Nina muttering, "Ugh, I can't see from behind East, I'm moving over," the *click!* of her seat belt as it unfastens.

"Nina, don't—" East starts to say.

The car gets closer, it fills up the road, and then the light is everywhere.

The world explodes and shatters into pieces that Leo will never be able to put back together, no matter how hard she tries.

AUGUST 17, 12:54 A.M.
23 HOURS AND 28 MINUTES BEFORE THE ACCIDENT

LEO DOESN'T FEEL Nina slip into her bed until it's too late.

She's asleep, dreaming about something that felt so familiar and safe at the time, something that she can't seem to remember once she wakes up. Those are the worst kinds of dreams, the ones where she has only absence, no memory, the void of something that whispers around the edges of her brain and then disappears as soon as she turns her head.

The first thing she realizes is that she's cold, and then that she's not the one who's cold, and she feels herself swim up from the deep end of her dreams, pushing up through the waves until she opens her eyes and feels her bed, her pillow, and her sister.

"Nina?" she whispers, then coughs because her throat is dry. Had she left the window open? It's open now in any case, and the air is damp and slightly cold, the coastal fog from a few miles away curling into the room.

"Shh," Nina says, then snuggles closer to her. "Mom's asleep. Don't wake her up."

"You're cold."

"I know." Nina tucks herself against Leo's back, giggling a little as Leo squirms away.

"Why are— Are your feet *wet*?" Leo whisper-shouts at her, then reaches back with a hand and tries to bat Nina away, but she only lands a few soft hits on her sister's duvet-covered hip.

"I lost a shoe," Nina says, then puts her toes between Leo's calves and pulls the duvet up so that her ear is covered. Nina always sleeps that way—has since she was a baby. "We had to run through the grass. It slipped off somewhere."

Leo sighs, pushes herself up, and turns over so that they're facing each other. Nina's eyes are mischievous, crinkled at the edges as she grins at Leo. Leo counts the crinkles. Seven.

"Scoot over," Leo sighs, pushing at her, and Nina moves just enough so that she can still warm her toes under Leo's legs. "What time is it?"

"Late," Nina says.

"Did you sneak out?"

"I think the more important part is that I snuck back *in*." Nina wriggles down a little, reminding Leo of when Denver had been a puppy, so excited about a treat or a walk that he would shake from his head down to his floofy tail.

"Where did you go?" Leo tries to stifle a yawn, fails.

"Just out."

"With East?"

Nina's eye crinkles go up to eight.

"You really need to meet him, Leo," Nina says. "You'd like him. You'd like him a lot. He's so much like you."

"I *have* met him," Leo points out. "We had math together last year."

Nina rolls her eyes so hard that Leo can practically hear it. "That's not exactly *meeting* someone. And I hate that my little sister is going to be in *calculus* and I still need to use my fingers to add things together."

Leo ignores the half-compliment. "I also met him when he came to pick you up that one time. Remember, in the driveway?"

"Oh my God, you are so literal." Nina rolls over onto her back so she can look up at the ceiling. The fairy lights that Leo had strung up on the ceiling several months ago were still there, illuminating the planes of Nina's profile so that to Leo she looked like a mountain range, something to be forged and discovered, something eternal that would live forever.

"I'm serious, you'd like him. He's a photographer. And not like, you know, the yearbook photographer, either. He's really good."

Leo pulls some of the duvet away from her sister, and Nina lets her. "A teenage boy with a camera? In *our* school?" She feigns shock. "How original. What an artist."

Nina reaches out and boops her nose, the only person that Leo would ever, ever allow to do that. "Don't be a baby," she says, moving her arm back under the duvet as she shivers a bit. Leo doesn't know if it's because of the cold or because of something else. Her voice is quieter when she speaks again. "He's special, Lee. He's special to *me*."

"Oh." Leo watches as Nina falls into her own thoughts, watches as her sister's face changes with the idea of East, and she realizes that wherever Nina has gone, she can't follow. Nina is suddenly completely unrecognizable to her, taking her first steps into love, or whatever love even is, and Leo watches as Nina's face grows soft and pliant under the lights. Leo doesn't know what that kind of new love feels like, and sometimes she fears that she never will know what that feels like, and she has a sudden stab of panic that Nina is not only growing up, but that she's going away. Going away from *her*.

Please, she thinks with a sudden urgency that surprises even herself, *come back to me*.

And then Nina rolls over again, grinning and tucking her hand under her cheek, wholly familiar once more. "There's a party tomorrow night. You should come with us."

Now it was Leo's turn to roll her eyes. "I'm not good at parties."

"You never *go* to parties."

"Because I'm not good at them."

'That's because you have no friends. You need to work on that, by the way."

"I have you."

"I'm your *sister*. That's not the same as a friend."

Leo stays silent at that.

"Just come with East and me," Nina continues. "We can get food beforehand, East will drive. If you hate it, then we can leave and just go hang out somewhere." Nina swallows then, blinking once as she gazes at Leo. "I really want you to like him, Lee," she said. "Can you at least do it for me?"

Leo already knows the answer. So does Nina.

Leo would do anything for her sister.

"Fine," she sighs. "But if anyone throws up on me——"

"You need to stop watching all those dumb nineties high school movies," Nina scolds her. "It's just people hanging out at a house. It's not like you think it is."

"And you're buying me food. In-N-Out."

Nina grins. "Oh, twist my arm then."

"And you're washing my sheets tomorrow," Leo adds as Nina puts her wet feet back under her sister's warm skin.

"Aye, aye, captain."

"What is——is that *grass*?"

"Probably a little mud, too. We had to run across the park when the sprinklers came on."

"Nina!"

"Relax, you're washable." Nina curls up again, resting her head against Leo's shoulder. "Mmm, you're warm, too."

"I *was*," Leo says, but she doesn't move Nina away, feels the pull of sleep reeling her back in.

"You know my favorite thing about East?" Nina whispers after a minute.

Leo just groans, a noise somewhere between "What?" and "I don't care."

"It's his smile," Nina murmurs, and Leo can feel her sister's chin press into her shoulder. "When he smiles, you just feel like everything's going to be okay, you know?"

Leo doesn't know, she has no idea what Nina's talking about, but she just nods and then turns her head, pressing a kiss against her sister's dirty hair. She smells like sweat and dirt and shampoo and coastal fog.

She smells alive.

"Trust me," Nina whispers. "You're going to love him."

"Um, are you going to your own bed any time soon?" Leo whispers back.

"Just give me five more minutes," Nina replies, then curls up tighter and sighs.

Leo turns over, feels her sister press her heart against her back, their pulses slowly synchronizing into the same slow beat. She breathes deep, smells the air, closes her eyes.

Leo holds on to her sister.

She doesn't let her go.

ACKNOWLEDGMENTS

Always and forever, thank you to my family for all of their love, support, compassion, and A+ senses of humor.

Thank you to my agent, Lisa Grubka, who has been guiding my career since 2006 with an incredible amount of wisdom and knowledge. Her professionalism is both perennial and astounding, and I am forever thankful for the stroke of fortune that led me to her. Plus she serves great cheese platters, so I am clearly wanting for nothing.

An immense amount of gratitude to the team at HarperTeen: my editor Kristen Pettit, Elizabeth Lynch, Kristen Eckhardt, Jessica Berg, Sabrina Abballe, Jacqueline Burke, and the national and regional sales teams. An extra special thank-you to Veronica Ambrose and Susan Bishansky for their eagle-eyed copy edits on this backward book. I promise to never put you through that again.

I have once again been gifted with a gorgeous book cover, and the immensely talented Corina Lupp and Philip Pascuzzo are both responsible for it. Thank you to them for finding such beauty inside these pages.

The writing world is both big and small, and I am grateful for the circle of friends who are always there to support me, including Anna Carey, Julie Buxbaum, Brandy Colbert, Katie Cotugno, Maurene Goo, Morgan Matson, Gretchen McNeil, Megan Miranda, Jessica Morgan, Maret Orliss, Liza Palmer, Jen Smith, and Elissa Sussman. To my friends with non-writing jobs: I love all of you more than words can say. Thank you for always having my back and letting me vent in the group texts, even when you have no idea what I'm talking about.

To the friends, colleagues, and total strangers who very kindly shared their personal stories, knowledge, and insight with me, thank you. This was a tough book to research and write, and your generosity and openness made the experience a little more bearable.

2022 marks the fifteenth year since I sold my very first book. It is a fact that still seems improbable to me, and I suspect that my sixteen-year-old self would be joyfully astonished by the life and career I've managed to build. Thank you to the librarians and teachers who continually put books into kids' hands, never stopping until they're holding the right one. Thank you to the bloggers, Instagrammers, TikTokers, whatever social media comes after TikTok, and book reviewers who have supported me on both Day 1 and Day 10,001. Thank you to the booksellers around the world who have championed my books, invited me into their stores, and taken me out for drinks and dinners afterwards. Thank you to the families who have sent me the most gorgeous, emotional notes about my books, especially *Far from the Tree*. I have saved every single one of them and they in turn have saved me. Thank you to everyone that

I've been fortunate enough to work with over the years, and to those who have shown me how kindness, diligence, faith, and success often travel together.

But most importantly, thank you to the readers. I am completely humbled by the way you've shown up for my books and for me over and over throughout the years. You have made me a better writer, but more importantly, a better human, and there are no words I could string together that could ever convey the gratitude I feel toward you. All I ever wanted was a small life where I could write books and send them out into the world, and I thank you every day for being there to receive them. I read all your emails, see all your comments, and hear all your words, and they make my heart sing. My grateful heart is yours for as long as you'll have it, and I hope we continue this adventure for many years to come.

From the bottom of my heart, thank you so, so much.